Shear Malice

Shear Malice
A Melanie Hogan Mystery

Rhonda Blackhurst

Books may be purchased in quantity and/or special sales by contacting the author at www.rhondablackhurst.com or rhondablackhurst0611@gmail.com.

Published by Lighthouse Press, Colorado
Cover Design by Isabel Robalo

Library of Congress Control Number: 2017906948

ISBN-13: 978-0991353262
ISBN-10: 0991353269

First Edition
Printed in the United States of America

Also by Rhonda Blackhurst

The Inheritance

The Melanie Hogan Cozy Mystery Series

- ➢ *Shear Madness*
- ➢ *Shear Deception*

The Whispering Pines Mysteries

- ➢ *Finding Abby*

To Clint

And to Ben and Alex

Shear Malice

Book Three

A Melanie Hogan Mystery

1

oday was going to be a fantastic day! The one I'd been waiting for, patiently impatient, for the past six months. Claire, my best friend as well as my business partner in a bustling hair salon, A Cut Above, was moving. Not to any old house, but to the house that was just across a big grassy field and past a few trees from my own. She was moving to the house that other people admired yet thought was an odd misfit to the lake home area where most were cabin-style or log homes such as my own. Nope, this one was a Victorian Claire-style house, the only one of its kind in a far-reaching radius. I chuckled. Wait until they met Claire. She was as unique and beautiful as her new home. Excitement surged through me.

Claire and I met years ago when we worked at an upscale salon that catered to high-end clientele. Neither of us liked it there much, with the hoity-toity ladies who thought the world was ending when they broke a nail, so we branched off into a business of our own. Despite well-meaning friends telling us we would regret it, that going into business together would ruin a friendship faster than anything ever could, we've proved them all wrong. In fact, the opposite has happened. We've gotten to be better friends, if that were possible. Not only are we besties, as Claire long ago coined our friendship, but both of us were only children. That made us the sister to the other that we never had. Not just sisters because we were thrown together by happenstance and didn't have a choice, but sisters because we did have a choice.

My phone rang as I headed out the door. I looked at the caller ID and grinned. "Hey, Claire."

"Hi, almost neighbor." Her sunny voice filled the invisible line.

"I hope you're not going to be one of those neighbors who's always knocking on my door for sugar, eggs, butter, or anything else."

"No, I'll send Sydney."

We both laughed. "She can come anytime she wants." Sydney is Claire's eight-year-old daughter, and the child I secretly pretend is mine, as creepy as that sounds. I can't have kids of my own, which is almost the only thing that can reduce me to tears. Sydney is all attitude, cute as a bug, and can pretty much get anything she wants from me. And she knows it.

"What time is Cole gonna be there with the moving truck?" Cole Mahoney is a police officer who has found himself thrown into my life too often over the course of the past year or so, whether he wanted to or not. He's also the lucky man who captured Claire's attention like no one else had ever been able to do. Not for lack of trying. She's had too many offers to count since her military husband died on tour, leaving Claire single and Sydney without a father. But since Cole entered the scene, she's been clearly off the market.

"He's stopping for coffee and bagels at Einstein Brothers first, so he probably won't be here until nine o'clock."

I moaned in anticipation of Einstein Bagels. "You better keep that man, Davis."

"You know it." I could almost hear her beaming.

"I'll be there by nine then. And don't take the only blueberry bagel."

"If you're here on time you won't have to worry about it."

"When am I ever late?"

"I won't answer that. Because I wouldn't be able to come up with a single instance."

"Just don't ask me the same question about you because neither of has that kind of time," I said.

"That was so not nice," she said with a giggle. "It's called free-spirited."

"Just call it what it is: Never-on-time-for-anything."

We hung up, and I threw a light blanket over my shoulders and brought my Bible and devotional book out on the balcony. Fall in Minnesota is the most gorgeous, breathtaking time of the year. The leaves are every shade of the spectrum in yellows, oranges, reds, greens. Even the shades of brown are beautiful. The lakeshore is just yards away from my balcony, and on the other side of the lake balls of red-orange fire were splashed among the green leaves as they continued to change color. It was the fourth of October, and despite the leaf-covered ground, the trees were a vibrant explosion of color.

After an early frost, it had been an unseasonably warm fall. Refreshingly cool mornings gave way to the upper sixties; a couple of times even lower seventies. Perfect weather for jeans and sweatshirts. My favorite. Actually, jeans and anything is my favorite. As long as I can wear my jeans, it doesn't matter if I have to wear a muumuu over them. It's all good. I pretty much wear heels every day, too, except days where I'll be stuck doing heavy labor. Like moving Claire.

A gust of excitement kicked up along with a slight breeze that began to pick up, swirling leaves around on the ground. I looked at the sky across the lake and beyond. There was supposed to be a front moving in late tonight or early morning, bringing rain and strong north winds. I only hoped we could be done with the outside stuff before it hit.

I rested my slippered feet inside the curly-q's of the black wrought iron fence that surrounded my balcony, one knee sticking through the hole of my old worn gray sweatpants that I couldn't get myself to part with. Sweats were like jeans. The more worn in and out they were, the more comfortable and worth keeping. And these were keepers.

I finished the chapter in Galatians that I was reading, highlighted one last passage to remember—not that I would, but figured the chances were better if I highlighted it—drained the last of my coffee and headed in, making sure to secure the lock behind me. After having two unwelcome visitors snooping in my house over the past year, I never assumed anymore that living in the country meant privacy. If anything, it gave the people who decided to be nosey the freedom to do it without being noticed.

I took the steps two at a time up to my bedroom in the loft of my small log home and changed into more presentable clothes—well-worn jeans, a hoodie, and my Nike tennis shoes. I tossed my hair back in a ponytail and was almost to the front door before I did an about face when I realized I'd forgotten to brush my teeth. Three minutes later I was locking the front door behind me and heading to Claire's house in the city. Her soon-to-be-vacated house. And as much fun as we'd had at her place, I couldn't wait to begin making new memories at her new house by mine out in the country. I imagined us having bonfires, sleepovers, walking across our yards with cups of coffee, not a care in the world.

It was nine o'clock sharp when I got to her house. Cole pulled up right behind me, honking and scaring me half to death, which he seemed to enjoy entirely too much. My eyes narrowed as I looked at him. He just grinned that much more. Guess the proverbial daggers I cast in his direction weren't menacing enough. I'd be sure to try harder next time.

Claire met us outside, bounding down the front steps like a child who's had too much sugar.

"Guess you don't need any more caffeine this morning," I said as she gave me a hug then turned to give Cole one. I gave him a smug look. "How's it feel to be second?" I asked him, smiling. Childish, I know, but all's fair in love and war, as they say.

7

Cole just grinned like a little boy on the morning of his birthday as he kept his arm draped over Claire's shoulders.

"Where's Syd?" I looked around Claire, expecting Sydney to come bounding down the steps and into my arms.

"With Tyler's parents. They came late last night to pick her up."

I tried to hide my disappointment, not to mention my surprise. I should have known I couldn't hide anything from Claire. "I know what you're thinking, Melanie."

"And what would that be, oh wise one?"

"First of all, you're gonna have to do with me. Second, she'll be just fine not being here for the moving part. She showed me which room she wants. Not that it matters because she'll probably be in mine every night anyway."

"She can stay at my house, too."

"Oh, I'm sure she will. Every time she doesn't get her way at home." Claire rolled her eyes. "I told her we would put all of her things in her room and she and I would unpack them together when she comes home in two days."

"What about school tomorrow?"

"They don't have any school tomorrow or Thursday. I think it's a teachers' workshop or something."

"School's barely just started for the year, and they already have two days off? What about Friday?"

"She'll be gone."

"Sure was different when I was a kid," Cole added.

Claire turned to look at him and asked him something, too quiet for me to hear.

"Would you like me to leave so you can talk freely?" I quipped.

"No need," she smiled and looked at Cole then back at me. "I was just making sure Levi is still coming."

I ran my hand through my hair and looked down at my jeans. Thank goodness these were the ones that only had the holes in the knees and not below my rear.

"Telling me that ahead of time would have been the nice thing to do."

"I am," she grinned, revealing the endearing gap between her front teeth. "He's not here yet, so technically, it's ahead of time. Another buddy of theirs from the police department is coming, too. How's that for telling you ahead of time?"

Cole laughed. "Come on, ladies. Let's have a little breakfast and coffee fuel before we get started."

"I think Claire's had enough," I tossed over my shoulder as I turned to go in the house.

Levi Wescott was the detective who worked the case last winter when my birth mother, Violet, was staying with me and set me up to take the fall for something I didn't do. I guess in fairness, I can't say she did it maliciously, but she wasn't exactly honest to exonerate me either.

There had been sparks of irritation between Detective Wescott and me at the beginning, which had turned into sparks of interest by the time the case wrapped up. I would like to think interest on both of our parts, not that I had any intention of finding out. My taste in men stunk to high heaven, and I wasn't about to take another chance anytime in the near future. But a little harmless flirting didn't hurt anything. In fact, it was good for a flailing ego. Especially when reciprocated, as was the case.

As if on cue, I heard a horn honk and Cole excused himself to go outside. I lifted the cover of the bagel box and snatched one of the two blueberry bagels. The screen door slammed, men's voices now in the porch.

"You know, you can just go in there if you want to hear what they're saying," Claire said.

"How do you know—"

"Because your ear practically stretches into the other room."

"Not true."

"So true!" she countered.

"Whatever."

Claire laughed, and I felt the blood rise to my cheeks with the embarrassment of getting caught. "He likes you, ya know. Levi," she added when I didn't respond.

"Good for him."

"It could be good for him if you'd lose your stubbornness."

"I don't have the time or energy to be in a relationship."

"Don't jump the gun. Start with friendship and see where it goes from there."

I looked up from my bagel, meeting Claire's enormous brown eyes, her flawless milk chocolate skin breathtaking. "I don't have the time or energy for what comes after friendship. And why encourage something I have no intention of pursuing?"

"Just don't turn away a friendship for something that *might* happen."

"Wouldn't dream of it." I chomped my bagel and looked away.

2

By the time we got the pleasantries over with and devoured all but two of the bagels, it was ten o'clock. The men began moving boxes as Claire and I packed the last minute things that somehow got left out of boxes, cleaning as we went along.

"You know," I said as I took a swig of water and wiped my forehead with my forearm, "This is pretty old fashioned and sexist."

Claire looked over her shoulder at me as she scoured the inside of the oven. "What is?"

"The men are doing the heavy work, and the women are doing the cleaning."

"I don't mind being old fashioned in this instance. I'm sure they wouldn't mind if you wanted to join in the heavy lifting. In fact, they might find it pretty amusing." She stuck her head back in the oven, scouring away.

"I'm sure they would." I watched as they each came in and took another box, five men in all by now. I looked around me at the almost empty house. "They're doing just fine on their own."

"You talk big, Melanie Hogan, but you're not that tough."

"Don't let anyone else know that, huh?"

She laughed and stood up, arching her back. "Sure. I'm kinda surprised you don't have your heels on today. You're all of, what, four feet without them?"

I threw my sponge at her. She put her arm up to block her face, laughing. "Five-two, thank you very much."

With the last of the things carried out and loaded onto the truck, Claire followed Cole and his buddy outside. "I'll be right back, Mel," she called over her shoulder.

"So you say."

I began toward the back of the house to give each of the rooms one last look over to be sure we did everything we needed to. Turning the corner by the bathroom, I heard the door swing open and ran smack into Levi before my brain could tell me to stop. Running into him was like running into a cement wall, sturdy, unmoving and unforgiving. The breath went out of me for a moment.

"What the—I thought you were outside with the rest of the testosterone."

"You thought I was or you hoped I was?"

"Both." I felt my cheeks flush. "I was just indulging in one last moment before closing this chapter of the story."

He followed behind me into the back rooms. "How've you been?"

"Good. You?"

"Same."

"Good thing we got that cleared up," I said.

I checked in closets, behind doors, under bathroom sinks, in medicine cabinets, until I found my way back to the kitchen. Levi stood on the opposite side of the kitchen island.

"What have you been doing for excitement since I've seen you last?" he asked. "Any more sleuthing?"

Merriment twinkled in those baby blues. I watched as he leaned a hip against the island, tucking his hands into the pockets of his jeans, looking ruggedly handsome in his flannel shirt and boots. A Minnesota Twins baseball cap covered his shaved head.

"Maybe," I answered, slyly. "Staying out of trouble, though."

"I was beginning to wonder if that was possible." He chuckled.

"Hey," I protested. "It's not like I go looking for trouble. It just finds me."

"Twice in a year. You're kind of a magnet for trouble. How's the salon?"

"Business is doing great. Gina and Maria are obviously gone, but Connie and Rubie are there, as well as Babs, our part-time nail and skin care specialist."

Levi tossed his head back and laughed. "Please tell me that isn't her real name."

"Can't. Because as far as I know, it is. It's on her paperwork she filled out to work there and everything."

"Poor kid." He almost looked pained. "Heard anything from Violet?"

I was impressed he remembered not to refer to her as my mother. Violet may have given birth to me, but she gave me up when I was four years old, which in my mind, by doing so she relinquished the right to be called mom, mother, or any other reference to the same. Thankfully though, she left me with my grandmother and granddad, because it was the best possible place for a girl to grow up. My grandmother, who I've always affectionately called Nana, was an angel sent from God to a lost little girl who needed an angel. There's not a day that goes by that I don't talk to her at least once.

"Violet sends an occasional letter. Generous of her, isn't it?"

"Is she begging for your forgiveness?"

"I don't know. I don't read them." I met his eyes for a split second before I tore myself away from them and looked through the window above the sink where Claire stood next to Cole, his arm draped loosely around her shoulders, both of them laughing at what I assumed one of the men said. "Why aren't you out there with them?"

"Because I'm in here with you."

"Poor you."

"I disagree."

I felt a flutter in my stomach and turned to look at him again. "In case I didn't tell you, thank you for working so hard at clearing my name last spring."

"You pretty much did that all by yourself. Our department could benefit from detectives as good as you. Maybe you should come work for us."

"Careful. I might be holding you to that if Claire gets sick of me and decides to kick me out of the salon by giving me a buy-out offer I can't refuse."

"She'd be lost without you."

"Probably."

"Yeah, she'd miss your humility." We both laughed, the moment of lightness feeling good.

Claire walked in, looking from me to Levi. "Am I interrupting?"

"Depends if you're asking us to work," Levi said, not taking his eyes off of me.

Claire looked at Levi. "Cole's waiting for you to ride with him in the truck over to the new house. The other guys went on ahead, and Melanie and I are going to meet up with you all."

"We'll give you a two-hour head start," I teased.

Levi tipped his baseball cap to me, grinned, and murmured as he walked past me. "You look good in green. Matches your eyes."

My heartbeat sped up. The smell of Irish Spring soap lingered in the air after he'd left, leaving me wondering how he could still smell good after working all morning. I hadn't been doing the heavy lifting he was, and I could tell you I certainly didn't smell Irish Spring fresh. But then I didn't shower this morning, either. It amused me that he did.

Claire rode with me in my car, reasoning that Cole could bring her back to pick up her car after we emptied the moving truck. My guess was he just wanted time with her alone, and he'd had enough. It was my turn to have some Claire time. Although, truth be told, by the time we finished I was looking forward to having a little R&R all by my lonesome at my house. It had been a chaotic day with a whole lot of interaction with people, and I was plum worn out.

By the time we unloaded the truck, a Northeast wind had kicked up, picking up leaves in mini swirling cyclones. The guys had gotten Claire's bed put together, and her chest of drawers carried in, while I put Sydney's bed together and

15

Claire unpacked some boxes in the kitchen. By the time we finished, it was dusk, and Claire decided to stay at her new house and unpack a few more boxes instead of going back into town for a final walk-through as she'd originally planned.

"Can you drop me off to pick up my car on our way into work in the morning?"

"If you're nice to me," I teased.

"When am I anything other than nice to you?"

She had me there. I wasn't sure I could give her a single instance to prove otherwise. As much as being nice was supposed to be a positive character trait, it was sometimes Claire's downfall. That and the fact that her feelings got hurt far too easily.

Everyone but Cole had left, and as Claire said goodbye to him, I snuck a glance at them from the corner of my eye. They were so cute together, but I couldn't help feeling the sting of envy, thankful it dissipated as quickly as it came. As nice as it would be to have someone to share life with, I did just fine on my own. I could eat and drink whatever and whenever I wanted, I could watch anything on TV that I wanted, I could leave the cap off the toothpaste—not that I ever did, but I could if I wanted to—and I could come and go as I pleased without any explanation. Just thinking about it made me realize it was pretty much all about me. Oofda! "Melanie, you're one self-absorbed woman," I grumbled.

Finally, Cole left, and Claire and I slipped on our jackets and hauled some empty boxes to the back yard to break them down and stack them beside the shed until she could arrange for trash pickup. The smell of rain blew in, and I could feel the damp cold against my skin.

"This is going to be the perfect place for Sydney," Claire said. "She can play outside, and I won't have to worry about traffic or the whole stranger danger thing—"

"Stranger danger?" I stopped breaking down the box I was working on and looked at her, trying not to laugh.

"It's what they call it in school when they teach the kids about talking to strangers."

I went back to working on the box. "Makes sense." I pulled a box cutter out of my jacket pocket and began working on the next one. "I gotta be honest; I worry a little bit about your liking it out here. You're so used to living in town. Even for me, when I first moved out here, the silence was deafening. And you know what else?" I stood and smiled at her. "We have bugs out here. Big fat ones."

"What you have are raccoons. Big fat ones," she added.

"Yeah, but they seem to like me too much to go anywhere else," I said dryly.

Those buggers are always scaring me half to death. One would think I would be used to them by now, but a loud crash in the middle of silence scares me every time. I have to admit they're cute, but they're a nuisance. After too many instances of picking up trash that they seem to like better on the ground than in the can, I finally got covers that lock in place so they couldn't dump them out anymore. It was a pain unlocking it when I bring a bag of trash out, but cleaning up the mess of overturned cans is a bigger pain.

17

"It'll be fun to take Sydney swimming in a freshwater lake instead of the saltwater ocean in California or in over-chlorinated pools. And hanging out in the boat!" She nearly squealed. "She can come out with us."

"I hope she has a bigger bladder than you do." I ripped the box cutter down another box, stomping it flat on the ground. "We should probably tie some rope around these, because with this howling wind they're likely to blow into my yard."

"That's one way to get rid of 'em," she said, laughing.

The shed door creaked on rusty hinges as I opened it.

"It freaks me out in here," I said, grimacing. "Something feels almost...sinister." I shivered.

I shined a flashlight until I found some twine lying in a corner on the dirt floor. Claire held the boxes together while I wrapped the twine around them and pulled tight, tying a knot to be sure it wouldn't come loose. Claire picked up one end of the bundle, me the other and we hauled them to the side of the shed against the back of the large lot where the trees began.

A gust of wind kicked up more leaves, blowing dirt right into my eyes. "Dang!"

I dropped the end of the boxes I was carrying and handed the flashlight that was in my other hand to Claire while I tried to clear my eyes of the debris. When I finally was able to open them, I saw the bundle of boxes lying on the ground, and Claire was running her hands against the back of the shed, shining the flashlight up and down, slowly.

"What's wrong?" I asked.

"Melanie," she whispered, making it nearly impossible to hear her above the howling wind. "Look at this." She tried to pry her fingernails in a small crack.

"Here, use this, don't use your fingernails." I handed her the box cutter. "Your nails are jewels, not tools," I said, reminding her of the phrase a manicurist said at the salon where we met. The phrase that irritated me to no end.

I looked on as she maneuvered the blade of the box cutter until a door opened. The smell of wet, musty earth poured out. Both of us shrank back until the smell evaporated into the wind.

"Well, this explains why the shed looks smaller on the inside than what the dimensions actually are. There's a secret room back here." The wind carried my voice, and I wanted to snatch it back before it reached too far.

Claire shined the flashlight inside along the walls and up on the ceiling, holding onto my arm with her other hand. "A secret room for what? Nothing's in here."

"Why would there be anything in here? If the previous owners were going to leave you a gift, they sure as heck wouldn't hide it back here."

"What do you suppose they kept in here?" She looked at me, her huge brown eyes reflected in the backlight. "It just feels so...I don't know. Kinda like we're not supposed to be here. Like we're trespassing or something."

Leaves rustled behind me. I turned to be sure (and hoping with all my might) that it was only the wind. I was straining my eyes to take in everything behind us when Claire jumped back and gasped.

"Oh, no!" she cried, her voice a harsh whisper. And anything harsh is never something that comes from Claire.

My attention snapped from what might be behind us to what was before us. Claire had the flashlight beam trained on the ground. But I wasn't prepared for what I saw. My breath caught in my throat as I looked up and met Claire's eyes. Sheer fear reflected back at me.

3

I took my cell phone out of my pocket, grateful for the flashlight app on it since Claire wasn't about to give up the real flashlight she clutched.

I shined the light on the ground just as the wind blew some leaves in, reminding us we weren't alone. I crouched and brushed a few of them from the surface so I could get a clear look. I ran my fingertips lightly across the smooth gray granite surface of one of the three gravestones that lay there. I shined the flashlight on them, one at a time, trying to read the writing, yet unable to focus. Despite the cold air that had blown in tonight and the cold dampness of this secret room, a bead of sweat ran down the center of my back.

"Did the people you bought the house from say anything about this?" I looked up at her, seeing how pale her face was against the night sky. She may be dark complected naturally, but these weren't exactly natural circumstances.

"No, they didn't. Maybe they didn't know about them."

The wind threatened to swallow the sound of her voice. "You don't have to whisper, Claire. These people are dead. You're not going to wake them up."

I didn't think it was possible, but her eyes got even bigger. "Do you think there are actually people here?"

"That's usually what a gravestone means."

"But this isn't a cemetery!"

"It is for these folks." I stood up. "The people who lived here before you bought it had been here since before I moved in. I wonder why they wouldn't have said anything?"

"Maybe they didn't know," she repeated. "They were just renting the place, after all. They didn't own it."

"Still, how could they not know, Claire? You've been here for all of a day, and we found it."

"Most people aren't as nosey as you are."

"Do I need to remind you that it wasn't me that made this grave discovery?"

Claire made a sour face. "That was a terrible choice of words, Melanie."

"I thought it was brilliant," I mumbled.

She shook her head. "I didn't see it when I looked over the property. And clearly neither did Cole. He would have said something. And you've lived out here for several years, and you didn't know about it."

"I usually don't make it a practice to go exploring on other people's property, much less looking in their buildings."

"Yeah, but you looked at it when I bought it," Claire argued.

"I didn't inspect the shed, for Pete's sake. A realtor would have caught this," I said. Do you have the phone number for the people you bought from?"

"Of course. It's in the contract."

"Call and ask them about it."

"I'm not calling them." She looked at me like I'd just told her to set fire to her hair.

"I will."

"Melanie, they obviously don't want me to know about it."

"Obviously, Sherlock. Which is all the more reason you should. If there's anything they're trying to cover up and they didn't reveal it in the contract, it would be grounds for you to get out of the sale."

I wanted to kick myself as soon as the words were out. I didn't want her to back out. I already had too many things planned for us as neighbors.

"But you wouldn't want to do that," I added quickly, "because this is going to be the perfect childhood for Syd, remember?" *Nice cover-up, Mel. Use the kid. Have you no morals?* I almost felt guilty. Almost.

"What am I going to do?"

"Nothing, that's what. Because I'm going to do it for you."

"What are you going to do?" She was back to whispering.

"Nothing illegal, if that's what you're worried about."

"I wasn't worried—"

"Yes, you were." I chuckled. "But with what I've done lately, I wouldn't blame you." It's not like I hadn't withheld critical evidence from the police in a murder investigation or broke into someone's house to investigate foul play. But really, is it considered breaking into the house when I didn't

23

have to break anything to get it? The door to that house was left not only unlocked but also slightly ajar. I had thought of it more as an invitation.

"Get me the number for the sellers, and I'll take it from there," I said.

I knelt down by the stones again, and took a picture of each one individually with my cell phone as well as all three together, inspecting the results after I clicked the picture. Even though I'd used the flash, the images were still quite dark. I looked a little closer, struggling to see the engraved names, dates of birth, and dates of death.

"Oh, my gosh, Claire." My breath caught in my throat, and sadness squeezed my heart as I zoomed in on one of them. "This one was just a six-year-old child."

I felt Claire peer over my shoulder as she inhaled sharply. "That's so sad."

Since Claire's heart is so soft that she tears up when she sees a dead animal on the road, I thought for sure she was going to start crying. I was in for a surprise when I was the one who felt dewy-eyed at the thought of a child dying before life even began. I was more determined than ever to figure out what happened to this family of three, especially the child.

I sniffled as inconspicuously as I could, knowing I wasn't fooling Claire for a second.

"You always put on such a tough girl façade. Why do you even bother," she said.

"Shut up." I lightly socked her in the shoulder. "Come on. You have a phone number to get for me, and I have work to get started on." I choked down a fresh wave of tears that threatened to erupt. What was my problem? Claire and I were trading places. I just hoped I didn't wake up a foot taller and Claire that much shorter, or we might be remaking the movie *Big*. Though, I could think of worse things than to star in a flick with Tom Hanks. I needed to call my grandmother and get a dose of reality. Some of her pure, totally unbiased love.

4

After a fitful night, it felt like I'd no sooner fallen asleep than my alarm clock went off. I hit snooze a couple of times before finally coming to terms with the fact that it had no mercy, and I would fare best by just getting up.

I lay on my back, looking up at the gray sky through the skylight that was perfectly placed right above my bed. I love falling asleep while gazing at the stars at night, watching lightning slash through the black sky during a storm, and the early morning sky lightens slowly before my very eyes. All from the comfort of my bed. Not to mention seeing the sky cry tears as raindrops splash heavily on the thick glass. It was one of the things that sold me on this house when I first saw it.

My ex-husband, Cain, hadn't lived here for more than a year before he left me for someone who could have children, not even waiting until he physically left before getting someone pregnant. Since the last year of our already short-lived marriage had less than pleasant memories, and I chose to blot them from my mind, I'd never thought of this as our house anyway, but rather mine.

My grandmother had wanted me to move in with her after my divorce, but I loved it out here too much. Besides, I was a thirty-four-year-old woman back then and moving back in with my grandmother would have made me feel weak. And there was no way on this side of heaven I was going to let Cain think he defeated me. I could only hope not on the other side of heaven, either, as I'm sure God wouldn't want to have to deal with the two of us together. I just hoped it wasn't me He left and Cain He took.

I got up and took my phone off the charger. I sat cross-legged on my bed to look at the photos again of the gravestones in Claire's yard. I studied them closely, zooming in on the first stone, studying each detail as if to commit them to memory. *Henry Swanson – Born September 13, 1950-Died October 31, 1992.* Halloween. I wondered what time he died on October thirty-first. Not that it mattered, but I couldn't help but wonder if it was midnight.

I zoomed in on the next one. *Norma Swanson – Born January 25, 1955-Died October 31, 1992.* Huh. Five years younger than her husband. Assuming Henry was her husband. I'd hoped for some identifier on the stone letting me know what kinds of things Norma liked, some word or picture. But there was nothing. Like her life was reduced to nothing but a blank slate, with no one even to know she was buried in some old shed in the middle of Nowheresville to visit her. Or did they?

My heart heavy, my finger lingered above the arrow for a moment before clicking on the next

27

photo. My eyes teared up ever so slightly before I blinked to clear them. *Zachary Swanson—Born December 25, 1986 – Died October 31, 1992.* Two months shy of his seventh birthday. He was younger than Syd. My heart ached horribly.

I set my phone down on the bed, tucked my hands between my crossed legs and gazed across the loft and out the window that looked out over the lake. *How did you come to die so young, little Zachary? What kind of life did you have?*

The wind from the night before had died down leaving in its wake an eerie, gray stillness that mimicked my mood. The lake was so smooth it almost looked like a thin layer of ice lay on top of it, but I knew it wasn't nearly cold enough for that. For October fifth, we'd had very few below freezing temperatures. I wondered what October thirty-first would be like, just twenty-six days away. I had to find out this little guy's story before then.

At that moment, I made it my vow to figure out what happened and make his young life count. Obviously, someone wanted it covered up, but I was going to uncover it if it was the last thing I did. And I knew I could count on Claire to help.

I looked at the blue numbers on the clock beside my bed. I didn't have any time to waste. I needed to get to the salon and get that number from Claire. Hopefully, she remembered to bring it. In fact, I hoped she would bring the entire contract. I wanted to go through it with a fine-toothed comb so that I could take in all of the fine print. I knew Cole read through it, but being a police officer wouldn't necessarily make him good at contracts.

Zipping down the back roads that led me to the highway, I merged into traffic in my little sports car, the music turned down so I could focus on my new goal. That of figuring out about one little Zachary Swanson. It broke my heart that he was buried in the back corner of a yard, locked up in a shed, no less, where no one knew about it. Not that he would know, but it was a shame, nonetheless, as if he were hidden away, locked in his room alone.

If I happened to have a light schedule today, I was going to do some digging around to see what I could find out. I wanted to know the background of the family and how they came to rest where they did. Was it even legal to bury someone in a backyard? I knew who to ask.

I picked up my phone. I knew better than to talk on my cell phone while driving, but my curiosity was stronger than what I should, or rather shouldn't, do. I punched the quick dial number.

"Wescott here."

"Sounding friendly as ever," I teased him.

"Hey." His voice instantly thawed. "Just—"

"Busy, I know," I said.

"You're without mercy."

"I just like to tease you is all. You make it so easy." I heard his low, sexy chuckle.

"So is this a friendly call, or do you need something?"

"Ummm...both?"

"Shoot. What can I do ya for?"

"Is it legal to bury someone in a backyard?"

"Why does that question worry me coming from you?"

"It shouldn't."

"I assume you're referring to the gravestones in the back of Claire's shed."

29

"Yup. Cole filled you in, huh?"

"He did. Despite being odd, it's not illegal. To have a private cemetery the land has to be surveyed, and the plat needs to be recorded with a deed. Unless it isn't permitted in this county, that is. And to be honest, I'm not sure if it is or not. If that were the case, if it's not, then the local zoning officials would have to be consulted. Of course," he added, "that's assuming it was a legal burial."

"How do I find out if that happened?"

"I have to ask why you care so much about this? Knowing you as I do, I'm pretty sure it's not because you're worried someone did something illegal."

"I want to make sure that little boy had a proper burial."

"He doesn't know it if he didn't."

"Levi!"

"I didn't mean that in a bad way, Melanie. I'm just saying that at this point, while it would have been wrong, there's nothing you can do to change it. Other than get yourself into trouble trying, that is."

"Well?"

"You could check with the town clerk for zoning laws for that area and ask if those names are recorded. I believe anyone can decide where he or she wants to be buried and it has to be carried out. As long as it's in writing, signature witnessed. Before their death."

"Obviously before." I heard him chuckle. "Don't you think it would be odd for there to be a document for the whole family? I mean, who would ever believe that the whole family would die on the same day?"

"Good point."

"And that's why I want to find out what happened. It seems odd."

"You know, when I first met you, which wasn't very long ago, you didn't so much like your life not to be orderly and perfect. What happened?"

"You saying my life isn't perfect, Detective?"

"I'm asking what happened to the woman who wanted things to stay status quo; life streamlined and—normal."

"Now I'm not normal? Are there any other insults you want to toss my way?"

"You know what I mean."

"I discovered I'm good at this investigation stuff. If I want crimes solved around here, I'm the one to solve them. I've proven that." I grinned at the punch I'd delivered, could just see his face about right now.

"I can't even dispute that statement."

"See?" I chuckled. "Think of it as me helping you with your job. So how can I get a copy of the death certificate?"

"You can't unless you have a tangible interest."

"Meaning?"

"You have to be related to the parties or somehow tied to them by blood or legally. Of which you're neither. Unless you can come up with a way around it, which I've no doubt you could." I heard him groan.

"Hmmm...could you get it for me?"

"No."

"Just no? Not even 'I'll think about it, Melanie'?"

"Just no."

"Why not?"

"Because it would be an abuse of my authority."

"So stuffy," I scoffed. He was anything but stuffy. In fact, he was incredibly hot. And if my track record in men didn't stink to high heaven I'd be much more likely to return his interest instead of running like a scared little girl.

"Call it what you want. And don't go getting any ideas of trying to get around the law and doing it yourself."

"Me?" I feigned hurt feelings. "I wouldn't even think about it."

"Somehow I don't believe you. You free for dinner tonight?"

"Guess I owe you for the information, huh?"

"Tell me you're teasing again."

I paused. Was I? Or was I trying to justify dinner with him? I didn't know. Apparently, I paused too long, because his voice changed when he spoke.

"Listen, you don't owe me anything."

"Yes."

"No, you don't."

"Yes, I'll have dinner with you."

"I'll pick you up at seven. Your house."

"Or I could meet you—"

"Or I could pick you up at seven."

"Or you could pick me up at seven," I agreed, giddiness washing over me.

When I pulled in the parking lot, and next to Claire's new, orange Honda CRV, I felt a surge of adrenaline pump through my veins. I trotted toward the door, as much as I could trot in heels, and hoped beyond hope that my schedule was light today.

Typically, I look at my lineup for the following working day before I leave the night before. I like to make sure I have all the supplies I need and get them all lined up. Claire makes fun of me for it, but that way I know if I need a little extra dose of serenity before I come in.

Some of my clients are more difficult than others, but as of a year ago, there was one less. Because she'd died while in my chair, on my watch, I'd expected to feel guilty for not being devastated. But Velma Johnson seemed to make it her mission to be a pain in everyone's rear end, and it ended up biting hers.

However, that was history I couldn't waste energy on right now. I had a curiosity to solve. The old saying "curiosity killed the cat" nagged at me; I just hoped in this scenario, I wasn't the cat.

5

Claire and I have been partners in ownership of A Cut Above for over six years, and it just keeps getting better.

Despite Claire's car being in the parking lot, the door was locked, and she wasn't in the salon.

I let myself in, making sure to re-lock the door behind me. Since the break-in that happened a year ago this past summer, we never left the door unlocked during non-business hours, especially when only one of us was inside. I went straight back to the office, dropped my shoulder bag on the desk, then went back into the salon area and behind the reception desk which housed the appointment book.

Wouldn't you know I had back-to-back appointments all morning, with a brief break in the action at two o'clock. That meant I had forty-five minutes to do a little Internet searching on my new focus or to do book work. I knew which I should do. But again, my curiosity won out. I had to stop that or I was going to get into trouble. This was uncharted territory for me—where curiosity won over logic—yet I kept finding myself here at an increasingly alarming rate.

Sitting at my desk, I crossed one leg over the other, laced my fingers and stretched them in front of me, my knuckles cracking. I logged onto the computer. I waited as it ground to life, the screen lighting up before me. I opened the search engine and began typing. *Zachary Swanson, Birch Haven.*

I waited while the search accumulated the results. Nothing. How could that be? Not even an obituary? I tried another variation. *Zach Swanson*, Minnesota. One item appeared. I read the short blurb beneath his name. *Zach Swanson, age six, died tragically in a fire at the family's cabin. The fire was ruled accidental as a result of faulty wiring.*

I sat back in my chair and took a deep breath, slowly exhaling, sadness tugging at my heart. Poor little guy. There was no other information, and I had more questions. I sat back up on the edge of my chair, fingers to the keyboard and typed in *Henry Swanson, Birch Haven, Minnesota.*

I waited for the search to complete, then took a sharp inhale, stinging my lungs. There were at least two-pages of hits. I scrolled down, speed reading the headlines until I reached one that looked like it was for this particular case in question. I clicked on it and waited for it to load, seconds feeling more like hours.

I leaned forward in anticipation as the screen settled on the article. *Henry Swanson, loving husband to Norma, and father of Zach Swanson, died tragically in a fire at the family's cabin on West Long Lake. The fire was ruled accidental as a result of faulty wiring.*

The exact wording as little Zachary's obituary. Hmmm...odd. Or was it? I'd never read obituaries for people who died together to know for sure.

I thrummed my fingers on the desk. The same person obviously wrote them both, but who? I sat back again briefly before sitting back up to read more. *The family was together at death and remains together in death at an undisclosed location for privacy purposes.*

For whose privacy? Didn't the little boy deserve to have visitors? My heart broke yet again for the little guy. I could smell a cover up, and it reeked. I scrolled through some of the other hits my search yielded, clicking on one at random. Domestic disturbance, Henry Swanson listed as the suspect.

My sense of curiosity ticked up a notch. I clicked on another. The same thing. I clicked on another, and yet the same. My breathing picked up pace, my heartbeat following suit. Had this man done something to his family? And if he had, would he have killed himself in the process? Call me naïve, but I would have expected that in a much larger city, but Birch Haven? Especially back in 1992. Maybe Henry's death was accidental and he just never made it out as planned.

My fingers on the keyboard again, I typed in *Norma Swanson, Birch Haven*, Minnesota, and waited for the results to pop up, my mind spinning cartwheels.

Finally, the search ended, yielding one page of hits. Again, I scrolled carefully and slowly until I found the one that matched what I was looking for.

Norma Swanson, loving wife to Henry, and mother of Zach Swanson, died tragically in a fire at the family's cabin on West Long Lake. The fire was ruled accidental as a result of faulty wiring.

I stopped for a moment and looked up before continuing, knowing what would come next. "The family was together at death and remains together in death at an undisclosed location for privacy purposes," I mumbled.

Again, the same, word for word. And, again, I wondered for whose privacy. I clicked on another article at random. Norma was the victim of domestic assaults that listed Henry as the suspect. The guy was a real winner.

I shook my head slowly, contempt for this man roiling in my gut. I clicked on another. The same thing. Another, the same. I read the headline. My breath caught in my throat, and I heard myself gasp. It was dated October 30, 1992. The day before the fire! I searched for the Birch Haven Press edition for that week, but it was suspiciously unavailable. How could that be?

I knew where I would be going after work. I had too many questions that needed answering. If I couldn't get them here, I would get them at the library. I was sure they still had microfilm—unless I was seriously out of touch with the advances in technology.

Claire rounded the corner, and I stifled a scream, my hand flying to my chest.

"Guilty of something?" she asked with a giggle.

"You won't believe what I just found." My eyes met hers over the top of the computer screen.

Her smiled faded. She dropped her bag on one of the chairs opposite the desk, sitting down in the other.

"Probably not, but I bet you're going to tell me anyway."

"Only if you want to know." I stared at her, my eyes pleading with her to be as invested in this as I was. She stayed silent. "I'd think you'd be more interested in knowing the story behind the gravestones in the back of your shed."

"Seriously? That's what you're working on? Melanie, I think you should let it be."

"You want them on your property without knowing why or how they got there?"

"No!" she squealed. "It freaks me out, and I'm not sure I'll ever be able to get a decent night's sleep. But it seems like it would be worse, like bad karma or something, to mess with that stuff." She visibly shivered.

"What stuff?"

"You know," she whispered, eyes wide, "the dead."

"There you go whispering again. Trust me, Claire. If the dead can hear you, it doesn't matter if you're whispering or screaming. They'll hear you no matter what."

"That's just creepy." She shivered again, wrapped her arms around her middle.

"I don't think it's creepy; it just feels wrong somehow. Something is not on the up and up." I turned the monitor toward her. "Look at all these hits that came up when I entered Norma's name. And there were at least twice that many when I entered Henry's name."

"I don't want to look at it, Melanie." She reached and pushed the monitor back toward me.

"It feels like we're snooping into someone else's life."

"I'm sure they won't mind." I began clicking away again, stopping on another. "If they do, there's nothing they can do about it anyway." I scanned another hit. I held up a finger. "Listen to this," I told her as I stared at the article. " 'Norma Swanson was arrested at her home today when officers were called out to a report of a child wandering outside without a coat or shoes. Police responded to the scene and found Ms. Swanson asleep on the sofa. The three-year-old child was taken to the hospital. The child remains in the custody of social services.' " I looked up at Claire, tears rimming my lower eyelids. "That's so sad."

"Why do you want to put yourself through this?"

"You, of all people, I would think should understand. You, who can't stand to see an injured rodent."

"This is different, and you know it."

"Burying your head in the sand pretending not to see it won't make it go away. This little boy deserves to have someone look into this and do right by him." I watched her as she processed what I said, something she typically didn't do. Claire was one to act off the cuff; not think too deeply about things. "Look, now that I've found what I have, I can't in good conscious just let it go. Can you? Really?"

She slumped back in her chair and let out a long sigh. "No. But doggone you, Melanie Hogan!"

"I know. You love me. You don't have to say it." I smiled sheepishly at her from over the computer monitor.

"I need to shake off the bad feelings you just gave me. I'm gonna put up the canopy on the bistro table outside. It's supposed to be nice today. Then I'm running down to the grocery store. Want anything?" The grocery store is on the opposite end of the little strip mall our salon is in.

I looked up and saw her looking down at me, waiting for my response.

"Oh, sorry. I was just looking at something else here." I placed my finger lightly on the computer screen, pointing to the article that now had my attention. "The fire investigation came under scrutiny for the way it was handled." I read on further as I heard Claire sit back down. "It doesn't give me a whole lot of information though," I said, more to myself than to Claire. I looked back up at her. "I'm going to hit the library after work today. Wanna come along?"

"Does this feel wrong to you at all? On any level?" I could tell she was struggling, her conscious seeming to waffle all over the place. "Don't you feel like you're butting into someone else's business?"

"I don't feel bad about it, if that's what you're asking. In fact, on the contrary. I feel like it's the right thing to do. For little Zachary." I knew I got her there. And every time I thought about it, it got me too. My inability to have children has always been my greatest sorrow. But it's also made me more passionate about other children. Like Zachary. I knew that unless I found out what happened, I would never rest.

"Ok fine. I'll go with you." She shook her head slowly in defeat, stood back up, reached into her bag and pulled out her wallet. "Want anything or not?"

"Thought you'd never ask. Whatever you're having."

"You don't know what I'm having."

"I know. But we like most of the same things." I glanced back up at her and frowned. "Wait. You're not getting mushrooms, are you? Because then I'd have to insist on whatever you're *not* having."

"If you ever tried them you'd like them."

I stuck out my tongue in disgust. "They're a fungus. And fungus is not meant to be ingested." And there was that Claire giggle I loved so much.

I grinned to myself as she walked out, calling over her shoulder, "Here comes your first appointment."

I put my computer to sleep, pushed my chair away from the desk, stretched my arms above my head, then went out to welcome, and introduce myself to, Michael, a co-worker of Levi and Cole's, and my first client of the day.

6

The day dragged on, and just when I thought it would never end, my last client of the day came in. Connie and Babs had already finished up and left. Rubie had just finished her last haircut, and Claire was blow-drying the color client she just finished. It had been a busy day at A Cut Above, with our new nail tech even putting in a full day—a rare occasion. Anyone who had that position either didn't stay very long before they left for something else or they didn't want to work very many hours. If we had a nail tech willing to put in the hours, she, or he, could have quite the business.

I had a feeling Babs just might be that person. She was miles apart in personality than the previous ladies had been. And she just...well, she just fit. I was beginning to think that position was jinxed until now. But I knew one thing for sure, despite looking like things might turn around with Babs on deck, you wouldn't catch me sitting at that station after the past year and a half.

At six o'clock my client was walking out the door, and my cell phone rang. I looked at the caller ID. "Oh shoot!"

"What?" Claire asked, startled.

"I totally forgot I told Levi I would have dinner with him tonight."

"You forgot?" she shrieked. "Go! We can go to the library tomorrow night. But I am curious, how did you forget?"

"Maybe I could reschedule with Levi for tomorrow night." My phone continued to ring.

"No, you will not," Claire scolded. "Pick up before it goes to voicemail."

I hesitated briefly while I tried to figure out what to do. My phone stopped ringing. "Oops," I said, surprised that I was truly disappointed. I punched the quick dial number to call him back, and he answered on the first ring.

After I had hung up, I turned to look at Claire who was standing still as could be, scowling.

"See you tomorrow night?" she asked, repeating what I'd just said into the phone.

"Eavesdropping isn't nice."

"You're in the same room as me. Guess I could have plugged my ears if you didn't want me to hear. Or you could have gone into the other room. Since you didn't, I assumed it was an open conversation."

"I have nothing to hide."

"Did you seriously choose to go to the library over going on a date with a hot man? And not just a hot man, but a hot man that seriously has the hots for you?"

"Stop scolding me."

"Well?"

"Well what?" The grin I'd been trying hard to suppress broke through. "He had to postpone because he was just called out to a crime scene."

"You are such a brat letting me think you canceled."

"You're just too quick to assume the worst about me."

"Not true."

"Says you."

"And you know it's the truth."

"Yeah," I grinned at her as I grabbed the broom from against the wall and began to sweep the pile of hair on the floor beneath my chair while Claire threw a load of towels in the washing machine.

"Why do you fight your feelings for him? Cole says he can't figure it out either. He says every woman at the department would give their right arm to have Levi notice them. What gives?"

"You'd have to ask him. How would I know why he doesn't notice them?"

"Melanie!"

A towel landed on my head, and I howled as I whipped it off, throwing it back at her. "Gross! That's a dirty one!"

"Quit being so impossible and answer my question."

"You know my choice in men leaves a lot to be desired."

"It has," she agreed.

"See?"

"What does that have to do with Levi?"

"I like him. Not just a little bit, but a lot. So what's wrong with him?" I looked at Claire in time to see utter confusion splayed across her face. "If I like him there has to be something wrong with him. That has happened to be the case with nearly everyone I've dated. And married," I added referring to my less-than-faithful ex-husband. "How do I know Levi doesn't have a secret life? That he's not married and playing me for a fool. That he's—"

"Stop it. You're super dramatic, and that's not like you at all. Besides, you know good and well he doesn't."

"Do I? Because I thought I knew Cain, too. And I thought I knew William. And then there was—"

"Point taken," she said, stopping me before I could continue down my list of miserable choices. "But you're wrong about Levi."

"I could hope," I muttered. "But hope doesn't a good man make."

"You're wrong," she insisted. "And you know it."

"Probably."

"And for the record, you didn't know William. Not really. It was one of your rare moments of impulsivity."

"See? There's a benefit to being slow in making decisions. To thinking things through. And how do I know going out with Levi isn't impulsive?"

"Other than the fact you used your one impulsive move for this decade? Your first meeting with him goes back over a year, Cole knows him well, and—oh," she said with a sigh and went back to emptying the lint trap in the dryer, "why am I even bothering. You're stubborn as a mule."

I cocked my head to the side, giving her words some thought. "Huh," I finally said. "Let's clean up and get going."

Rubie came out from the ladies room. "Where are we going?"

"To the library. Wanna go?"

"Are you kidding me?" She looked at me like I'd just told her we were going to the dentist, asking her if she'd like to come along for a good shot of Novocain. "No, thank you."

"Your loss."

"What are you going to the library for?"

"Melanie's trying to get information on the people that are buried in my backyard shed."

"Have you heard of the Internet?"

"Yes, I have, smart aleck. But there's a specific issue of the newspaper I can't find on there, and it happens to be the issue from the day after the fire that claimed the Swanson family. I'm going to see if it's on microfilm."

"Microfilm?" Now she looked at me as though I'd just told her I was going on a dinosaur hunt. "Is that even still a thing?"

"They don't put things on microfilm anymore, but I'm sure what was converted to microfilm remains. I can't imagine they'd just purge it all into oblivion."

"Well," she said as she picked up her jacket, "you two have a jolly old time with that. I'm going to see what kind of fun I can find. The kind of fun that doesn't have to be quiet. Like in a library."

She came around the desk and gave me a quick hug and peck on the cheek, leaving me with the scent of Loves Baby Soft, a fragrance I didn't even know was still manufactured until I'd met Rubie. She crossed the floor and did the same with Claire.

"Ciao, ladies," she said. And she bounced out the door. Literally bounced. I've never known anyone with more pep in her step than our Rubie. Not even Claire.

"Is she Italian?" Claire asked after the door closed behind Rubie.

I couldn't help but laugh at my sweet friend. "No, she's not Italian, Claire. She's Swedish."

"Oh," Claire was still watching the door as if pondering why Rubie would have spoken in Italian if she was Swedish.

I slowly shook my head and chuckled. "Come on. Let's go. Or it's sayonara to you." I walked toward the door and looked over my shoulder at Claire. "And no, I'm not Japanese. Just in case you were wondering."

The library was quieter than I ever remembered a library being. Of course, the last time I'd been in a library had been in college when I thought I wanted to be a journalist. How I ended up going from that to cosmetology is beyond even me.

Anyhow, given the fact that was more than twenty years ago, I guess it was possible I'd simply forgotten what it was like inside of the ultimate house of books. The familiar smell of all those books made me feel nostalgic as I remembered the security I used to feel among the shelves and shelves of books that could transport me anywhere I wanted to go. Whenever I wanted to forget about Violet, it was the library that made that happen the fastest. Except for my grandmother's kitchen, that is.

I inhaled deeply, the smell of paper and books, that unique grassy mustiness, the smell of imagination and ideas, filling my nostrils and lungs. Instant peace. Why didn't I come here more often?

Just for grins, I slid a book from the shelf and opened it, a puff of dust disappearing into the air. My fingers lingered on the smoothness of the pages. I slipped the book back into place, a dust bunny escaping. Apparently no one had checked this book out any time recently.

I was lost in the moment as I looked around me at the artificial trees strategically placed, the massive skylight overhead in an otherwise windowless room, and rows of desks with small lamps begging to be used. Ahhh, I was in heaven.

"Melanie?"

Claire's voice jerked me back to the present. "Let me have my moment," I said, irritated to be plucked from my reverie. Until I remembered why we were there. Momentum flooded back.

Feeling like a bloodhound, I led us quickly to the microfilm area but found myself at a loss as to how to operate the new machines. For being an ancient method of looking up information, the technology that made it possible sure had advanced.

Once I finally figured it out, Claire sat to my right, looking on as I searched the database for anything that would shed some light on the dark mystery of Zachary Swanson.

I looked around for the librarian and saw her studying the computer monitor behind the desk. She looked every bit the part of the librarian I remembered from elementary school. Her hair was swept up in a severe knot at the nape of her neck, her narrow reading glasses perched on the end of her nose, attached to a tarnished silver chain that hung around her neck. She had a gray cardigan sweater draped over her shoulders. I wondered if she had on hose and the flat librarian shoes I'd remembered the librarian from grade school wearing. I fought the urge to peek, afraid she would have me arrested for being a creeper.

"I'll be right back," I told Claire as I got up and walked over to the librarian. If they even still called them that these days. Secretaries were now called administrative assistants and housewives were now domestic engineers. Perhaps librarians were no longer called librarians.

"Ma'am?" I loudly whispered when I reached her.

"I may be old honey, but I'm not deaf," she said quietly. "I can hear a normal whisper."

I felt my cheeks warm with embarrassment. "Sorry."

"No need," she said. Even her smile was prim. "How can I help you?"

"I was wondering if you could help me find an old newspaper from November of 1992."

"Of course. From what day and which paper?"

"The *Birch Haven Herald*. Or the *Minneapolis Tribune*. Either would do."

"What's the exact date you're looking for?"

"The November first issue."

She came out from behind the desk and walked back to the drawers that housed the microfilm. I followed her, studying her nude hose and black flats. She began rifling through the contents of the chosen drawer and pulled out a white paper sleeve, sliding out the contents.

"I assume you have an article, in particular, you're looking for?"

"Yes. The one about the Swanson family."

"Oh!" She turned and looked at me over the top of her glasses still perched on the end of her nose. "Why didn't you say so? Whatever you can't find here my assistant, Bert, can help fill you in."

My heart skipped a few beats. "Why's that? Did he know the family?"

"Know the family," she shook her head as if remembering the sad, tragic event, "he was the family. Henry's family, anyway. Follow me." She turned and strode quietly, reminding me of a cat, to the back corner office. "Bert?" The man's head lifted from what he was looking at so intently on his desk.

"Yup?"

"This here is—" she turned to look at me.

"Melanie Hogan."

She turned back to Bert. "This here is Melanie Hogan. She is looking for information on the Swanson fire from 1992."

"What about it?" he practically growled.

"Ms.—what is your name?" I asked the woman who stood beside me.

"Mrs. Allen."

"Mrs. Allen told me you're related to the Swansons?"

"Sure was. Henry anyway. Why do you want to know?" His voice was gruff and loud in the quiet surrounding us.

"Can I ask how you're related to him?"

"Tell me what business it is of yours first."

"My best friend," I paused and pointed toward Claire who was now standing a couple of feet in back of me, "just moved into what I'm assuming was their home."

"Henry was my brother." He looked from me to Claire, then back to me again as if trying to

50

decide if what I said was true. "Why would you assume it was their home?"

Was this some test? Or could it be he truly didn't know? Claire and I exchanged a look, her eyebrows raised.

"Because their headstones are in my backyard shed," Claire said, her statement sounding like a question.

Bert removed his glasses, took a deep breath then cleared his throat. "Yup. That'd be the house all right." He looked at Claire with suspicion. "You wanting them moved? Is that what this is about? Because I'm pretty sure you can't do that. Though can't say as I'd blame you."

"No offense, Bert. But nothing was mentioned in the disclosure about people being buried on the property. I'm pretty sure there are consequences for not disclosing that," I said.

"The people rented it before you moved in didn't seem to mind. In fact, don't think they even knew."

"Had they known, they may have wanted something done about it. Or probably wouldn't have rented it to begin with. Who owned the house?" I asked, changing my focus to Claire. "I never did see the closing documents."

Claire gave me a look and said to Bert, "I'm not asking that they are moved. I just want to know the story is all. Or Melanie does, anyway."

He looked at me with what appeared to be a sharp accusation. "Why would you care if it's not your house?"

"What happened to Zachary?"

"He died in the fire. That's no secret." He sat on the edge of his chair and rested his arms on the desk, toying with his glasses. Emotion tugged at the corners of his lips. It was so brief I wondered if I'd seen it at all.

"How did they come to be buried on the property instead of a cemetery?"

"My brother wanted to be sure and keep his family together where they lived."

"Even in death?"

"I know what you're thinking, Ms. Hogan."

"No, you probably don't. Because I'm not even sure what I'm thinking."

"My brother had his problems, but that wife of his wasn't blameless either."

"And Zachary? Did they take out their—their—shall we say *issues*, on Zachary?"

"What parent doesn't spank their child?"

My heart sank a bit, threatening to fall if my rib cage wasn't there to hold it up. "Did they ever do more than just spank him?" I asked, my voice little more than a whisper.

"My brother loved that boy."

"Some parents have odd ways to express their love." Violet instantly came to mind.

"He may have gotten a little rough with Zach a time or two. But Zach always knew how much he was loved. And Norma—well, Norma was a piece of work. She did whatever she could to push my brother's buttons."

Apparently, jerkism ran in the family, because this man took the prize. He wasn't about to let his brother have any consequences for his actions. Apparently, it was all Norma's fault.

"Can you tell me about the arrest the night before the fire?"

"How'd you find out about that?"

"The Internet is a wealth of information."

52

"For snoopers," he scoffed. "Norma threatened to leave him. He said over his dead body was she gonna leave. She said that could be arranged. He put her in her place, and she called the cops. What would of you done?"

"Where was Zachary when all this happened?" I asked, ignoring his question.

"In bed I s'pose."

"Yeah, I suppose," I said.

"Now, look here, Ms. Hogan. Don't go gettin' all high and mighty. You don't know what my brother had to live with with that woman."

"No, you're right, Bert. I don't." I looked at him, my stomach sour with contempt. "Thank you. I found out all I need to know."

I turned on my heel and left, nearly running into Claire who'd been so quiet I'd forgotten she was still there. "Come on Claire," I said. "I'm suddenly feeling the desperate need for fresh air."

My mind had traveled miles away to a little boy who'd been failed by his parents. Hot tears stung the backs of my eyelids. I dropped my library card, which I'd still been clutching. As I bent down to pick it up, another library customer beat me to it. I reached for it as he held it out to me. "Thank you," I said as I looked at him and forced a smile.

"My pleasure."

As I reached the door, I turned to Claire. "Who was that guy?"

"I don't know. Why?"

"I think I've seen him before."

7

By the time I was halfway home I was in full-on depression mode. My typically cynical mind was even more so, if that were possible, and I was coming up with all kinds of things I'd like to do to the people responsible for the misery in little Zachary's short life. I had to find a way to let it go. At least the part that was eating at me. It was like a flesh-eating disease that was leaving me raw and wounded all over.

I knew what I'd do. Call my grandmother. She was the perfect antidote to stop the disease. She was the perfect antidote to everything.

I followed Claire, slowed as she turned in her drive, then proceeded to mine, my headlights illuminating all the leaves that had fallen just since that morning. They continued swirling down from the nearly naked branches, landing in soft piles of the leaves that had fallen before them. It's a lot of work raking them, but there was nothing better than the smell of burning leaves on a cold evening.

For a brief moment, as I was transported by memories of standing around a burning leaf pile, the thoughts that had been dogging me all but disappeared. But only for a moment. My heart was heavy again when they reappeared seconds later.

I parked my car in the garage and made my way to the house, the high yard light illuminating the way. The sky was black as could be tonight, the stars hidden behind clouds I couldn't see. The moon wasn't even visible.

I shuddered as the chill of the night seeped through my jacket, my step picking up the pace until I reached the bottom of the concrete steps that led to my front door. I took them two at a time, fumbled while unlocking my door, and re-locked it quickly behind me. I'd become a little more vigilant of my surroundings since the summer before last when I had a menacing visitor here, permanently changing my life.

My phone rang before I had a chance to set my things down. I looked at the number before answering, and my spirits lifted.

"Hi, Nana."

"Hi, dear. I just wanted to check to be sure you're home safe."

"Aw, and here I thought you were calling because you missed me." I smiled to myself, slipped out of my jacket one arm at a time and hung it neatly on the back of a chair.

"That too."

I could almost see her smiling as she always does, her long, silver hair in its single braid, cornflower blue eyes twinkling. "You're a swell liar."

"If I was lying, which I'm not. How was your day, dear?"

"Busy. I didn't even have time to get into any trouble." I slipped out of my usual black high-heeled boots and set them on the mat by the door.

"Saved me from getting any more gray hair, did you?"

I chuckled. "You have the most gorgeous silver hair of anyone I know. And with my clientele, I know lots of them."

"I just happen to have a very good stylist, don't cha know."

"Nana? Do you remember a family by the last name of Swanson? They died in a house fire in '92."

"Why, yes, I do remember that story."

"Did you know them?"

"Not well. I knew *of* them. It made quite the news around here."

"Hm."

"Why do you ask?"

"No reason."

"That's not true, and you know it."

"I'll come by day after tomorrow. I'd rather talk to you about it in person."

"What did you go getting yourself into?"

"Nana, I'm insulted," I teased, thinking of some way to divert her attention to something else. "I have a date tomorrow night."

"It's about time. Is it with that fine detective?"

My heart did a little dance. "Yup. Do you approve?" I turned out the lights and began climbing the stairs to my loft bedroom.

"You know I do. And I want to hear all about it when you come over next time."

"Of course. Even if I didn't want to tell you, you'd find a way to drag it out of me." I heard her laugh.

"Get some sleep, dear. I love you."

"I love you too, Nana."

I tossed my phone on the bed, slipped out of my clothes and into a pair my flannel PJ's and sock slippers. I sprawled across my bed and lay looking up at the blackness of the sky through my skylight, my eyelids heavy.

When I opened my eyes, I felt a moment of panic when the sun was streaming through the skylight that had only a moment ago been pitch black. Or so it seemed. Not only couldn't I remember falling asleep, but I also woke up in the exact position I last remembered. I hadn't moved a single time all night. How was that possible? I must have been wiped out!

My panic subsided, and I lay back again and took a long, slow breath, stretching from the tips of my fingers to the tips of my toes. I remembered my upcoming dinner with Levi, surprised to find myself as calm about it as I was. Being in his company wasn't only fun, it was comfortable and entertaining. A good mixture for one who has lived life for far too long in the safe zone.

The rest of the morning, thoughts of Levi and our upcoming dinner invaded my usual morning routine. It never ceased to amaze me that rather than feeling anxiety about it, I was looking forward to it. That in and of itself should have caused me grave concern given my usual demeanor of finding something to worry about in any given situation. After numerous failed attempts to keep my mind on the task at hand, my prayer and meditation, followed by reading the newspaper, I gave up, heading to the salon earlier than usual.

Claire waltzed into the office at eight thirty, just as I finished putting together the last of the product order. I waited until she flung her bag on the chair and started folding a load of towels from the day before.

"You know," I told her, "I don't think I've ever folded a towel since we've been in business."

"I can leave it for you if you'd like. But then we may be taking towels straight from the dryer to use."

"I'm not complaining. It was my backhanded way of saying thank you. Hey, you know that guy from the library last night? The one that picked up my library card and I thought I remembered him?"

She took an armload of towels, plunked them in one big heap on top of the dryer and began folding. "Yeah?"

"I remember where I know him from."

"Are you going to tell me or make me guess?"

"He was my first appointment yesterday. A new client."

"Did it seem like he remembered you?"

I sat back in the desk chair; the comfortable squeak sounded as expected. I rocked back and clasped my hands behind my head. "I don't know. Guess I had other things on my mind."

"So what do you make of that whole thing anyway?"

The bell jingled above the door in the salon, followed by Rubie's sunshiny, sing-song voice.

"Happy Thursday, ladies!" She appeared around the corner, fresh-faced, blew me a kiss and then Claire. "Why so serious? Who died?"

"No one died. We're just talking about last night," Claire answered, folding another towel.

"What could have possibly happened last night? You were at the library. Nothing happens at the library."

"We met the brother of Henry Swanson," I said.

"Who?" Her face scrunched in confusion.

"The dead guy buried in the back of the shed in Claire's backyard."

"Oh, that Henry Swanson." She looked at me and winked. "What'd his brother say?"

"Not enough, enough, and too much," I said. Claire and I exchanged a look.

"Okay, I may not be the brightest bulb on the tree, but I'm not stupid. And that made absolutely no sense whatsoever."

I told her about our conversation with Bert, Claire filling in where I'd forgotten anything. When we finished, Rubie's eyes were moist. I thought she might start crying. Oh, jeez! There was no time for that. She yanked a tissue out of the container on my desk and dabbed her eyes.

"That poor, poor boy," she said. "And nice job. I'm going to start off the day looking like a raccoon from my mascara running." She sniffed and tossed her tissue into the garbage can. "So now what? You guys going to continue your search for info after work? I wanna go. Who knew the library could be so interesting?"

"Can't tonight. I'm going to dinner with Levi." I tried to suppress my grin but couldn't.

"It's about time the two of you go on an actual date. I thought the plane was going to run out of fuel as it circled."

Claire and I both laughed out loud. "Did you think of that one all on your own?" I asked.

"Naw. Heard it on an episode of *Castle*." She blew a big, pink bubble. "Well, the next time you guys go somewhere, library included, count me in. I'm relieved you're not going tonight, though. If you were to spend a Thursday evening at the library, making it two nights in a row, I'd have to label the two of you big geeks."

"We invited you last night, but you rejected us."

"Well, I didn't know you were going to actually do something."

"Claire, did she just call us boring? I'm pretty sure she just called us boring." I shook my head in disbelief.

"Yup, I heard it," Claire agreed.

"I just meant that—"

"Stop while you're ahead, Rubie." I held up my hand, palm facing toward her and she smacked it down. "You slap like a girl." It felt good to laugh after the heaviness of the last couple of days. "Hey, guys, Sunday is supposed to be an Indian summer kind of day. Want to go biking on the Paul Bunyan trail?"

"I'm in!" Claire yelled, causing me to jump.

"Biking?" Rubie raised an eyebrow. "That sounds like a whole lot of work."

"Come on. Stop being such a princess and try it."

"I'll have you know there's nothing wrong with being a princess."

"There is if it stops you from having fun."

60

"I have fun!" she argued. "Just not the library kind of fun you apparently have."

"Shopping does not count as fun," I said.

"Says who? Shopping is fun. And it's darn good exercise, I'll have you know."

I made a face and pretended to stick my finger down my throat. Claire laughed. "You're losing this one, Rubie. Neither Mel nor I like to shop much."

"You guys don't know what you're missing. Okay, fine, I'll try biking if one of you has a bike I can use."

"You can use Syd's. It's pink and everything," I said. "It even has the little pink and silver pompom thingys on the handlebars." One look at Rubie and I knew she didn't think it was as funny as I did. "Okay, jeez! I'm kidding. I have an extra big-girl bike you can use. I even have an extra helmet."

"Yeah, it's Mel's because she doesn't use hers." Claire's tone and her look were equally as accusatory.

"Sunday it is," I said and stood as the bell announced the arrival of the first customer. "Hey, Claire?" I called as she turned the corner into the salon, peeking her head back into the office.

"Yeah?"

"Nothing." I looked down.

She shrugged. "Okay." And she was gone again.

I needed more time to figure out how to broach a subject I was dying to bring up with her. I had a feeling she wasn't going to like it one bit, but it was something I had to do. I wouldn't ask that she join me if she didn't want to, I just needed her to allow me access to do it.

8

evi called at three to confirm our plans and let me know he'd be picking me up at my house at seven. My stomach did a little flutter. This was different than what I'd experienced with any others I'd dated over the years, including my one-of-a-kind ex-husband. In part because I enjoyed Levi's company so much. He treated me better than I'd been treated by any other man, and yet it all felt so comfortable and uncomplicated. Usually, when something felt too good to be true, it's because it was. I didn't dare say as much to Claire, because she'd accuse me, as usual, of being too cynical. Which, to her credit, I knew I was. But she could call it what she would, I believed it to be nothing other than realistic in this case.

The next time I was able to come up for air and look at the clock, I was shocked to realize it was six o'clock. Connie and Babs had left for the day. Claire canceled her last appointment and was slipping into her jacket to head home, claiming an oncoming migraine.

"You're just afraid I'm going to ask you to go to the library again," I teased her.

"Not true. I know how to say no," she said.

"*That* is what isn't true. You haven't figured that out yet, and you know it."

My question from earlier balanced on the tip of my tongue, threatening to tumble out, but I couldn't ask it. Not only didn't I want to feel like I was taking advantage of her not being able to say no, but I also didn't want to ask in front of anyone else. Not even Rubie. In fact, if Jack were here I probably wouldn't even ask in front of him. Jack is the third part of our trio, the trio that is becoming a quartet with Rubie. Almost. I still protect the bond that Jack, Claire and I shared.

Half an hour later, Rubie was right behind me out the door, already late for her date. I zipped home to change clothes before Levi got there to pick me up.

I jogged from my garage to the house, dropped my bag and keys on the kitchen table as I ran past it, and took the stairs two at a time up to the loft. I rifled through my closet and found a clean pair of jeans, the knees fashionably shredded, a white cashmere sweater, and my usual black high-heeled boots. I swept my hair up in a loose up-do, letting wispy strands curl loosely around my face and on my neck. I slipped in a slightly larger set of hoop earrings, my simple Celtic cross necklace on its silver chain that hung just above my rib cage. I'd just applied a pearl-tinted lip gloss when my doorbell rang. I took one last look in the mirror and headed downstairs.

I opened the door and stood motionless for a moment. Or should I say breathless?

"You clean up good, Detective Wescott," I finally managed to utter. I smiled and stepped aside for him to come in.

"Are we back to being formal with the whole 'detective' thing?" He extended a bouquet of white Gerber daisies, one green rose in the center, and a bottle of Martinelli's Apple-Cranberry sparkling cider. Daisies were my absolute favorites.

"Ah," I smiled and sniffed the flowers. "A man who has done his homework."

"Well, I am a detective."

"Indeed you are. And a good one at that. Although you'd be much better if you'd get me the death certificate I asked for."

"I have boundaries, ma'am."

My jaw dropped open. "Ma'am? That's taking a mighty big risk." By now I think every officer in the police department knew better than to call me ma'am.

"I'll dispose of the 'ma'am' if you will shed the 'detective.' Deal?" He held out his hand, a slow grin spreading on that gorgeous face of his.

"Let me think about it," I teased him. I filled a vase with water, loosely arranged the daisies, and set the bottle beside it on the counter. "I'm curious—I've never seen a green rose before and with my grandmother's green thumb, I've seen a lot."

"Green supposedly represents hope and optimism."

"How did you know that?"

"I thought we already established that I'm a detective."

"I don't buy it. That you knew what it represents."

"The florist told me. I just liked it because it matches your eyes."

I laughed. "That's more like it. Ready to go?"

"I am." He opened the door for me then waited for me to close and lock it before he went to my car door and opened it for me. I slid onto the beige leather seat of his Toyota Camry, the interior of the car toasty warm and smelling of spice. I might start drooling if I wasn't careful.

Levi folded his six-foot-two frame into the driver's seat. My heart beat a little faster as I felt his presence so close in the small interior of the car. I looked at him out of the corner of my eye for a moment and took in his black leather blazer jacket and his jeans, his shaved head covered with a beanie. So entirely different from what I'd chosen in the past, yet so completely...me. I suppressed a satisfied grin.

"What?"

I startled, not realizing he'd been paying attention to me. "What do mean, *what*?" I feigned ignorance.

"I dressed for the occasion, in case you're wondering."

"I wasn't wondering that at all. I just didn't pin you like the Camry kinda guy. I expected you to show up on a Harley."

"It's at home in the garage. It's unseasonably warm, but I didn't know if you'd be up for it."

"Aha!" I grinned. "So you do have one."

He looked at me as if I'd stated the obvious. "Of course." Then he smiled that delicious smile of his.

"Where we going?"

"Any suggestions?"

"Nope. It's all on you."

"I'm good with that as long as it's not a test."

"A test for what?" I asked.

"Whether I choose the right place or not."

I did my best shocked look. "Would I do that?"

He chuckled. "Yes, you would."

"Well, Detective, it's not a test."

"Well, then, ma'am, prepare to be surprised."

I smiled, buckled my seatbelt, and prepared to be surprised as suggested.

The conversation was light and easy for the first twenty minutes until I realized we'd gone into town and then out the other end.

"Where we going?" I looked around me at the landscape passing by in the darkness, then at him.

"I told you it's a surprise."

"Patience isn't my strong suit."

"You're all of forty years young. Not too old to learn."

"Forty-one."

He smiled and reached over and took my hand in his; his large, warm, rough hand dwarfing mine. My heart didn't only skip a beat, I think it stopped entirely for a moment. I felt butterflies in my stomach. Darn it! Despite this not falling within my comfort zone, I was enjoying it far too much. What in the world was happening to me? It was like I was evolving into an entirely different person over the course of the past year and a half.

"What are you thinking?"

His deep, soft voice startled me.

"I'm not ready to bear all my secrets," I murmured, giving him a small smile.

"Some would be okay."

"Careful what you wish for."

"How about starting with telling me about why you call your mom by her first name? Back when I asked, you said it was a story for another time. This is another time."

"Wow, you have a good memory for a man."

"I'm a—"

"Detective, I know." I laughed softly. I paused for a moment trying to figure out where to start, finally deciding that the short to-the-point version would be the best. I stared out the front windshield in front of me, focusing on the headlights illuminating the road in front of us. "Violet left me with my grandparents when I was four years old. She went to Hollywood to become a movie star." I felt him glance over at me. "She said she was going to come back for me when she'd made her claim to fame. By the time I was seven I knew that was never going to happen."

"But you still hoped."

"I still hoped." I felt a tug at my heart even now as I said it. His hand tightened around mine. "By the time I was ten, twelve, somewhere in there, I started to be afraid that she actually would come back for me. Life with my grandparents became my home, and I didn't want to leave. My grandmother was—is—the most amazing woman in the entire universe." I leaned my head back against the headrest and smiled as I thought of her. "She has an unshakable faith, she's kind, smart, hardworking, and she devoted her whole life to granddad and me."

"What about your father?"

"Never knew him." He squeezed my hand gently.

"Were you close to your granddad?"

"I was. He used to let me hang out in the garage with him while he worked on old cars. That's how we bonded." I smiled at the memory of my granddad, feeling for a moment like I was back in that garage with him, grease smeared on my face and hands. "He died when I was twenty-three. Heart attack."

"I'm sorry."

His deep voice was so tender it brought the threat of tears to my eyes, but I willed them away. "I had a good life with my grandparents. But Violet—well, Violet lost the right to be called anything other than her name."

"I could think of a lot of things I'd like to call her other than Violet," he said under his breath.

"Like felon?" I said, my all-too-frequent sarcasm raising its ugly head. Last spring Violet found herself in a vat of hot water. Levi is the advisory witness for the prosecution in her trial. "Any news on her by the way? Or on her trial?"

"Sounds like they may be reaching a plea deal."

"A plea deal?"

"They're going to offer her a lesser charge. If she accepts that, then the original charge will be dismissed."

"Is that good?"

"For Violet, it means less mandatory time in prison. For you, it would mean not having to testify." He looked over at me.

I let my head lay against the headrest again and processed the news.

"Thoughts?"

"It would be nice if I didn't have to testify," I said, my voice barely more than a whisper.

"And?" His voice was gentle.

"I don't love her. In fact, I don't think I even like the woman. But despite all that, she gave birth to me. It's because of her that I'm sitting here at all. I don't want to be responsible for putting her in prison."

"Melanie," his voice was a sharp change to that of just a moment ago, and it startled me. "You are not responsible for her going to prison. Violet and only Violet is responsible for that." I heard the anger in his voice, something I'd only heard once before, and that was when he was talking to me about her after he'd interrogated her last spring. "She tried to pin a murder on you just to get herself out of the hot seat. While I'm grateful she did at least one thing good, which is to have you, I'll never forgive her for what she's put you through."

"My grandmother says forgiveness is the key to peace. And I've finally been able to forgive Violet."

"Your grandmother is a very wise woman. I'm glad you were able to find it in yourself to forgive Violet. But I'm afraid I may never be able to live up to that."

I looked at him, realizing I'd never felt safer anywhere in my life. This time I squeezed his hand. "It's okay," I said quietly. "It took me a very long time."

Inside the car, it was completely silent except for the whisper of the heater blowing. Not only did the warmth feel good, but it also enhanced the smell of the spice cologne he had on.

In fact, his cologne was a perfect match to the square liquid air freshener gizmo that was stuck on the steering column. It wasn't overpowering, but perfect and pleasing. Levi's hand remained on mine. He laced his fingers through mine. I was sure I was precisely where I was supposed to be, and it felt amazing.

The next fifteen minutes were spent talking about Claire and Cole, more about my grandmother, and about A Cut Above.

"It sounds like you and Claire complement each other well. Not a lot a friends can pull off being business partners and stay such good friends."

"We get each other. And that's a huge reason why it works so well. I know I get on her nerves sometimes with my stubbornness and sarcasm, and she has gotten on mine a time or two. But that's to be expected. And not only do we get over it fast, we know *how* to get over it."

"Kind of like a good marriage."

I snorted before I could stop myself. "Yeah, I wouldn't know anything about that." I concentrated hard out the front window.

I felt his gaze shift over to me for a moment. "You just haven't found the right one yet."

"Don't expect I ever will. I'm totally okay with that."

"Are you really?"

"Yes, I am. Really."

"Don't be so quick to write it off." His hand squeezed mine again, and that flutter took residence in my gut again. "Cold?" he asked, looking at me. "I can turn the heater up if you want."

70

"No, it's perfect." And perfect it was. Right here, right now. My skeptical Doubting Thomas self was resting peacefully, and I was enjoying it immensely. "So tell me why you shave your head."

"My nephew was going through Chemo and lost his hair. I did it to support him and just ended up keeping it shaved. Like the no-hassle."

Impressive and totally sweet. "And the pierced ear?"

"I worked undercover for a few years. Couldn't catch the bad guys if I didn't try fit in by looking the part."

"Hm."

He looked over at me, clearly amused. "Hm? Are you complaining about my bald head and pierced ear?"

"On the contrary." I turned my head so he wouldn't see the smile I couldn't stop. "Tattoos?"

"One. So where are you on your investigation into the family buried in Claire's backyard?"

My pulse quickened at the mention of my new mission. "I'm going to find some way to get a copy of the little guy's death certificate."

"You know I would help you if I could."

"I know." I looked at him and smiled. "I wish you could, but I can do it on my own. I'm a big girl."

"Not so much. Five two and a hundred pounds soaking wet doesn't qualify as a big girl," he teased.

"A hundred and fifteen dry." He laughed a sexy sound that made my heart pitter-patter.

"What are you hoping to find on the death certificate?"

71

"I want to see the official cause of death. I also want to check hospital records to see if he was ever admitted for suspicious injuries."

"I think you'll run into one brick wall after another with that. I don't think you'll have a problem with HIPPA since he's deceased, but Federal Law still protects privacy rights after death. You'll need to find out if there's a named personal representative. There are privacy rules in effect, but I believe—don't quote me on this—that healthcare facilities can release medical records to the named representative or someone deemed a personal representative by state law. Of which you are neither, so that doesn't help you."

"Well, aren't you encouraging?"

"I aim to please. Seriously, though, it's not easy, if even possible, to get someone else's medical records."

"I have to try at least." I watched him as he looked in the rearview mirror, turned on his signal, did a brief check over his left shoulder, and changed lanes, changing back again when he was sufficiently ahead of the car he passed.

"Jeez, do yourself a favor and never be in a car with me when I'm driving."

"I've seen the results too many times to count of people who don't look before changing lanes."

"Touché," I mumbled.

"What?"

"Nothing." I was in no hurry whatsoever to tell him I was in an accident several years before, resulting in a hospital stay and chronic migraines, because I failed to do that very thing.

"Tell you what, I'll see what I can find out at work from the old-timers who worked the case and who were around back then."

My heart leaped with joy. "You'd do that?"

He looked at me and smiled, his diamond stud glinting in the headlight of an oncoming car. My heart melted into a puddle of goo. "I'd do anything for you as long as it won't get me fired." He looked out the windshield again before he added, "And then I could probably even be convinced."

I couldn't suppress the grin that made me feel like I'd just won a marathon. "Hm. Mr. Wescott, I can't decide if that's flattering or foolish. We'll go with flattering."

"Happy to see I've graduated from Detective to Mister."

"What would you say if I told you I want to dig up Zachary's grave?" My hand flew to my mouth. "And I totally cannot believe I just said that out loud." My cheeks were burning.

"I can't either." He glanced at me, his face grim.

"It's just that—" I took a deep breath. "Well, it's just that I want to be sure there's even someone buried there."

"Don't do it," he said, his voice stern.

"I wouldn't be able to anyway without Claire's consent. I can't think of a single time she's said no to someone who needs something, but—"

"But this isn't you needing something. It's a foolish idea."

"Huh," I grumbled, "the man just called me foolish." But I couldn't disagree with him. I knew he was right. "Are we almost there?"

"You sound like my son."

73

"It seems like we've been driving a long time."

"Are you complaining?"

"I'm not, but my stomach will be soon. I'm starving."

"Perfect." He smiled and flipped on his signal and turned into the dirt parking lot of a small picturesque red barn-looking structure. The parking lot was packed, and the sign read simply The Red Barn.

"You're taking me to a hoe-down?"

"I'm taking you to a place that serves the best burgers, hot dogs, and fresh sweet potato fries you'll ever find this side of heaven."

My night just got a whole lot better, if that was even possible. My stomach grumbled its impatience at the mouth-watering cuisine Levi had just mentioned. He came around and opened my door, held out his hand to help me out of the car, put his arm loosely around my waist, his hand resting easily on my hip, and steered me toward the barn door.

He held the door open for me, and I turned to look at him before moving forward. Well, well, well. Just behind Levi, coming through the door, was a familiar face. I put my hand on Levi's arm and pulled him down, standing on my tip-toes at the same time, and whispered, "Don't look now, but Henry's brother, Bert, just walked in behind us. I may have to strike up a casual conversation."

"And our pleasant dinner just turned into business for my date."

"It will still be pleasant," I assured him with a smile. "I'll be on my best behavior."

"That's what I was afraid of and hoping for at the same time." He shook his head slowly and turned to give the woman at the desk our name. But not before I saw him smile.

9

I pulled into the parking lot at the same time as my first appointment. Guilt tried forcing its slippery little claws into my happy place that I'd been in since early last evening. I braced myself for the barrage of questions from Claire and Rubie.

"Well, look what the cat dragged in, Claire," Rubie said the minute I pulled open the door.

"I was wondering which of you would be the first to criticize."

"Oh, no criticizing going on here, sister," Rubie said, grinning from ear to ear. "There'll be a whole lot of something going on, though, if you don't fill us in."

I held the door for my client. "Hi, Edith." I smiled at her and gave her a hug. "Thanks for coming to my rescue."

"What ya need rescuin' from?" she asked, her northern accent heavy. She flung her coat on a chair and waddled her way over to my stylist chair.

"From us wanting to know what happened on her date last night," Rubie answered.

Edith turned and looked at me and raised an eyebrow. "Well, then, I'm 'fraid I won't be rescuin' ya. I want details, too, don't cha know."

"Ladies, I'm not one to kiss and tell."

"Ah-ha!" Claire squealed with delight. "So you kissed!"

"Is nothing sacred with you guys?"

"Nope," Rubie said with far too much delight.

"And we're not afraid to admit it, young'un," Edith added.

"Thanks. You're no help at all, Edith." I watched as she squeezed herself into my stylist chair and wiggled to make herself comfortable before I fastened the cape around her neck. "Color and cut, right?"

"Don't change the subject," Rubie said. "Friends don't keep secrets."

"Not spewing my personal life all over the walls of this place isn't the same as keeping secrets."

"Forget the walls and spew your personal life all over us. We want to live vicariously through you," she said.

"Live your own life," I quipped, unable to stop from giggling. I felt like a high school girl who had gone on her very first date. If first dates still happened in high school these days. The way things were progressing, I wouldn't be surprised if it had changed to junior high. All I knew for sure was that I felt like I was still on an emotional high. And for someone who was more often than not emotionally stable and flat, this was all new territory for me.

I managed to ward off further interrogation while I applied the color to Edith's hair, and yet again when I had a walk-in wanting a hair cut while Edith's color processed.

Business was non-stop for all of us, including Connie and Babs. The room was filled with people talking and laughing, the calming white noise of blow dryers and stationary hair dryers, a fine mist lingered in the air from the aerosol sprays, and the smells of color and artificial nails were thick.

I was able to skate from further curiosity until late afternoon when a white van pulled up, and a woman came in with a floral delivery, the most amazing bouquet of daisies of every possible color, even a black one that looked soft as velvet.

"Melanie Hogan?" she called.

My stomach fluttered. It was a feeling that was getting enjoyably familiar.

"Yes?"

"Delivery."

She set the flowers on the counter, the little rectangular envelope that held the card sticking out from the top, teasing me with the mystery of its message.

I opened the register and took out some cash for a tip.

"Looks like someone has an admirer," she said as she turned and left.

"And it looks like someone has something to tell me," Claire said as she looked on over my shoulder.

I pulled the card from the little forked holder and held it to my chest. "Privacy please," I teased her. I looked at her as she rolled her eyes.

"Gimme a break! I remember back in the day when you used to tell me things."

I laughed. "Oh puh-lease. You're so dramatic."

"Hey, I know!" Rubie said. "How about girl's night out after work? Grizzley's Tap House? I'm buying."

"Are you trying to buy information from me, Rubie?"

"Whatever works. Entertainment is never free anymore. The good stuff costs a lot of money."

I laughed at her, impressed that she was still so fresh and bubbly at the end of a busy day. "I promised my grandmother I'd go over there later so I only have time for a quick soda."

"Tell you what. We'll drink while you talk. That will make it faster. Deal?"

We locked the door at six o'clock, put the money in the drop box we'd just had installed a year ago, did the fastest cleanup ever, and each headed to our respective cars.

I turned the ignition, my engine smoothly coming to life when I noticed a piece of paper tucked under my windshield wiper blade. A corner flapped in the breeze. At first, I thought it was nothing more than a gum wrapper that had blown there and gotten stuck, but on closer inspection, I saw it was haphazardly folded in fourths, and I could make out faint writing on it.

I looked around me. Claire and Rubie had already left. This end of the parking lot was vacant except for my car and another several parking spaces down. Thank goodness it wasn't completely dark yet. I opened my door, reached my left arm through the opening between the door and the windshield, pulled the note from under the wiper blade and sat back in my car, closing and locking the door. I looked around once again and still saw no one. I unfolded the slip of paper and looked at the unfamiliar writing.

Malice: The desire to inflict injury, harm, or suffering on another because of a hostile impulse or from deep-seated meanness. Malice will be yours if you don't mind your own business. Leave the boy alone.

A chill cut through me to the bone. I shivered, a sinking feeling in the pit of my stomach. And yet, I felt oddly validated. I was right. Someone had something to hide, and they would obviously do anything they had to so their secret was left unrevealed. With one last scan of the parking lot and the salon, I left to meet the girls at Grizzley's.

I pulled my car into the parking space next to Rubie's car, Claire's car directly across from mine. There was safety in numbers, and if someone was watching and saw me here, they would likely leave me alone if I were with a group.

I waited a moment until I saw a couple walking toward my car. Right after they passed my door, I quickly got out, locking the door from my key fob, and fell into step behind them. Close enough to be safe, far enough behind so they didn't think I was a stalker. Once we reached the door, I walked past them and to our booth, the same one we more often than not managed to snag. Claire with a club soda with lime on the table in front of her, and Rubie with a Tom Collins, the cherry already gone.

"What took you so long?" Claire asked.

I pulled the slip of paper out of my jacket pocket and handed it to her. I watched as she read it and her already huge brown eyes grew even bigger, her mouth a perfectly formed "O." Rubie snatched it from Claire's fingers. She read it and gasped.

"When did you get this?" Rubie asked.

"And from who?" Claire asked.

I looked at Rubie then across the table at Claire, feeling strangely calm at the moment. "It was on my windshield when I left the salon. I don't know who, but obviously it's from someone who has something to hide."

"Who all knows you're checking into this whole thing?" Rubie asked.

"You guys, Levi, Cole, the librarian, and Bert, the old man from the library. Henry's brother."

"Henry's brother," they both said in unison, nodding their heads.

I shook my head. "I don't think so. If his nephew had been harmed in some way, why wouldn't he want justice for him?"

"You heard how he acted when you were talking to him," Claire said. "He's not the nicest guy and is defensive of his brother."

"But at the expense of his nephew, a six-year-old child?" Rubie asked.

"I saw him at The Red Barn last night," I said.

"Oh my gosh! He's following you," Claire gasped.

"I don't know for certain. He appeared pretty familiar with the place, so maybe it's just his hangout."

"Did he say anything to you?"

"No. I don't think he saw me. It was pretty packed."

"I can't believe you didn't talk to him and get him all wound up," Claire said.

I shrugged. "Thought about it. But then I decided I could probably learn more by watching

81

him when he wasn't aware I was. That turned out to be a bust. I learned nothing."

"Did you tell Levi about it?"

"Of course, I did. He was there, goofball."

"I meant about the note," Claire said.

"Oh. No. I just got it. And then I came straight here. I didn't want to call him until I've had time to process it."

"You have to tell him."

"As a police officer or as a—friend?"

"Tell us what happened last night," Rubie said, the note all but forgotten.

Looking at Claire's knit brow, her usual smile absent, I could tell she was still hung up on the note. So was I.

"I had an okay time," I said, being as evasive as I could, knowing it was driving Rubie nuts. When she slapped my arm with her red cloth napkin, I knew I succeeded. "Okay, fine. I had the best time I think I've ever had on a date. Ever," I repeated.

"Is he a good kisser?"

"I don't know," I lied, knowing it was killing Rubie. "The jury's still out. I have to give it another shot or two to be sure." A girl can't kiss and tell all.

That finally shook Claire out of her troubled state. At least a little bit. "Well, be sure to let us know when the verdict is in. And be sure it doesn't take too long. The verdict, not the kiss," she said with a distracted smile.

"He was every bit the gentleman," I said. My stomach fluttered as I thought about him and the kiss that just barely grazed my lips. Soft but teasing.

"Well, that's disappointing," Rubie said, pouting. "Gentlemen don't win in the end. Doesn't he know that?"

"Well, then, my friend," I said, shaking my head, "it sounds like you're the one who should be reporting to us."

"Or not," Claire said with a grimace. "Some things are better left unsaid."

"Hey!" Rubie said. "I take offense to that."

"Get over it," I laughed. "I don't want to hear about your escapades, either."

I pulled from my pocket the envelope that had been attached to the flowers and handed it to Claire across the table. She pulled the card from the envelope and read it.

"That is seriously the sweetest thing ever," she crooned.

"Well, don't keep me out," Rubie complained, reaching for the card. Seconds later, she, too, was crooning. "What a romantic."

"Yeah," I agreed. "I would never have guessed that."

"Why?" Claire asked. "I tried to tell you he was an amazing guy."

"Yeah, but you heard that from Cole. Of course, he would have said that. They're best friends."

I looked at the card and read it again. *This bouquet reminds me of you—full of color, beauty, strength, and so enchanting. Had a wonderful time last night. L*

"You know," Rubie said, "I wouldn't have guessed him to be the romantic type either. The shaved head, pierced ear, the tat he tries to hide—"

"Wait! You've seen his tat?" I asked, leaning back to look at her. I wasn't sure why, exactly, I was shocked. Rubie notices everything about a good-looking man.

"Yeah. It's on his bicep."

"When did you see it?"

"How could you not have seen it?" she asked in awe. "Those biceps are incredible!"

"I did see it. I was just trying to figure out when you would have," I said, struggling to remember when he had on short sleeves or his jacket off, for that matter. I hadn't seen it until he showed me last night.

"What's it a tattoo of?" Claire asked.

"It's a footprint and a boy's name," I answered.

"His son's name?" she asked.

"Either that or he's Jack's type," Rubie said. "Since we know it's not the latter, it's probably safe to assume it's his son."

I laughed. "You should be helping us solve this case with Zachary," I said, sadness tugging at my heart at the thought of the little boy. "Yes, it's his son's name," I told Claire. "Good thing it's not a woman's name. It's so tacky when guys do that, and it would be a deal breaker."

"Oh, dear God!" Rubie squealed. "That is just too sweet. And perfect! What's the catch? That's what I want to know." She grabbed my arm, her fingers curling around my bicep, and she leaned into me.

"I'm still trying to find it."

"Stop looking, Mel." Claire shook her head. "You're looking for a reason for it not to work."

"No, I'm only looking for why it can't work."

"Same difference."

"There's no such thing."

Rubie rolled her eyes. "You two stop your bickering."

"She started it," I said, sounding all of five. "I'm just realistic."

"No, you're self-sabotaging," Claire said.

"I agree with Claire."

"What do you know," I said, pulling away from Rubie and glaring at her playfully.

"A lot more than you apparently think I do."

"Traitor." I nudged her with my shoulder and smiled.

The waitress was back at our table with another round before we'd finished our first.

"Compliments of the table over there under the neon Miller sign." She nodded her head toward the responsible table as she set our drinks down, another club soda for Claire, a Tom Collins for Rubie, and a red wine for me this time instead of the diet Pepsi I had the first round.

"You might be driving, Claire." I twisted around to look at the table, my heart beating in my chest and my cheeks flushing as I saw Levi, Cole to his left, and another man on his right. The man on his right had a crew cut, square jaw, and looked military. *Hmmm...he looks familiar*.

"Well, well," Claire said, beaming like a little girl who just saw Santa Clause. "I didn't know Cole was planning on coming here."

"Did you tell him we were? He probably followed you to make sure you were where you said you were going to be."

"He so would not do that." She gave me a scowl.

"I know he wouldn't. But it was fun to see your reaction." I grinned.

"You're a brat, and you know it," she said, her brows furrowed. "Besides I didn't tell him anything. We didn't even know we were coming here until right before we left the salon."

"True. Lighten up, kid. I was teasing anyway."

"I wanna know who the cute guy is that's with them," Rubie said, looking star struck.

"It seems like I should know him, but have absolutely no idea," I said as I looked over at the same time Levi looked at me. We shared a secret smile. Or I thought it was secret.

"As Syd would say," Claire chuckled, "get a room."

I looked at Claire in horror. "Syd better not be saying that."

"She heard it on TV and thought it was hysterical."

"Why would she be watching that kind of stuff on TV, first of all. Second, what does she think it means that she thought it was funny?" To say I was concerned was an understatement.

"Now it's you that needs to lighten up. Stop going off on tangents," she said, chuckling.

"Wanna ask them to join us?" Rubie said, still stuck on the third party at their table. I was pretty sure she had no idea Claire and I had just had an entire conversation about something serious. Anytime Sydney is involved in a conversation, it's serious. I love that girl.

"It looks like you do," I told Rubie and laughed. "You and Shane have been split up for all of a month, and you've been hitting the circuit like there's no tomorrow."

"I was ready the day I saw that jerk with his secretary. The only problem is, everyone I've met so far has been a loser. Fifteen minutes into the date and I'm making some excuse about why I have to leave."

"Was Shane seeing his secretary before you even split up?" Claire asked.

"Yup. Like I said, he's a jerk." She rolled her eyes again and shook her head.

"Want me to go ask them?" Claire asked, looking toward Cole's table.

"Knock yourself out. I can't stay much longer though. I promised Nana I'd see her for a little bit tonight. It's already seven-fifteen."

The words weren't even out of my mouth, and Claire was halfway to their table. Rubie was dragging a chair to the end of our booth, while I sat and watched the transitions happening.

Levi stood and began to cross the floor to our table then stopped at another table on his way where two women were sitting, one putting her hand on his arm. He said something, one of the women tipped her head back and laughed, and the other touched his arm as well and said something back to him. Lip reading wasn't my strong suit, and I was irritated with myself that I even felt the need to try. *Insecure much, Melanie?*

I looked away and watched Cole as he slid in the booth by Claire, planting a gentle kiss on her cheek as he put his arm around her shoulders. Rubie extended her hand toward the man that followed Cole to the table.

"Hi! I'm Rubie," she said, her blue eyes sparkling with energy.

The man took her hand in his own, his attention lingering on her pink glossed lips. "Hello, Rubie. I'm Michael. It's a pleasure to meet you."

Ahhh...Michael. That's twice now I hadn't recognized him. Maybe I'm not as good as I thought I was at this detective stuff.

I shook my head slightly and looked at Levi as he slid into the booth beside me. Rubie slid back in next to him, strategically placing herself on the end and close to Michael. Levi's hand reached for mine under the table. He laced his fingers through mine. I looked at him, and he winked. His eyes were so soft I felt like I could fall ten stories into the depths of them and land safely.

"Hope we're not crashing your party," he whispered, his breath warm against my ear. Shivers rippled to the tips of my toes.

"We just stopped to have a quick one before I go to my grandmother's."

"Tell him about the note on your car, Mel."

"Claire, I—"

"What note?" he asked, looking at me and waiting for me to answer.

"It's nothing," I lied.

"Yes, sir, it is," Rubie argued.

"Someone left a note on Melanie's car tonight at the salon," Claire filled in. "Show it to him, Mel."

"Yes, show it to him, Mel," Levi said, giving my hand a light squeeze before he let go and held his hand out for the note.

I reached into my pocket and withdrew the note, putting it in his waiting hand. He unfolded it, read it, folded it back up and put in his pocket.

"Wait, you're keeping it?" I said, my jaw dropping.

"It would appear so. I want to do some checking."

"Let me see it," Cole said, holding out his hand across the table. Levi gave it to him. Cole read it and raised his eyebrows. "This is something to be taken seriously, Melanie."

"I realize that. But I'm not going to—"

"You're not going to what?" Levi interrupted me.

"I need to know what happened to Zachary Swanson."

"At the risk of your safety?"

"I'll be fine."

"Can we at least talk about this?" His voice was low and quiet.

"We can, but not right now. I need to get to my grandmother's."

"I'll walk you out."

Rubie slid out of the booth, followed by Levi, then me. She sat back down, staying on the end to be closer to Michael.

"Bye, Levi," called one of the women at the table he'd stopped at earlier. She said something to the woman sitting with her, and they both laughed.

"Fan club?" I said, embarrassed that my sarcasm sounded like raw insecurity.

"Jealous?" He put an arm around my waist, and half smiled, amused.

"Nope."

He tipped his head back and struck his hand on his chest. "You just put an arrow right through my heart."

I chuckled. "You'll live."

"She's my cousin."

"And the other one?"

"Her best friend and someone she has been trying to set me up with for years."

"And?"

"Not interested."

"Can't say the same for her."

His arm tightened around my waist as he pulled me closer to him. "I'm only interested in you and keeping you safe. Will you let me do that?"

"I'm used to being independent."

"I can live with you being independent. In fact, it's darned attractive." We'd reached my car, and he pulled me close to him. He looked down at me, cupping his hand under my chin. "But don't be so independent that it puts you in danger, taking you away before we even get started."

He leaned down until his face was mere inches from mine. I was sure my heart was going to leap right out of my chest and take off at a dead run. He hovered there for a moment, my pulse racing until I didn't think I could stand it another minute before passing out. His lips brushed mine so lightly I wondered if I'd imagined it.

"Drive safe." He straightened up and opened my car door. My knees were so weak I nearly fell into the driver's seat.

"Thanks for walking me out."

"My pleasure." He smiled a lazy smile, the tiny diamond stud in his earlobe sparkling in the lighting that illuminated the parking lot. "I'll see what I can find out from your visitor earlier and call you when I find out something."

"You won't call unless you find something?"

He smiled at me, his eyes twinkling, and he closed my car door. As I pulled out of the parking lot, I looked in my rearview mirror and saw that he was still standing there, watching my car.

10

I pulled into my grandmother's yard at eight sharp. I inched the front of my car as close to the garage door as I could, my car bathed in the porch light. I told myself I wasn't being paranoid, just cautious and vigilant. I let myself in before my grandmother had a chance to open the door.

"Hello, dear." She smiled and wrapped me in a tight hug. For such a small woman, she had a heck of a grasp on her. "I'm glad you were able to make it." She pulled back and held me at arm's length, her eyes narrowed. "Have you been drinking and driving? I smell wine."

"Says the woman with the nose of a bloodhound. Levi bought me a glass of wine, and I drank maybe a quarter of it." I gave her a quick peck on the cheek. "Don't worry so much." She took my arm and led me to the kitchen counter, pulling an embroidered dishtowel off of the most delicious sight. My stomach grumbled its delight. "Cranberry-Cherry."

"Sit, and I'll cut you a slice."

"Uh-uh. How about you sit and I'll cut us a slice."

"That's my bossy child," she said, her smile broader than ever as she took a seat at the table, her back to the wall.

I cut two pieces of her masterpiece and placed them on white china plates. I fetched two forks, balancing one on each plate, and put one in front of her, the other on the table in front of the chair to her right, closing the curtains before sitting down.

"I love how cozy it is in here in the evenings, Nana." I looked at her as I sat down and felt guilty as I just now noticed for the first time that she was in her flannel robe, her long silver hair loose from its usual single braid. "Were you going to bed?"

"Not this early."

"Are you feeling okay, Nana?"

"Yes, child," she laughed softly. "Stop thinking I'm more fragile than I am."

"You're stronger than anyone I know. I just want to be sure you stay that way." I took a bite of the slice of heaven that only she can make, closed my eyes and moaned my approval. "This is sheer perfection." I opened my eyes to see her eyes radiating glee.

"You're biased."

"I'm smart."

We both savored a couple of bites in silence until she spoke.

"What's with the questions you were asking about the Swanson family? What are you up to?"

I feigned hurt feelings. "Me?"

"Yes, you."

I chuckled. "You know me too well." I played with my fork, pushing around a piece of crust on my plate before placing a cherry on my tongue.

"I'm beginning to wonder what happened to the Melanie Hogan I used to know so well."

I winked at her as I swallowed. "She's evolving into a more well-rounded person." She took another small bite before putting her fork down, waiting for me to continue. "How well did you know them?"

"As I told you before, I didn't know them. Not really. I just knew of them. The man has a brother or two that lives around here somewhere."

"I met his brother Bert yesterday. He's a piece a work."

"Where did you meet him?"

"He works at the library. I went in there to see if I could find something on microfilm. I asked the librarian for help and when she found out what I was looking for, she introduced me to him."

"I suppose I did hear something about him working there," she mused. "Was he able to give you what you needed?"

"Enough to know that Henry was a hotheaded wife beater and that anger issues seem to run in the family."

"Melanie," she said, frowning, "it's not nice to speak ill of the dead."

"I'm not saying anything that's not true. Henry racked up quite a record of domestic abuse and assault. Norma even had a child neglect accusation. It breaks my heart to think of what that little boy had to live with."

"What did Bert say?"

"Among other things, that I didn't understand what his brother had to put up with living with that woman." I took another bite of my pie. "I mean seriously? What a sexist thing to say." I expected her to say something about talking with my mouth full, but she didn't. I finished chewing and swallowed before continuing. "What did you hear about them? The Swansons."

"I would rather not repeat gossip."

"It's not gossip if it's true."

"Since I didn't know them I can't know if it's true or not."

"Nana—" I shook my head slowly and smiled. How could I get frustrated with her for being the better person? "Okay, what did people say that we'll assume isn't true?"

"I suppose it wouldn't hurt to tell you so long as you don't take it as gospel."

I held up two fingers and did a mock salute. "Scout's honor."

"You weren't a Girl Scout—"

"I know. What is it with you guys?" I rolled my eyes. "Claire feels the need to remind me of that, too. I always wanted to be, though, if that counts for anything." I grinned at her. "You were saying?"

"People wondered if the fire was deliberately set and then covered up."

"Was there any speculation as to who might have wanted to hurt them?"

"Sure there was. People are always quick to accuse the spouse. But since both were killed in this case, I don't see how it could have been Henry. They apparently had a tumultuous marriage, and when I was working at the hospital, Norma was a patient there a time or two. In fact, the boy was seen a time or two for taking some falls."

"Do you believe he fell?"

"I didn't have anything to tell me otherwise. And I wasn't the doctor, just the nurse."

"A nurse who knew more than any of those doctors. Were you his nurse, Nana?" I thought about my grandmother tending to and comforting the little guy.

"Just once." She smiled as she remembered. "Some patients you just don't forget. He was one of those."

"What was he like?"

"A very sweet little boy, so quick to hug. But I remember ..."

A shadow clouded her usually sunny disposition. "You remember what?"

"When his mom was in the room he was talkative. But when his dad came around, he was like a different kid. He went into a shell."

"Do you think the bodies are actually buried in the back of that shed in Claire's yard, or do you suspect it's just the gravestones?"

"Hard to say. And I imagine you'll never know."

"Yes, I will. I've been trying to get up the courage to ask Claire if we could dig up one of them. Just Zachary."

"Melanie, don't go—"

"I'm not borrowing trouble, Nana. Maybe he's not even buried there. Maybe, just maybe—"

"Melanie Hogan..." Nana warned.

"I'm just finding justice for this boy, Nana. If it was an accidental death, then there's no harm done. But I'm sure that's not the case, or someone wouldn't be trying to—" Oh shoot! I squeezed my eyes shut as I realized the mistake I'd just made. I opened them and saw Nana's eyes were narrowed.

"Someone wouldn't be trying to what?"

"Nothing."

"You best tell me right now, dear."

"It's nothing to worry about, Nana. Really."

"Let me be the judge of whether I should worry or not. What is someone trying to do?"

I sighed, knowing she wouldn't let it rest until I told her. "Keep me from finding the truth."

"And how exactly are they trying to do that?"

"Threats. Intimidation. You know, the coward's way."

"Turn it over to your gentleman friend. The detective. Or Claire's boyfriend. They're trained for this kind of thing, don't cha know. And you stay far away."

"I told both Levi and Cole about it. In fact, Levi's on it and will call me as soon as he finds something out."

"And you'll leave it alone?" I didn't say anything but rather looked down at my half-empty plate. "Melanie?" she said, her tone stern.

"I need you to trust me, Nana."

"I do, you know that."

"Just not about this."

"I trust you, dear. It's the person who's trying to keep you quiet that I don't trust."

"I promise I'll be careful and keep Levi and Cole in the loop on anything and everything that happens. Deal?"

"If that's the best I can get I guess it'll have to do."

I covered her hand with mine and looked deep into her cornflower blue eyes, noticing the light there dimmed just a smidge. "I promise."

I told her about Violet's possible plea deal as I ran some water in the sink, added a few drops of Dawn, collected the forks and plates, and washed them up. When I told her what Levi said, about how it would impact her sentence, sadness dimmed the light in her eyes a bit more. I sighed from the weight of my heavy heart. I had done nothing but cause her grief tonight.

I sat down and took her hands in mine. "I have to go, Nana. I'm exhausted. Are you going to be okay? I can stay overnight if you want me to."

"You know I'd love nothing more than for you to spend the night, but I'll be fine, dear."

"You don't want me to stay?" I teased, trying to lighten the mood.

"You know I do. But I also know you love your home. Go there. I'll be perfectly fine. It's you I worry about."

"Well, we're quite a pair, aren't we? We worry enough for all the mothers out there." I leaned over and gave her a hug. "Don't get up. I'll let myself out and lock the door behind me."

As soon as I got in my car, I locked the door before I even started the engine. As it hummed to life, I turned the heater on full blast. I couldn't decide if the chill was from the air, exhaustion, or the thrill of Levi invading my headspace again. He had a way of weaving his way into my thoughts every few minutes over the past thirty-six hours. A whole lot longer than that, if I were to be completely honest with myself. But why start now?

I had only gone maybe half a mile when I looked in my rearview mirror and noticed a set of headlights that shone blue light. I'd seen a few cars with those particular lights, but when they were in the car following behind me, they were annoying. I adjusted my mirror to accommodate the nighttime, so the lights were muted and didn't shine in my eyes, blinding me with their glare.

I turned on my radio, Carly Simon keeping me company as I turned through the city streets that eventually led me to the highway.

I turned onto Oak Street and saw the same blue lights make the turn a few yards behind me. My pulse quickened. I continued on Oak until I reached Pine Street and hung a right. By the time I reached the end of the block, the same blue headlights were making the turn onto the street. Not to be outdone, I turned left onto Birch Street.

Lo and behold, moments later I saw the blue headlights appear behind me again. By this time, I knew this was no coincidence even if I did believe in coincidences. My palms began to sweat.

I picked up my phone from the center console and punched in the speed dial number for Claire. It went to voicemail. Knowing her, she had already turned in for the night. I couldn't imagine she'd still be at Grizzley's Tap House. I decided to drive there to see, just in case. The parking lot was only half full of lingering vehicles, Claire and Rubie's cars not among them.

I glanced in my rearview mirror as I pulled out of the parking lot and saw a dark sedan style car sitting on the side of the frontage road that led in and out of Grizzley's. I turned toward the car and passed it trying to get a look in the window, but the tint was too dark to see through during the daylight, much less at night.

I'd just gotten to the end of the frontage road when I saw the blue lights illuminating the darkness in front of the car I'd passed moments before. I looked just as the car did a U-turn and was once again yards behind me.

My pulse picked up yet another notch, and it felt like my heart was thrumming in my throat. The only thing I could think of doing was continue to drive around town. I couldn't lead him on the highway or to my house. I called Levi's number. He answered on the second ring.

"Wescott."

"Levi, it's Melanie." I might be in luck. "Are you at work?" I hardly recognized my voice, a harsh whisper as if the person in the car following me would be able to hear me if I spoke any louder.

"Melanie, what's wrong?" The concern in his voice was unmistakable.

"I'm being followed."

"Where are you?"

"Driving around town. Right now I'm on College Drive. I don't know where to go so I don't lead him toward my house."

"Do not go home, Melanie. I'm at the police department. Either drive here, or I'll meet you where you are. It'd be better to lead him here. Hopefully, I can see the car."

"K. I'm only a few blocks away now."

"I'll be waiting for you outside the front door. Pull right up to the door. Stay on the phone with me, though. Have you been able to get the license plate?"

"No. He's staying far enough behind me that I can't see it. Plus he's got those annoying bright blue lights blinding me when I try to look."

"He? Did you see who it is?"

"No, the windows are tinted dark. I couldn't see."

"Lead the sucker here so I can nab the make and model of the car." His voice was so tight I thought it might snap. "I'll radio one of the officers to where you are."

"I'll be to the police department by then." I looked in the rearview mirror again and wasn't sure if I should be frightened or relieved.

"Melanie? What is it?"

"He's gone." I glanced back again. "His car isn't behind me anymore."

"Come here anyway. Speed if you have to."

A block away from the police department, on the backside of the building, the car appeared in front of me, stopped at the end of the block taunting me. I slowed, then stopped, my heart beating a million beats per minute. I was so close to the police department. Is this as close as I would get?

I looked behind me. What were the chances I could do a quick, sharp U-turn and outsmart him by going back and up another block to get to the department? There were no cars on this side street and no street lights, everything around me black except the interior lights on my dashboard, my headlights and the headlights of the mystery car shining down the street perpendicular to the street I was on.

Rather than turn around, I started backing up slowly. The car turned on my block, now facing me, and inched forward. I began backing up again, slowly, until I saw headlights of another car turn and come up behind me. The car in front of me quickly backed up and zoomed off, his tires squealing. I let out a long breath I hadn't realized I'd been holding. The car behind me honked to get me moving. The driver probably thought I was drunk, crazy, or both, sitting in the middle of the block. But I didn't care. I wanted to blow him or her a kiss for saving my behind, then decided a mere wave might redeem my mental state. Or not. Again, I didn't care right now.

When I pulled up to the police department, Levi was pacing the sidewalk. He strode over and opened my door.

"Why did you hang up the phone? I told you to stay on the line with me."

"I assumed it was okay to hang up once I told you he wasn't behind me anymore. The threat was gone. Or so I thought," I added as he folded me into a hug. I felt so safe and warm there; I hoped it never ended. But as all good things do, it did. Too soon. He pulled back, keeping a gentle grasp on my arms.

"What do you mean 'or so I thought'? What happened after you hung up?"

"He wasn't behind me anymore because he outsmarted me and got in front of me. I took a side street to get here faster, but apparently, he knew what I would do."

"How'd you get away?"

"Another car happened to come by, and the creep took off."

"Did you get his license plate?"

"Again, no. Either he was sideways, or his lights were shining right in my eyes. I couldn't see anything."

He pulled me close to him, holding me tight. "Melanie, this has got to stop." His breath was warm on the top of my head.

"I apparently struck a nerve with this guy. I won't be safe until I find out what he's hiding. Whatever it is, he doesn't want me to know."

"You won't be safe until you stop trying to find out what he doesn't want you to know."

I pulled back and looked up at him. "Levi, I won't be safe as long as he's out there, and neither will other people. This jerk thinks it's okay to intimidate people. Well, it's not. He might be a killer."

"It's not for you to stop him."

"Then who?"

"The police."

"The police didn't know anything about this until I started asking around about the Swanson family."

He sighed and looked up in defeat. "I'm not winning here, am I?"

"It's not about winning or losing. It's about doing the right thing."

"Despite you being in danger because of it?"

I smiled up at him. "Nothing will happen to me because I've got you looking out for me."

He slowly shook his head and looked down at me, cupping my face in his warm, weathered hands. "I'm not with you 24/7, kiddo." Our eyes held for a moment until he dropped his hands and slid them into his coat pocket. "Okay, fine, have it your way. But I'm staying at your house tonight in case this bozo manages to follow you home." I opened my mouth to speak, but he put his hand up and interrupted me. "No objections. I'm not suggesting I stay in your room, so relax. I'll sleep on the couch. But I'm staying. Either that or you stay at my house."

"I wasn't going to object. I was just going to say thank you and that I appreciate it."

His eyebrows raised and his jaw dropped open. When he finally regained his composure, he turned his head slightly sideways, squinted, and continued to watch me. "What's the catch?"

"What'd ya mean?" I asked innocently.

"You don't agree that quickly."

"Detective Wescott, I'm insulted. Are you saying I'm difficult to get along with?"

"You can be, yes."

I laughed. "I may be difficult to get along with, but you're brutally honest."

He chuckled and put his hand on the small of my back, leading me into the lobby of the police department. "I'll be right back. I just need to grab a file."

"You trust me to stay here by myself? You're not afraid I might do something?"

"We have cameras everywhere. Don't try anything."

A mere two minutes later he came back through the door leading to the lobby and waited for me to go in front of him. I started walking to my car and could hear his boots in step behind me.

"My house or yours?" He asked.

"What kind of lady would I be if I went to your house?" I teased.

"A smart one."

"Mine."

I heard him snicker and mutter, "Of course, yours."

"But remember you promised you'll sleep on the couch."

"How could I forget?"

"Can you keep that promise? Cause otherwise, the deal's off." I stayed looking forward so he couldn't see me grinning from ear to ear.

"It won't be easy, but I'll manage."

"See that you do."

I heard him snicker again as he opened my door for me. "I'll follow you."

When I finally turned in for the night, Levi was at the table doing some work. I lay in bed but sleep wouldn't come. I struggled to listen to every sound that drifted up the stairs. I wondered what he was doing, what he was thinking, and even if I would see him at the top of the stairs. Would I be strong enough to say no? I wasn't so sure.

When the lights went out downstairs and all was quiet, I tiptoed to the top of the stairs, cringing when a floorboard squeaked.

"You made me promise, Mel," I heard him say in the darkness. "If you come down here, all bets are off."

I grinned and tiptoed back to bed, not saying a word. Instead, conflicting thoughts tumbled around in my head until I finally fell into a fitful sleep.

11

The next morning I woke to the sweet smell of maple syrup and freshly brewed coffee. My mouth watered. It took a minute to register where I was and who was in my kitchen. And then I was wide awake within a matter of seconds. I hadn't fallen asleep until well into the early morning hours, and when I finally did, it was a deep sleep riddled with vivid dreams.

I looked at the clock on my nightstand, got up and wrapped my big thick white terrycloth robe around me, tying the belt snugly. I went into my bathroom, looked in the mirror at the circles under my eyes. *Great!* I ran a brush through my hair, brushed my teeth, and as quiet as I could, tiptoed downstairs and into the kitchen. I leaned against the wall in the arched doorway that led into the kitchen and watched Levi scanning some papers in a file at the kitchen table, a cup of steaming coffee in one hand. I cleared my throat, catching his attention.

He looked up, his eyes gentle. "Good morning, Sleeping Beauty."

"Morning. How'd you sleep?"

"I think you might have to get a different couch if I stay another night."

"Claire has never mentioned the couch being uncomfortable."

"Claire's not over six feet tall."

"I have a spare room you could have stayed in."

"She tells me after the fact," he muttered and shook his head. "If I recall, the spare room wasn't offered. Just the couch."

I smiled at him. "Sorry." I really was. I hadn't even thought of the spare room. His being in the same house as me overnight had thrown me for a loop. "You won't have to stay another night anyway. I'll be fine."

"Let's wait and see what you get yourself into today before you decide you'll be fine, shall we?"

"I see you made breakfast. You didn't have to, you know."

"I know I didn't. But I was hungry." He smiled and winked at me. "Help yourself."

I hated to admit it, *really* hated to admit it, but it was fun having him here. That scared me to death. Was it Freudian that my feet were cold and I wished I had on slippers? *Don't go getting attached, Melanie. You don't know how to do the relationship thing*

"Thank you, but I can't. I have to get going."

"Doesn't the salon open at nine? It's only six thirty."

"I know. I have to stop off somewhere before I go in." I turned to leave the room and said over my shoulder. "You don't have to leave yet if you don't want to. You can just lock up when you leave."

I reached the top of the stairs when I heard his voice at the bottom. "What just happened?"

I turned to look at him standing at the bottom of the stairs.

"Nothing. Why?"

"Because within a matter of seconds there was a twenty-degree drop in temperature in the kitchen."

"I'm not sure what you're talking about." I shrugged, trying my darndest to look innocent. "I just have to get going, is all."

He looked at me, his eyes making me squirm. "Okay then. I'll be ready to leave when you do."

"You don't have to—"

"Yes, actually, I do. I have to get to work."

"On a Saturday?"

"On a Saturday," he repeated as he disappeared back into the kitchen.

After a steaming hot shower, I donned my usual jeans and a pair of my many high-heeled black boots, a red sweater, and silver hoop earrings. I dried my hair and pulled it back into a loose braid, bangs brushing over my forehead. As I entered the kitchen, Levi stood and reached for his leather coat.

"You look good in red," he said, his voice telling me he was a million miles away.

"Thank you. I don't wear it very often. I save the bright colors for Claire."

"Why's that?"

"Because she looks so good in them. They suit her."

"Don't sell yourself short."

My stomach fluttered. Darn it! I'd allowed things to get way out of control and it had to stop.

"—afternoon?"

My attention snapped back to the present. "I'm sorry?"

He came and stood in front of me, the faint smell of his cologne candy to my senses. He put his finger under my chin and lifted gently, so our eyes met.

"What happened this morning?" His voice was deep but soft.

"Nothing."

"You and I both know that's not true."

I tried to look down, but he kept his finger under my chin.

"I'm just—I—Levi, I don't know if this is such a good idea."

"If what is a good idea?"

"Us."

He exhaled long and slow. He removed his hand and began to gather the papers on the table, placing them in the open file. He closed it, slipped into his coat he'd just a moment ago hung on the chair before coming to stand by me.

"Well, I guess that's something you'll have to figure out for yourself. If you need space, I'll give it to you. Let me know when you figure out whatever it is you need to."

I could hear the sting in his voice.

"Thank you for staying last night. I appreciate it."

"No problem."

He waited while I slipped into my jacket. I grabbed my shoulder bag from the stool beside the door, clutching it tightly as I passed by him, stepping into the brilliant morning sunlight. He pulled the door closed behind me and started to his car.

"I'll check in with you later this afternoon," he called over his shoulder. "If you need something before then, call."

I pulled into the parking lot of Birch Haven Senior Living Community at seven thirty sharp. I scanned the building, almond siding lined with white French windows along the entire front side of the first story. The upper stories had white French doors that opened onto balconies.

Claire found and gave me the name and address for the people who had sold her the house. The same people who'd arranged for the man to show her the property and meet with her to sign the paperwork. Since I couldn't fall asleep last night, I'd researched the facility on my iPhone, finding out that the individual units didn't have kitchens, but rather an industrial kitchen complete with a chef and a dining room on the main floor. I had called to find out what time the residents would be coming down to the main floor for breakfast and planned my visit accordingly.

I milled about the lobby, watching as geriatrics dawdled into the eating area, some with canes and walkers, a few in wheelchairs, and several walking independently. A few were fortunate to have each other still, walking together with steps perfectly in sync from many years of practice.

I wasn't exactly sure who I was looking for, and it wasn't like I could ask the staff what they looked like. They'd likely call security on me, and if I ended up arrested, I'd be talking with Levi a whole lot sooner than either of us anticipated.

As it was, all I had to go on was an old photo I saw in one of the news articles from around the time of the fire. It was likely they'd changed a whole lot in fifteen years, but hopefully there would be some identifiable characteristics. If nothing else, I could base it on one of the couples walking together. That narrowed it down significantly given that was only about a third of the residents. If that.

The dining room area was almost full, and I was just about to give up when I looked down the hall and saw two vaguely familiar people shuffle in my direction. Hope resurfaced. Could they be the ones from the old photograph?

I waited until they were closer before I was certain they were exactly who I had come to see. The woman's hair was now yellowish-gray, but it was the same short shag as in the photo. The man wore the same thick black square eyeglass frames and suspenders holding up his trousers. I looked at my watch. I had exactly twenty minutes to talk with them before I had to get my tail to the salon.

I stood and went to meet them as they were almost to the doorway of the dining room.

"Mr. and Mrs. Oliver?"

They looked at one another, then at me. "Yes?" the man said, none too happy that I was interrupting his mealtime.

"I was wondering if I could talk with you for a moment."

"What about?" he grumbled.

"Hank," the woman scolded lovingly. "Where are your manners?" She looked at me and smiled sweetly. "I'm sorry dear. What did you want to speak with us about?"

"About your neighbor's house on the lake."

Hank's head snapped to look at me, his eyes clearly letting me know he didn't want me there. "What in God's name do you want to talk to us about them for?"

"Did you know them very well?"

"Well enough," he grumbled. "That man was a weirdo!"

I hid my amusement at his description of Henry Swanson.

"Now, Hank," the woman said, "You know good and well they was in a bad way. Money was tight and having that boy—well, it ain't easy when money's tight and you have a family to raise."

"When did you buy the house?"

"Right after the family left."

I tried to hide my surprise. "Why did you buy it?"

"For an investment," Hank grumbled. "What's it to you?"

"Just curious, is all."

"You know what they say about curiosity killing the cat," he said, looking at me over the rims of his glasses then at the dining room. "We have to get moving, young lady. Meals are served at a certain time. We miss it; we don't eat."

"Just one more quick question?" I asked, touching his elbow. He jerked his arm away. "Did you know about the gravestones in the secret room of the shed in the back yard?"

"Secret room?" Henry scoffed. "You been watching too many of those mystery shows. We rented that property since the day we bought it. Can't see that anyone woulda done something like that. Now scoot." He took hold of his wife's arm and turned her toward the dining room.

"Did they stay at the cabin much?" I blurted. "The one where—"

"The one that killed 'em?" Hank asked point blank, turning to look at me, now beyond irritated. "No. From what I heard it was his brother's place. He let 'em use it once in a while."

"His brother's place?"

"That's what I said." He looked down his nose at me as if I were a bug he would have loved to swat out of his way. "Why you being so nosey?"

"His brother Bert?"

"I don't know his name," the woman said, appearing to try to remember what she couldn't.

"It ain't none a her business anyway, Gertie."

"Are you aware of Henry's criminal history?" I asked, knowing I was pushing my luck with Hank. But Gertie didn't seem to mind talking with me. Hopefully, she could give me something useful before Hank shut her up completely and pulled her away. It was darn close to that as it was.

"That poor boy had to see his dad do some terrible, terrible things," Gertie whined, shaking her head slowly. Her eyes took on a distant look and I wondered if I'd lost her.

"People have said they don't believe the fire was an accident. Do you believe it was an accident?"

"Oh, dear," Gertie came back to me. "Why would people think it wasn't? Of course, it was an accident." Tears sprang to her eyes.

"See what ya done?" Hank grumbled. "We moved here to get away from all that stuff and here ya are, bringing it to her. Now scat." He moved his hand as if he were shooing away the bug he saw me as only five minutes ago. I'm sure he would have crushed me if he could.

A staff member heard Hank's raised voice and came over to him, placed one hand on his arm, the other on his back. She gave me a dirty, accusatory look.

"Hank? Are you okay?" she asked.

"I better be going," I said before Hank could answer. "Hank? Gertie? Thank you so much for your time."

I turned and left as Hank grumbled something about busy-body nosey people having no right to poke around in other people's business. I had to wonder how mobile Hank actually was. He wasn't one of the residents with a cane or walker. In fact, he was the steady one of the two, with Gertie holding onto him for balance. Was he still able to drive?

12

Claire and Rubie were already at the salon when I pulled up. Connie and Babs would both be in later. Holding my Caramel High Rise from Caribou Coffee in one hand and my keys in the other, I scanned the parking lot as I walked to the front door. I didn't see either of them through the large windows, so I was surprised to find the door unlocked.

"Hello?" I called as the door closed behind me.

"We're in here," Claire's voice came from the office.

Since I'd been in such a hurry to get out of there the night before, I had forgotten to check my lineup for the day. Again.

I glanced at the open appointment book. Perfect! My first client wouldn't be in until nine thirty. I turned the corner into the office and saw Claire perched on the edge of the desk and Rubie in the chair across from her. They both looked up.

"Why's everyone so serious? And why was the door unlocked when you were both back here?"

"I spaced out locking it again after Rubie got here."

I slipped my keys into my shoulder bag and set it on the floor in the corner. I looked at Claire, then at Rubie. "Anyone wanna fill me in?"

"Sure," Claire said, hesitating a moment too long.

"Spill. What's going on? You're starting to worry me. Is Sydney okay? When is my little bug coming home, anyway?"

"Hopefully not until this craziness stops," Claire said, her eyes huge pools of concern.

"What craziness?"

"The craziness you started when you insisted on digging up stuff you shouldn't have. Quite literally."

"Claire, what are you talking about? Can you honestly tell me you're okay with people buried in your backyard? Without even knowing the story? Furthermore, given what I've found out so far, don't you want to know if the fire was an accident or not? I, for one, want the person held responsible if little Zachary—well, if it was intentional. He deserves someone to out the killer if that's the case."

"I just wish you wouldn't have started your little investigation to begin with. The fire wasn't even in Birch Haven."

"On the outskirts. Pinewood Lake."

"How did you find that out?" She closed her eyes and held up her hand. "Wait! I don't even want to know."

"Nana," I said, ignoring her request of ignorance.

"Oh." Claire's resistance softened. "Is she okay with all this?"

"She knows I can't rest when a child's welfare is concerned."

"It's not exactly a child's welfare when the child is already—well, already gone," Rubie said with a shudder.

"Don't tell me you're against this, too," I said, looking at Rubie.

"I'm not against anything. I'm just for the path of least resistance."

I sighed and shook my head. "I can't let this go, guys. Especially now that someone dangerous is out there threatening me. Now that he or she knows I know something, the danger won't end until I find out who it is. You guys both know that."

"You're right and I know you are," Claire said. I could tell it was killing her to admit it. "It's just that what I found this morning is more than a little disturbing. It's terrifying."

"What'd you find?"

"Someone was on my property last night. I went out to put a little teddy bear on the boy's headstone. There were footprints all over back there and the shed's back door was left open. And what's worse? There was a headstone with your name on it! A real headstone, Melanie!" Tears brimmed her lower eyelids, her eyes glistened. "With the rain last night, it wasn't hard to see the footprints in the frosted grass all over back there."

I took a deep breath and leaned against the door, my legs feeling a bit wobbly. "Someone is obviously telling me they'll go to any measure to shut me up," I mumbled to myself. Once I regained my bearings, I looked up at Claire. "Why didn't you call me?"

"Calling you wasn't top of my list. Getting the heck out of there was. Besides, I was on my way to leave for work and I just assumed you'd be here when I got here. Where were you? You're always here before anyone else."

"I made a stop on my way in."

"Do I dare ask where?"

"Birch Haven Senior Living Community."

"Rose isn't thinking of moving?"

"No!" I answered quickly, putting her fears to rest. "She's nowhere close to needing that place. You told me Hank and Gertie are the couple who owned your house. Well, they're also the couple who used to live in the blue house by yours when the Swansons lived in your house. After the Swansons died, Hank and Gertie bought that house, eventually selling it to you, and have been renting out their own house since moving to Birch Haven Senior Living."

"Why would they rent out such a beautiful house instead of living there?" Claire asked, flabbergasted. "That old blue house they lived in doesn't even compare to mine."

"Right? You know what they say, different strokes for different folks. Anyway, I stopped in to ask them a few questions about what they might remember."

"Did they remember anything?" Rubie asked.

"The man was a grumpy butt but the woman, Gertie, is the sweetest little thing. She seems to think the fire was purely accidental. That might just be innocence on her part though. She did say how sorry she felt for Zachery because he had to see his dad do some terrible things."

Claire's eyes grew wide. "Did she tell you what kind of terrible things?"

"No. And I didn't get a chance to ask. Hank was too busy giving me the third degree."

"Well, do you blame him?" Rubie asked, her blonde curls pulled up in a high ponytail. "Someone comes out of nowhere and starts asking questions about something they'd probably rather forget. He's probably suspicious of you, if anything."

"Suspicious of what? And what makes you think that?"

Rubie looked away from me and stood up. "I don't know. Just a thought."

"There must be something that made you think that."

"There's not. I don't know why I said that. Forget I mentioned it." She bounced up, skirted past me and was out the door.

Forget she mentioned it. Yeah, right. What did she think Hank might be suspicious of?

"Did you call Cole?" I asked.

"Yeah. On my way here. He's going to have some guys go check it out and see what they can find."

"It's trespassing, but not unless we can find out who it was."

"We? How about 'they,' Melanie. Stay out of this one and let them do their job."

"I will."

Claire's jaw dropped open. "Did I hear you right?"

"Yes. I won't interfere with their investigation on your yard. About this," I added. She breathed a sigh of relief. "Claire, we should start riding to work together. It's silly for us to each take our cars when we start and end at the same location. On the days we're working, that is."

"That's a good idea," she said as she stood up and came over to give me a hug, her five-foot-six frame dwarfing my five-foot-two one. "Heck, the way things have been going, I might be taking up residence in your spare room. Cole told me about your follower last night. I can't believe you didn't call me and tell me yourself."

"I tried to. It went to voicemail. So then I called Levi. He was at the station, so I drove there to meet him."

"Cole said Levi stayed the night at your house." She smiled at me like the cat that swallowed the canary.

"Wow! Is nothing sacred? Cole tells you everything, doesn't he? Apparently, I need to have a talk with the detective about keeping his mouth shut. For your information, he slept on the couch."

"Seriously?" Rubie asked, her jaw hanging open. "If I had a man like that staying at my house there's no way I would have let him sleep on the couch."

"What are you doing eavesdropping? And had he known that he would have stayed at your place instead of mine."

"Yeah, right," Claire scoffed, shaking her head. "It's you he's hung up on."

"That alone tells me the man has a serious problem. And I suppose Cole told you that, too, huh? That Levi is 'hung up on me' as you stated. I'm beginning to think the three methods of communication are telephone, telegraph, and tell-a-Cole."

Rubie let out a yelp as she laughed, making me jump.

"What is up with you two this morning? I can already tell this is going to be a weird day." I shook my head and turned to leave the office to get my station set up. Claire began folding towels and Rubie went into the ladies room. "We're still on for biking tomorrow, right?"

"I am," Claire answered, her voice muffled from her head nearly buried in the dryer as she reached for the last few towels.

"If I don't get a better offer," Rubie's voice traveled through the bathroom door.

"She'll be biking with us," Claire said, laughing.

"Hey, Claire," I said, "slumber party at your house tonight?"

"Cole would feel a whole lot better if he knew I wasn't alone. I'm just not so sure it would make him feel better if he was aware that it was you with me."

"And what exactly is that supposed to mean?"

"That you can't protect yourself much less someone else."

I turned to stare at her, insulted. "Excuse me, but I've done an okay job of keeping myself safe."

"Really? Because I haven't seen that lately. You've gotten yourself into a whole lot of unsafe predicaments."

"That I got myself out of, I'll have you know." I started walking away from her. "Besides, there's safety in numbers. Even Cole knows that. That's police work 101." I stopped after a few steps and turned toward her. "Letting them do their investigation about my impending final resting place in your shed doesn't mean you can't fill me in on what they find, right?"

"I'll let you know what I can when I can," she said, clearly not happy being reminded.

I smiled sweetly and winked at her as she rolled her eyes.

Before long the bell announced incoming and outgoing customers, and my concern all but disappeared. Voices rose over one another, the air was ripe with chemical solutions, and blow dryers hummed. It was the perfect remedy to anything that ever got me down. This place—the business Claire and I built—and Nana's kitchen were my very favorite places in the world.

Shortly before noon, I was doing the finishing touches on a comb-out. Claire tugged my arm and nodded her head toward the office. I rested my hand on my client's shoulder and leaned in toward her.

"I'll be right back, Phyllis."

I set the can of aerosol hairspray on my station and followed Claire.

"Did you find out something? What's been taking them so long?"

"They've been trying to find something. Seems the guy—or woman, whoever it was—knew what they were doing."

"Well, they found something, didn't they?" Concern edged its way into the pit of my stomach.

"About all they found was that it's a size 12 boot print. Likely from The North Face."

I leaned against the wall, ran my thumb along the teeth of the comb I still grasped.

"Okay, so the person who's after me has big feet. And a boot that probably ninety percent of the men around here wear." I sighed.

"Yeah. There's that. But at least we have something. That's better than nothing." Her voice

121

sounded like she was giving Syd one of her pep talks.

"No fingerprints?"

"None."

"They were probably wearing gloves that every Tom, Dick, and Harry around here wear too."

"Look on the bright side, Melanie," she said, smiling sweetly. "At least we have something to look for, right?"

At three o'clock I took a short break and walked down to the grocery store to get something for all of us to eat. I took my phone and called Levi on my way there. Just as I thought it would roll into his voicemail, he answered.

"Wescott."

"Either I always catch you at the wrong time or you have caller ID and know it's me. How's your day going?"

"Never better."

"And here I thought sarcasm was my department."

"Sorry."

"Wanna talk about it?"

"Not now. Later?"

"I'm staying at Claire's tonight. Maybe you could stop by her house?"

"As much as I like Claire, three's a crowd when it comes to a personal conversation."

"How personal is it?" My stomach did a somersault.

"Personal on my end, but it's something that could potentially affect you."

I frowned. "That sounds serious. Is everything okay?"

"I can't get into it right now. How about I meet you at your house to talk. You'd be able to be to Claire's by eight."

"Yeah, I guess that should be okay. I'll let her know," I said. "Cole was planning on going to her house to check her backyard anyway. He wants to install a camera under the eve of the shed."

"It's a deal then. Six thirty-ish?"

"I'll be there. And Levi? "

"Yeah?"

"What kind of boots do you own? Other than your black tactical ones?"

"I don't own anything that resembles The North Face, and sure in the hell not a size 12."

"I knew that. Just had to ask."

I heard him chuckle. "Of course you did. See you about six thirty."

I followed Claire on the way home from the salon. I honked my horn as she turned into her driveway, and I went ahead to mine, the next one down from Claire's. When I pulled in, I saw Levi's car parked in the front yard. A quick glance at the clock on my dashboard surprised me. It was already six fifty. I hadn't realized we stayed as long as we did after closing. Rubie bailed on us when she got an offer to go out for a drink from her last customer, Joey.

As I opened my car door, Levi got out and met mc. He took my hand, holding it loosely in his own, and walked side by side with me to the front door. Neither of us said a word, and as much as I was dying to find out what he wanted to talk about, there was a fair amount of fear as well. What was weighing on him so heavily?

"Can I get you something to drink?" I asked, as I set my bag and keys on the chair by the door and slipped out of my boots.

"Beer?"

"You're in luck. I think I have a couple left over from the last time Jack was here. Let me check." It had been a while—too long—since Jack had been to my house, so I looked in the very back. Of course, my refrigerator wasn't exactly stocked, so it didn't require looking too hard to see two bottles lying down on the bottom shelf. I took one out and handed it to Levi, catching his surprise. "What?"

"Remind me to bring a six-pack the next time I come here."

"Levi Wescott," I snickered, "are you a beer snob?"

"I just like to drink a real beer when I have one and not carbonated water."

I reached for a wine glass, opened the bottle of the apple-cranberry sparkling cider he brought me the evening of our date, and began pouring. I leaned over and peered around the island at his feet.

"If you suspect me at all, you'd better know enough not to let me in your house."

"What are you talking about?" I asked, feeling my cheeks warm.

"I'm a trained—"

"Detective, I know," I interrupted. "Can't get anything by you." I smiled at him sheepishly. "I don't suspect you. I'm just practicing my detective skills."

"I'd prefer it if you left the detecting to me."

His eyes met mine and held there. I swooned. Man, I could so get lost in those eyes. It took some work to snap myself out of it. "So what did you need to talk to me about?"

He took my hand and led me into the living room, sitting beside me on my overstuffed, caramel and chocolate-colored plaid couch. He kept his fingers laced through mine, focused on his finger lightly caressing the top of my hand. Finally, he looked up at me. "My ex-wife has been talking about moving to the East Coast for quite some time."

My head started pounding in my ears. Were they getting back together? Suddenly my hand he'd been holding now circled my wine glass. "And?" I cursed myself for asking when I really didn't want to know.

"She called me this morning to let me know she found a job and is moving in two months. She's going out there to find a realtor and to look for a house at the end of this month."

"What does this have to do with me?" I hardly recognized my voice. He reached for my hand and I quickly tucked it under my leg to still the trembling before it became noticeable.

"I need to know where we're going here. With us."

"Not to the East Coast. I mean not for me," I added quickly. "I can't tell you where you should go."

"I'm not talking about us individually, Melanie. I'm talking about us together. As in sharing time, life, you name it." He sat back and sighed. "Is hoping for there to be an 'us' a waste of my time?" I couldn't speak for fear of what would come out of my mouth. "Because for a while I thought there was an 'us.' In fact, I was sure of it.

But then this morning you did a one-eighty and it confused the hell out of me."

I took a sip of my sparkling cider. What I really wanted to do was magically turn it into wine and drink straight from the bottle to alleviate the growing discomfort. In fact, I was so focused on it that I hadn't realized he was waiting for me to answer him.

"I honestly don't know how to answer, Levi. Or frankly, what to think." I played with the stem of my wine glass. "This has come so completely out of the blue." I felt a lump form in my throat.

"I haven't been secretive about my feelings for you. In fact, I think I've been pretty open in my fascination with you since last spring. Then again, this is all new territory for me, so correct me if I'm wrong."

"Meaning?"

"Meaning I don't typically fall for someone this way. Hence the reason I'm still single after being divorced for over seven years. Hell, I haven't even dated more than a handful of times during those years."

"Why me?" I looked at him, fear bubbling to the surface. Did I really want to go any further with this conversation? The old me wanted to shut it down before it got started. But the old me kept getting buried. I shuddered when I realized how someone wanted me buried. Literally.

"I don't know." He began peeling the label off of his bottle. "There's something about you that—well, you're fun, strong, smart...." He looked at me and grinned. "You're kind of hot, too."

I cocked my head to the side and narrowed my eyes. "Ditto."

"You think you're kind of hot, too?" He winked at me and placed a finger against my lips as I began to protest. "I'm just trying to make this situation we're in right now a little lighter. Humor me."

I hesitated before I smiled. "So you don't think I'm hot?"

His head tilted back and he let out a hearty laugh. "Oh, no, I didn't say that."

"Well, good thing, because I was just gonna show you the door." I took another sip of my cider and studied him for a minute. "So what does any of this have to do with the East Coast?"

"I have an opportunity to get on with a police department near the city where my son will be living."

My heart sank to my toes and I swear I felt it hit the floor. That'd be a good bruise to overcome. "Tell me more," I said quietly.

"If you're willing to give us a try, I can fly back and forth, and fly my son out here for vacations and the summers."

"And if not?"

He began to peel at the label on his bottle again, working the edges loose. "I might take the job to be closer to him and make things easier."

The lump in my throat grew. "That's a lot of pressure to put on me."

He took my hand in his, his grayish-green eyes looking deep into mine. "That's not my intent at all," he said. "If you'd be willing to give us a shot, it's worth flying back and forth to the East Coast. Hell, I could even take you with me if you'd be willing to go."

I felt the backs of my eyelids get hot and I looked away from him before he read something there I didn't want him to.

"Melanie—how do you feel about me? About us? It's time to be honest."

"Why wouldn't I be honest? Should I be insulted with that statement?"

"You're trying to change the subject. I know you well enough to know you get uncomfortable talking about real feelings. And that you keep people at arm's length when you feel them getting too close. Except for the people in your circle, that is." He put a finger under my chin and gently lifted my face to meet his. The look in his eyes was so intense yet so tender I wanted to take refuge there. "I want to be in your circle."

As much as I knew it was time that I put on my big girl panties and lay it out there, it was far from easy. And yet the words tumbled out before I knew it.

"What has transpired between us has been completely unexpected. In fact, it scares the pants off me." I took a deep breath, exhaling slow and long. "I've only dated a handful of times since my divorce. Not only because I didn't want to, but I've never met anyone worth taking the risk. What happened with William last spring was simply a challenge. Nothing more, nothing less." I took the risk and looked into his eyes. "But, Levi, my success rate in the relationship department stinks. Frankly, I don't know how to do a relationship."

"I don't agree with you."

"Look at my past. My history. It's not exactly conducive to a successful relationship. Violet's genes, her blood, run in my veins—"

"You're nothing like Violet." His eyes sparked, anger toward my mother evident. "Rose is the one who raised you. It's Rose that taught you how to love. How to live."

"What she and my granddad had is something I've always aspired to have but—"

"It's not too late for that. You just haven't found the right person yet."

Until now. I was grateful God was in control of my tongue right now, because I knew that was the last thing I should say at this moment. I knew what I had to do and he wasn't going to like it. Nor would I, for that matter. It would be the hardest thing since...well, since I couldn't remember when. I looked at my wristwatch.

"I really need to get to Claire's, Levi. It's already eight."

"All I'm asking is you think over what we've talked about and let me know."

I leaned over and gave him a hug with my one free arm, the other still clinging to a now empty glass. He held me close. "I'm glad we had this talk," I whispered. "I really am."

13

When I got to Claire's house, Cole was just getting ready to show Claire his handiwork.

"Come on," he said to me, "I'll show you, too."

"You're pretty proud of yourself, aren't you?" I asked.

"Yes, I am. Because if this person comes sneaking around again, we're going to find out who it is." He looked over his shoulder at me. "I would think you would be a little more worried about this. It wasn't a fake headstone, Melanie. It was a real one. With your name, date of birth, the whole shebang."

Oh, I was scared, alright. But not as scared as a few moments ago when Levi stirred up the fear of God in me by facing all that emotional crap.

"I never said I wasn't concerned. But at least it didn't have my date of death engraved on it, right?" I said with false gaiety.

"Well, now we'll find out who it is before we're forced to add the date of death."

"Unless he's been watching you install the camera. Then he won't be back."

He shot me a look. "You're positivity is killing me."

"I aim to please."

Claire and I followed him outside to the back of the shed where the camera mostly hid under the eve, only a small part of it visible. Not enough, though, for anyone to see in the dark unless he knew what he was looking for.

"Impressive, Tool Time Tim," I said.

Cole was all too pleased with himself. "*Home Improvement*! Used to be my favorite sitcom back in the day."

"Home what?" Claire asked, her innocence cute as could be.

"It was a sitcom years ago. I have to admit it was quite good," I said.

"You don't watch TV. How would you know?" she asked.

"I used to watch it with Granddad. He loved it." Warmth spread through my insides as I remembered my granddad and I watching it together. It was one of my favorite memories of our time together.

"Well, I'll walk you ladies back to the house and then I need to get going. You can't have a girls' night when I'm around."

"Got that right," I teased. Looking at Claire, I said, "Too bad Rubie couldn't make it. Now you're stuck with me all to yourself."

"Some nerve that she would choose a date over time spent with us."

"Well, we'll have to pummel her with questions tomorrow and get details."

Cole let out a half-laugh. "Give the girl some privacy. If she wants you to know she'll tell you."

"Or we could just ask," I countered.

As soon as Cole left, Claire locked the door and watched as he drove out of the driveway. Once out of sight, she closed the curtain on the window she'd just been looking out of.

"Popcorn?"

"Naw."

Her eyebrows raised. "Since when have you ever said no to popcorn? Everything okay?"

I looked at her brown eyes, brimming with concern. Our time together had been limited lately, and I missed her like crazy.

"Feels like we haven't talked in forever. I mean really talked."

"Right? I was telling Cole that I was so excited for tonight because I need to get caught up on what's going on in your life."

I kicked off my tennis shoes and set them on the rug by the door then hung my jacket on the back of the kitchen chair. "You're getting this place whipped into shape," I said, looking around.

"Yeah, it's getting there. I want to have it done completely by the time Syd gets back. That gives me exactly two more days."

"On a Monday? What about school?"

"It's been fall break this past Wednesday through Friday, and she'll just have to miss on Monday. Thank goodness she's young enough that it won't set her back too far by missing a day."

I sank into a kitchen chair. "I sure don't remember having as many days off from school when I was a kid as they do nowadays."

"Yeah, but they don't get out as early now either. Plus they start in August instead of after Labor Day like it was when we were kids."

"Good point."

She walked over to the light switch and flipped it off. "Come on, let's go into the living room where it's more comfortable." I followed her, curled up on one end of the sofa, and hugged a pillow in my lap. "I'll be right back. I'm gonna go get some sweats on, too," she said.

She was gone before I had a chance to say anything more. I looked around the room. It looked so Claire-like. It was exactly what I needed tonight. Comfortable and familiar.

I looked at the aqua-colored sofa I sat on and the two teal and beige club chairs to the right, a side table between them, each with a beige, teal, and peach throw pillow, an exact match to the one I clutched against me at the moment. I put my slippered feet up on her cottage style coffee table, the feminine lines, the distressed finish and the turned legs so typical of Claire.

I realized all over again how different we are, from our clothing to our home decorating styles. My home is classic rustic and log while hers is cottage all the way. And this house is Victorian on the outside, whether she wanted it or not. She wears her signature brightly colored head scarves and lots of long dresses or bouncy flouncy miniskirts in multi colors and flats, many of them glitter and glitz. I stick to jeans, high heels, and most often a black or white top of some sort, my hair hanging loose or in a loose braid or ponytail. And yet when it comes to friendships, there is none stronger than ours.

Finally, Claire came back into the room and sat down on the opposite end of the sofa.

"I thought you decided to go to bed," I teased lightly, laying my head against the cushion.

"Not a chance. We're way overdue for a real talk. Spill."

"About what?"

"About whatever has you in such a funk. I'm not sure I've seen you like this in a long time. Want something to drink?"

"Do you have any seltzer water?"

"I do. Cucumber mint?"

"I'll get it," I said as I stood and went into the kitchen and opened the fridge, retrieved two cans, handed one to her before I sat back down. "Levi might be moving."

"Where?" Her eyes grew wide.

"The East Coast. New Hampshire to be precise."

"Why? When will he know for sure?" She slipped her head scarf off, her curls springing wild.

"He's waiting for me to give him an answer."

She breathed in sharply, her breath held there. "An answer to what? Don't tell me you're—"

"No!" I exclaimed realizing what she was thinking. "I'm not moving."

"Then what?"

I took a drink of my water, set the can down on a coaster, leaned back hugging the pillow to my chest and sighed. "His ex-wife is moving there for a job and taking their son. Levi has an opportunity for a job close by."

"Melanie, that's awful!"

"You haven't heard the worst part yet," I said, my voice pained. I took a deep breath and exhaled slowly. "He wants to know if there's a chance for us. If there is, he wants to stay here and fly back and forth, flying his son out here for vacations and summers."

"Well, that's good, right?"

"No."

She frowned and shook her head as if clearing away the confusion, a curled lock of hair springing up and down. "Why not? I see the way you look at each other and how happy you are when he's around. I haven't seen you like that in a long time. If ever."

"We haven't known each other nearly long enough for him to make a decision like that."

"Melanie, the length of time you've known each other isn't the issue here. You've allowed Levi to see more of you than you've allowed anyone except me, Jack, and of course Rose. That's huge for you."

I smiled as I thought of him and the fun we'd had in the short time we'd known each other.

"He makes me feel good about things. He makes me laugh, he's fun, he's kind, tender, and best of all, he's real. But that's also the part that scares me the most."

"Why? Melanie, sometimes you frustrate me. It's like you want to be miserable. If you find gold, you're determined to conclude that it's nothing more than fool's gold."

"I'm not miserable without him. I have a good, full life."

"Don't you want to share that with someone?"

"I share it with you, Jack, and Nana. And kind of with Rubie."

"You know what I mean," she said, her voice gentle. "Melanie, you're so afraid of getting hurt. You've got to get past that. Not everyone you let in is going to leave you."

"Levi is. He has to."

"Not if you'll give him a reason not to."

"I can't." When I looked at her, sadness reflected in her eyes. "I really like him, Claire. I mean *really* like him. It's something I can't explain even to myself."

"Why do you need everything to have an explanation? Just let it be what it is. A gift."

I took another deep breath and let out a sigh of frustration. "I can't! Don't you get it, Claire?" My voice rose. "I know what it's like not to have a father. I know what it's like to have a parent who doesn't put you first. I can't and won't ask Levi to do that to his child. Dear God, his child would eventually be as screwed up as I am." I tilted my head back, closed my eyes and groaned.

"You said he could fly back and forth and—"

"I can't ask him to do that. Not for me."

"What, you don't think you're worth it? And you're far from screwed up, by the way."

"No, I'm not going to be responsible for taking a parent away from his child. Flying back and forth wouldn't be the same as being physically present for his son. He would miss school activities, school conferences, soccer games, day to day life that makes up the whole and creates the unique relationship between a father and son." I stopped, brushing away tears that burned the backs of my eyelids, a stray rolling down my cheek. "What the heck is up with how soft I'm getting, anyway?" I angrily wiped my cheek.

"Honey," Claire whispered, scootching over and taking my hand in hers, "don't you think it should be Levi's decision whether he moves to New Hampshire or not? He's not asking you to make the decision for him, just to give him the information he needs—that only you can give him, by the way—for him to make an informed decision. It's his decision, Mel, not yours to make for him."

"I can't—I won't be responsible for him making a decision that he will someday regret. And he will regret not being as much a part of his son's life as is humanly possible. And then he will resent me. It's a lose-lose situation. I have to back off, so he won't stay."

I sat unmoving, trying to absorb what Claire had said. Wise words, they were. But they didn't change my mind. I knew what was right. I would not be responsible for another kid being screwed up from not having his father around.

"Before Levi left my house I asked if he'd be able to run a criminal history on Henry and Norma. He said he'd do it tomorrow," I said, changing the subject. It wasn't a subject that was lighter than what we had been talking about, but it was different nonetheless, and right then I needed different.

"How long does it take to get the results back?"

"He said he'll know tomorrow if there's anything worth knowing. Other than the obvious already stated in the newspapers."

We spent the next two hours talking about the salon, Jack and Bryce and their crumbling relationship, and ruminating on Rubie's date.

And finally at midnight, with both of us unable to keep our eyes open, we turned in so we could get some sleep and summon the energy to show Rubie the time of her life biking on the Paul Bunyan trail in the wilderness. Neither of us gave another thought to the camera in Claire's backyard.

14

Sunday morning came too quickly, but as soon as I remembered we were going biking, I jumped up, making sure to make plenty of noise when I made the coffee so Claire would wake up. She was such a light sleeper that it didn't take much noise before she came stumbling into the kitchen, eyes still half closed, yawning, her hair sticking up in every which direction.

I looked at her, jumped back and screamed dramatically. "Who are you and what did you do with Claire?"

"Ha Ha. You're hysterical," she said, yawning again. "Why are you up? It's not even light yet, and it's freezing outside."

"It is so light. You just have to open your eyes to see the sun."

"Someone had a good night's sleep," she said through another yawn. "Me, I could use another few hours."

"Actually, I didn't sleep much. My mind wouldn't shut down." I poured Claire a cup of coffee and set it on the counter in front of her.

"Well, then pray tell, why are you so full of energy this morning? Or should I say mischief?" She plunked down on a stool, propped her elbow on the counter and leaned her head into her hand as if holding it in place.

I took a sip of coffee, turned and looked out the window in front of me, my hands circling my mug. "I think it's called delirium. I'm too tired to think clearly."

"Well don't fall asleep on the ride today. We aren't able to carry you back home."

"I love the fact that you've got my back." I turned around to face her, leaning against the counter behind me. "Rubie is meeting us at my house at ten. I'm going to head home, change, check the tires on the spare bike, so she doesn't have an excuse not to go. I'll see ya around ten?"

"I'll be there. Awake even."

I gave her a wave, slipped into my shoes and jacket and headed out the door, pulling it closed tightly behind me.

Before going to my car, I circled Claire's house to the back to check on the camera and if there was any sign of a visitor during the night. Finding the camera undisturbed and nothing I could immediately see indicating we'd had company, I circled the other side of the house just to cover all bases and got in my car. It would have been easy enough to walk here last night, but given the circumstances and the fact that it was dark, I had been just fine driving, thank you very much. Plus, if Levi had had any suspicion that I had planned to walk, I suspect he would have tied me to the chair and refused to let me up.

Thinking of Levi brought back the dilemma he served for play in my court yesterday evening. I wanted to scream *Don't Go!* But that would only result in catastrophe for him and his son as well as for us. Our relationship would be doomed before it even got off the ground. In fact, when I thought about it, we were doomed either way. Despite the lack of sleep and losing at something I wanted badly, I felt better about it this morning. However, once the few hours of sleep I actually got wore off and I found myself in his presence again, that whole feeling better thing had the potential to take a serious nosedive into the great abyss.

As if on cue, my cell phone began playing its happy tune, and Levi's name popped up on the screen. Not quite yet, I told myself. I need some space and time to think. Besides, I wasn't ready to get booted out of my happy place yet. If he'd come up with the criminal history on Norma and Henry already, it wouldn't change any before I called him back later this afternoon. In fact, if it changed at all during any span of time would be cause for great concern given the fact that neither of them was able to change it. That would be a problem on a whole new level.

By the time I was done pumping the tires and checking for leaks on the spare bike, Rubie was pulling into the driveway, and Claire was riding her bike across the expanse of field that separated our houses. We only had to travel about two miles before we could hop on the paved trail that went for hundreds of miles.

As predicted, the sky was clear, the sun shining brilliantly, beating warmth against our shoulders, alleviating the sting of the cold. Rubie had on gray compression leggings, a matching gray long sleeve shirt with pink trim, thumbs peeking through the thumb holes, and a gray and pink half-zip hoodie tied around her waist. Her nails were perfectly manicured and polished pink, her hair done to perfection, and she wore pink lipstick to boot. I stared at her, my jaw gaping open.

"We're going biking on a trail in the woods, not to some hotty totty aerobics class."

"I know that, genius. But does it hurt to want to look good while I work out?"

I looked at Claire, shook my head slowly and snickered. "Nope, not at all. But I have a question for you, *genius*," I repeated, "how are you going to keep your hair looking like that when you put a helmet on?"

"I'm letting you wear the helmet. I wouldn't want to take it from you."

"She doesn't wear one," Claire said, looking pointedly at me.

"Well, I don't want to wear one either."

"So you're both going to be idiots?" Claire asked in disbelief before she looked at me. "You're a horrible role model, Mel."

I shrugged. "Rubie, you'll want to put your jacket on. Once we get moving, you're going to freeze. Let's hit the road, ladies." I gave each of them a bottle of water, locked the door, and led the way out of the driveway.

We stayed one behind the other while we were on the road, Rubie bringing up the rear, trying to talk to us. I heard Claire say something to her a time or two but I pretended, mighty well, I might add, that I didn't listen to a word. There was nothing like time spent in nature, smelling the moist soil and tree bark, listening to the dry leaves rustling as they spiraled together off of the baring limbs onto the leaf-packed ground.

We'd no sooner turned onto the trail than Claire zoomed up beside me.

"Hey, you," she said, "you may want to think about slowing it down a little."

"Can't keep up?" I teased knowing full well she could ride circles around me. Claire had the athletic build I envied, to begin with, her muscles toned to perfection. Add to that her workout regime, and—well—she made me look like a pansy.

"Rubie's going to croak after another mile at this speed."

"Oops, sorry. Hadn't thought of that." In fact, I really hadn't thought of anything at all once we started except how good it felt to get on the bike and ride as if I were escaping from all of my problems.

All of a sudden I heard Rubie scream, a sound that could wake the dead. I jumped and turned to look. She was coasting, her legs high in the air.

"You didn't tell me there were snakes out here!" she squealed.

"You didn't ask," I hollered back, now laughing hysterically.

"It's not funny!" she yelled, now peddling faster than I thought she ever could, until she was by my side, gasping for air. "Are there a lot of them out here?"

"There can be," I answered, trying to keep my cool so I wouldn't scare her into turning back. "They like laying on the asphalt in the sun because it's warm for them." I glanced over at her. "They're only garter snakes, Rubie. They're harmless."

"Don't tell me you're not afraid of them." She looked at me skeptically.

"Nope. I hate 'em." I shuddered. "But they don't seem to care. They come out anyway."

"I knew this was a bad idea," she grumbled.

I giggled and sped off, hearing Claire laughing behind me.

Every time I looked at Rubie for the next several miles, her head was down, focusing on the ground. Once she almost ran smack into an oncoming bike that swerved to miss her.

"Rubie!" I said, my voice sharp. She jumped and looked up, nearly taking both of us out when she turned sharply. Her front tire barely missed getting snared with my rear tire. "You should have worn the helmet," I mumbled and rolled my eyes. If we all returned unharmed, it would be a miracle.

Another five miles farther along the trail Rubie pulled up beside me, flanked on the other side by Claire.

"Rubie's tired," Claire said. "Maybe we should turn around before we get any farther and she's not able to make it back."

"We've gone about seven miles. Are you able to go a few more before we turn around Rubie? There's a little coffee shop up ahead about three miles."

"How far do you guys go?" she asked, winded.

"Claire can go forever, probably until she reaches Canada," I answered, the probable truth tampering my sarcasm. "I usually go about thirty."

"Miles?" she gasped.

"Yeah. Round trip, though."

"Well, I can go another three if it means coffee," she said as she peddled faster with a renewed spark of energy.

Minutes later there was a loud pop to our right.

"What was that?" Claire called from behind me.

"It sounded like a gun." I had to admit I was a little concerned. "It's too early for deer hunting season. I suppose someone could be shooting small game or waterfowl."

"You mean we could get shot?" Rubie squealed, her eyes huge.

"We won't get shot. Between Claire's hot pink helmet, the pink on your jacket and vest and my orange and black jacket, I'd think we're safe."

"You *think* we are? Why does that not make me feel better?" she asked.

"We'll be fine, Rubie," I said as if I were talking to Sydney. "We're almost to the coffee shop."

"Well, let's hurry it up, shall we?" she said, her voice at the end of her request a full octave higher.

She sped on past me, and Claire pulled up beside me. "Guess she's not tired anymore," she said.

We both glanced over to our right as we heard something rustling through the brush. "Good thing Rubie didn't hear that," I said.

"I did!" she called back over her shoulder. You'd think we just told her the sky was falling. "Like you just happened to forget to mention there're bears out here? My trust level with you just plummeted to zero!"

"Ouch! Harsh," I grumbled. Claire giggled. "I didn't forget; I just chose not to tell you," I yelled ahead to Rubie, the breeze carrying my voice to her.

"Melanie!" she screeched as she peddled even faster.

Claire and I both laughed.

"That was funny, but it was mean," Claire said.

"We'll know how to get her to go faster on the way back home."

"She'll never go with us biking again. Ever!"

"We'll probably have to go shopping with her to make up for it." I grimaced. I hate shopping almost as much as I hate those pesky little garter snakes.

By the time we caught up to Rubie, she had found the coffee shop. She slid off her bike and nudged the kickstand down with her foot, then winced and rubbed her behind with both hands.

"I'm pretty sure I won't sit down again for at least a week," she groaned. "And my legs feel like rubber bands that have been stretched too far. Like, seriously," she said, shooting me daggers, "I swear I won't be sitting down again anytime soon. My bum is killing me!"

"Well, that ought to be interesting getting back home then." I chuckled.

We didn't bother chaining our bikes, but rather kept them close together. Claire gave me her order, a chai tea latte, and stayed outside while Rubie and I went into the shop.

As I stood at the counter giving the woman my order, I heard Rubie talking with someone in a small alcove off to the left. I poked my head around the corner to see who she'd found. The girl could strike up a two-way conversation with a pillar.

"Melanie," she said when she spotted me craning my head around the corner, "look who I found hanging out? Do you remember Michael?" I must have had that deer-in-the-headlights look. "Michael," she said again, staring at me as if she couldn't believe I didn't remember. "He was with Levi and Cole when they stopped by Grizzley's the other night."

"Of course I remember Michael," I said. I smiled at him, extending my hand. "The third of the Three Stooges. What brings you out here?"

"It's somewhere I can go and not worry about running into any of the town's delinquents."

"Well, we just put an end to that for ya, didn't we?" I said.

He laughed. "What brings you ladies out here?"

"Claire and Melanie talked me into biking with them today." Rubie looked at me, her eyes narrowing. "And never again. I'm lucky I made it here alive." Her lips, freshly colored with pink gloss, protruded in a perfect pout. Man, she had that down better than Syd.

He looked her over from head to toe. "You don't do this much, do you? This whole bicycling thing."

Rubie's cheeks colored to match the trim on her hoodie. "Not really my thing. Especially with all the little critters we've come across. And one that wasn't so little."

I looked at Michael and rolled my eyes. "There was one little snake and a potential bear."

His eyes sparkled with amusement. He looked at Rubie and said, "Don't feel bad. I would be afraid of a bear, too. Even if it was just a potential one." She looked at me with a silent *aha!* "Do you ladies care to have a seat and keep me company?"

"Claire's outside guarding the bikes. I'm just waiting for our drink order."

"You go right ahead and be rude, Ms. This-Whole-Outdoors-Thing-Is-So-Fun-You're-Just-Gonna-Love-It." She sat in the stuffed café chair kitty-corner from Michael, wincing when her behind touched the cushion. "I'd love to," she said, smiling at Michael after she settled in. "When you guys are ready to get going," she said to me, the smile disappearing, "come back in and get me."

"Deal." I snickered. Okay, so maybe I was unfair. But she was so darn cute when she was mad.

I lingered by their table listening to Rubie tattling about how I laughed at her with the snake until she finally moved on to something else. Finally, the barista called my name. I snatched Rubie's hot chocolate off the counter and set in front of her at the table, then turned to get mine and Claire's. "Nice to see you again, Michael," I said as I looked over my shoulder.

He nodded. "You, too. Take care, now."

I picked up my almond latte and Claire's chai tea and pushed the door open with my hip.

"Where's Rubie?" Claire asked looking past me.

"Apparently her date didn't go so well last night. She found a new boy toy." Claire squinted at me against the sun as I sat down in the chair opposite her. "She's choosing his company over ours." I chuckled again. "Maybe I was a little hard on her."

"Ya think?" Claire tilted her head back and laughed. "She's fine. She's just a lot more girly than you're used to."

"I love her to pieces, Claire, but we couldn't be more different. Heck, all three of us are as different as three people can be." I marveled over that for a minute.

"That's why we get along so well," she said, kicking my foot under the table. "Now be nice to Rubie on the way back or that could change."

"Yes, ma'am," I grumbled.

We sat in silence, enjoying the warmth of the sun and the smell of the crisp fall air. All was quiet until Rubie came through the door and sat down gingerly on the chair next to me.

"Bum still hurting there, Petunia?"

"Yes." She winced as she scooted back in the chair.

"Where's Michael?" I asked.

"He had to run."

"Hm," I said, looking around me. "I didn't see him come out."

"He went out the back. Said he always parks back there."

I drained the last of my drink. Claire had finished hers already. Rubie came out empty handed, so I assumed she'd finished hers as well.

"Should we get going?" I asked without making a move. I was more relaxed than I'd been in a long time.

"Can you guys go and come pick me up with the car?" Rubie asked.

"No," Claire and I both said, Claire's voice much gentler than mine.

"You can do this," I said.

"Think how good you'll feel when you're done," Claire said.

"I won't feel anything if I'm dead."

I laughed. "Dramatic much? Think about the sense of accomplishment you'll have."

"I'll try," she groaned, stretching to each side, arms over her head, fingers laced together as she did. "Shopping is just so much easier. Not to mention more fun."

"For you," I mumbled. "It's all a matter of perspective." I stood and wrapped an arm around her. "Come on. I'll be a good girl. Promise."

On the way back, in the same place that we'd heard the rustling on the way to the coffee shop, we heard it again. I glanced over, peering through the dense brush as I rode. And then another *pop!* This time at the same time as the *pop!* the front of my bike skidded out from under me, and I tumbled down the ditch, the weeds cushioning my fall. Claire yelled my name, and Rubie screamed. It all happened so fast and all at the same time that I couldn't be sure what happened. I sat up, rubbed my hands, my scraped palms burning. Claire scrambled down to me, kneeling by my side.

"What in God's name just happened?" I asked.

"Melanie, your bike tire is flat as a pancake!"

Claire wrapped one arm around my shoulder and took my hand with her other, helping me up, then assessing a scrape on the side of my forehead. "This is exactly why you should wear a helmet."

"Apparently." I crept back up the incline to the path and inspected my bike tire, a sliver of fear piercing my previously peaceful demeanor. I looked at Rubie, then Claire, and whispered, "Ladies? I've been shot."

15

The three of us hovered toward the ground, each scanning a different direction. I cursed my timing at cutting electronic ties by leaving my phone at home. Rubie clutched her hot pink phone tightly in her hand; I was afraid all the bling on it would cut her fingers. There was no way of prying it loose, either, without serious injury. Thankfully Claire didn't go anywhere without hers and was already on the phone with Cole.

"Why were you whispering?" Rubie asked Claire when she hung up. "Whoever shot at Melanie's bike obviously knows exactly where to find us anyway."

"Let's not jump to conclusions," I said, trying to rationalize. "It's possible it was just a hunter with lousy aim."

"Um, yeah. Let's go with that," Claire said hesitantly, then looked at me. "Girl, you sure go getting yourself into a lot of messes lately."

"That sounds exactly like something Jack would say. Besides, if it was a hunter it had nothing to do with me anyway."

"Do you really think it was just a hunter? Because I don't. And I don't believe that you really do either," Claire said. "It's not deer season, and I'm pretty sure waterfowl don't traffic the trails."

"And here I thought I was the queen of sarcasm," I whispered. "Besides, it doesn't matter what I think. The fact is it could have been. And even if it wasn't, there's a good chance it had nothing to do with me at all. Someone who just wants to be a pest."

"It's possible, but not probable."

"Whatever happened to your hopelessly positive outlook on things?" I asked. "And why are we still whispering?"

We were now hunkering down in the ditch that ran alongside the bike path. I nudged Rubie.

"You okay?" I'd never known her to be quiet for so long. I looked at her studying the long grass around her feet. I would have said "snake!" just for grins but she would have screamed bloody murder, and that just might be what it would have been if that happened. I still wasn't sure what we were dealing with. Besides, I promised I would be nice on the way back. And that was one thing for which I could be counted on, keeping my word.

I looked at Claire. "I never asked, and you didn't say, but I'm assuming Cole is coming to the rescue?"

"Him, Levi, or both."

"Let the cavalry arrive," I said. I hoped Levi was coming. I could use the security he gave. Guilt nipped at the heels of that thought. Is that what I was doing, using him for my benefit? Is that what I'd succumbed to?

"—out here."

Rubie's still-panicked voice cut into my thoughts. "What?"

"I said I can't believe no one else has come by yet. Wouldn't you think there would be other people out riding today? Or are we the only crazy ones."

I glanced down at the Garmin exercise watch Claire talked me into getting months ago.

"It may seem like we've been hiding out in this ditch for hours but it's actually only been ten minutes."

"It's so quiet out here," Claire said. "No more gunshots, leaves rustling, or anything. It's almost eerie."

"I don't hear anything either," Rubie whispered, her eyes still wide. She'd probably sleep with her eyes open tonight. "Is that a good thing or a bad thing?"

If the circumstances weren't so serious right now, I might have laughed at her question, not sure if it warranted a verbal answer. Instead, sarcasm kicked in. Again. At least I was consistent on that front. "I'm not sure if it's good or bad for you, but I'm sure glad no one is shooting since I can't outrun a bullet on foot."

"Listen," Claire whispered, a smile tugging at one side of her lips. "I can hear the siren."

Sure enough, here he, or they, whichever the case may be, came to the rescue. But lights and sirens? Really? It seemed a little overkill considering we weren't even sure if this was an intentional hit or an accident.

When the sirens got to the nearest cross road that connected to the trail, flashing lights slowly got closer. The trail was barely wide enough to accommodate the cruiser.

"It's Cole," Claire said, her eyes brightening when she recognized him behind the wheel. She stood up and walked out to him, Rubie right behind her, followed by me.

"Just so you all know," Rubie announced, "this will be the last outdoor excursion I ever go on with you guys. In fact, it just might be the last one I go on ever," she said with dogged determination. "I'm sticking to shopping and playing bingo."

Cole enveloped Claire into a brief hug and began looking around, beginning with my bike tire. "Melanie, Levi wants you to call him when you get a minute."

"Did he stay at the station?" Claire asked him.

He looked up at her from his kneeling stance by the bike tire. "He got called out to a homicide."

"Glad it wasn't mine," I answered.

"Melanie!" Claire said, looking at me in disapproval.

"Lighten up. It was a joke."

"Jokes are funny, not demented."

"Yeah," I mumbled. "I guess I could use a little work on that." I looked at Cole, now standing and looking around, one hand resting on his service weapon holstered on his duty belt. "What do you think?" I asked.

"I think it's not going to be what you want to hear."

"You think someone intentionally meant to hit me?"

"I think if someone has such bad aim that he would mistake a biker for small game or fowl, he's not a hunter, and everything else is out of season." He frowned. "So, yes, I think it was more than likely intentional. My guess would be to scare or intimidate or they would have hit something other than your tire." He looked directly at me, his eyes unwavering. "You obviously peed in someone's Wheaties to make them this mad."

"Seems I've been doing nothing but stepping on toes lately. I'm getting pretty good at it."

"Too good." He looked at Claire. "I'm just glad Sydney wasn't out here with you guys."

His statement was sweet, his tone fatherly, but guilt pierced my heart, dead center. What if Sydney had been here? I had to figure out who was trying to keep me from finding out the truth, whatever that truth may be, before Sydney came back on Monday. I swallowed the fear that threatened to rise to the surface and reached for my phone to call Levi before remembering I left it at the house.

"Claire, can I borrow your phone, please?"

It rang twice before the familiar voice answered.

"Wescott."

"Hogan," I said, attempting to be as gruff as he sounded when he answered.

"Hey there." His voice softened. "I didn't recognize the number. You okay?"

There was a lot of commotion in the background on his end. "Yup." I swallowed hard. Was I going to get emotional now? Seriously? "Cole said you'd been called out to a homicide, so I won't keep you. Just doing what I'm told."

"That's a first," he teased lightly.

"Is it a bad one? The homicide." *Stupid question, Melanie.*

155

"They're all bad. I just wish I could be with you right now."

"I'm fine. Really." I swallowed again.

"Call you when I'm done?"

"Sure. That works."

"You sure you're okay?"

I hesitated before answering him. Telling him anything other than I was fine would interfere with his ability to concentrate on his investigation. I forced myself to smile, hoping it would reach my voice. "Yeah, I'm sure."

"Okay, then."

Apparently, I wasn't successful, because I could tell he wasn't convinced. "Hey, Levi?"

"Yeah?"

"Thanks."

"For what?"

"For—for—just for being you," I blurted and hung up.

"Where's your helmet?" I heard Cole's voice behind me.

"I must have forgotten," I lied.

"Good thing you landed on your hands and arm when you fell and not your head."

I touched the burning on my forehead. "Yeah, for the most part anyway. My head is too hard to have done any damage, so it's a non-issue." In truth, my mind was whirling with "what if's" tumbling all over one another, unable to complete an entire "what if" question.

Cole radioed in some backup to go through the woods surrounding where we had been to see if they could find anything. Next, he loaded two of the bikes on the bike rack that was affixed to the back of his cruiser and put mine in his trunk.

"As soon as the guys get here I'll give you ladies a lift home."

"I'm staying," I said.

Cole looked at me as if he was unsure how to proceed. "No, you're not." Apparently, he decided shooting straight was the way to go. Pun intended.

"Actually, I am." I could tell he was getting frustrated. "Look, Cole, I'm not trying to be difficult. But someone just took a shot at me. Maybe I'll remember something I saw or heard as we're searching and canvassing the area." He still didn't appear to be convinced. "I'll behave, okay? Jeez! What do I need to do, swear an oath? Swear in blood?"

His phone buzzed, and he snapped it free from the belt clip, looked at the incoming number, and answered. "Hey, Wescott. What's up?"

I listened as he mumbled, "Uh-huh. Okay. Sure. Yeah." He looked at me, and I felt my cheeks get warm. He was talking about me but trying not to let me know it. Like it was that hard to figure out. There was another, "Yeah, sure. Okay. Yeah, see you then." He hung up and pressed his brows with his thumb and forefinger as if he were pressing away an impending headache. Likely the one I was giving him.

"Tell me, Mahoney, what was that all about?"

Cole chuckled, slowly shaking his head and mumbled under his breath, "Wescott has his hands full with you." He looked up at me. "That was Levi."

"Obviously. I kind of figured that out."

"Officers Johnson, Holliday, and Mendoza will be coming soon. As well as Detective Wescott.

He's pretty much done what he needs to at the crime scene and got someone to relieve him for the rest of it."

As if on cue, three patrol cars pulled up and parked along the side of the narrow dirt road just yards from one side of the bike path. The driver's door opened on each of the cars, the three talked for a couple of minutes, and then a black unmarked car pulled up behind them.

"I thought only three officers were coming, not the whole department."

"Me too," he answered.

The odd man out walked with the three uniformed cops, his cap pulled low. Something about him looked familiar. If I could just see his face.

"That's Michael!" Rubie said, her mood brighter than it had been since we left the coffee shop. "What's he doing here?"

The four of us stood watching until they reached us.

Cole took a step forward. "Thanks for coming out, guys. Mikey, you got called in on your day off?"

"No." He smiled at Rubie then looked at Cole. "I was in the area—at the coffee shop the ladies were just at to be exact. I heard the call come through on the radio."

I watched him as he spoke. Something wasn't sitting right with me, but I couldn't put my finger on what it was. Claire distracted me for a moment as she gave me a hug, followed by Rubie, before they climbed into Cole's patrol car. I watched as he backed out of the trail and back onto the crossroad where he disappeared down the narrow dirt road and past the line of patrol vehicles and out of sight.

Despite Cole already filling in the crew on what happened, I explained again from a first-hand perspective. I told them where the shot had come from, where each of us were, the shot we heard before we reached the coffee shop, and the rustling we'd heard and assumed it was deer or, heaven forbid, a bear.

Officer Mendoza ran point. "I'll look north; Johnson, you go south; Holliday, east. Larson," he called as he began his northerly route, "if you want to help, take west."

"I'm on it," Michael answered.

"Ms. Hogan," Michael said, "you take it easy and hang tight while we look for some answers. You needn't worry yourself with cop business."

Cop business? I fought to wipe that stupid smirk off of his face as he turned and walked away. The smirk he tried to conceal but couldn't quite do it. My fists clenched at my side, and I bit my lower lip. I kept my sights on him as he shuffled his feet in the brush, ducking and swerving as he made his way through. Other than being an annoying little gnat, something seemed off with this guy. Familiar, but in an uncomfortable way. What was it?

16

Forty-five minutes after Cole left with Claire and Rubie, Levi's navy blue department car turned onto the trail where Cole's car had last been. He got out, put on his BHPD (Birch Haven Police Department) cap, and strode over to me, a man on a mission.

"What happened?" His voice and eyes were gentle, contradicting his actions.

"You haven't heard from Cole or the other officers?" I looked down, embarrassed, the unfamiliarity of that making me squirm. I forced my eyes back up to face him and his half smile, which was amused. "Sorry, I didn't mean it the way it came out. I was just surprised Cole hadn't filled you in on the details. He tells you everything else on the planet."

"He told me everything he knows. Including that I have my hands full."

"I'm sure he did," I grumbled.

He chuckled and shook his head. "I want to hear it from you. First-hand."

"That you have your hands full?"

"Melanie, you're making this lighter than you should. Someone shot at you," he scolded, gently.

"I don't know why everyone assumes the person shot at me. In fact, I might not have had anything to do with it. Not everything is about me."

"Tell that to this guy," he grumbled.

I sighed, then I launched into the story from the time we left, even getting a grin out of him when I told him about Rubie's debacles, and continued the story until the bullet hit my bike. He looked at my scraped hands and the bump on my forehead. He touched my cheek gently, briefly. My heart raced.

"Do you need medical?"

Yeah, for an inevitable broken heart. I took a breath. "You of all people know I'm a whole lot tougher than that," I scoffed.

He smiled at me. Directly at me. And my knees turned to jelly. "Yes, I do know that. But I have to ask. It's my job."

"It was Cole's job and every other officer that came out here, too, apparently."

"That'll teach you to wear a helmet from now on."

"Or not," I said in defiance. "Or probably," I mumbled, knowing I was wrong for not wearing one to begin with. Hardheaded or not, it was a bonehead move on my part not to wear one.

"Let me go talk to the guys real quick, and I'll give you a ride home."

"That'd be nice since my bike isn't only broken but in Cole's trunk."

He winked at me then strode over to Officer Mendoza, the one clearly in charge. Mendoza

161

pointed toward the east, his index finger traveling around to point in my direction, Levi's gaze following. Then he pointed at something on the ground, kicked his foot around in the brush to clear an area, and Levi looked down, squatted to look closer, then stood back up. He said something else, Mendoza laughed, and then he began walking back to me.

"Appears you didn't stay put when they asked to do. Why am I not surprised?"

"I wasn't just going to stand here when I could be doing something useful."

"Of course not. Knowing you as I do, I would expect nothing less. Are you ready to head out?"

I walked to the passenger side of his car and reached for the door handle, but he beat me to it, opening the door for me. As I fastened my seatbelt, he walked around the front of his car to his door, waved at Officer Mendoza, and got in.

"Did they find anything?"

"A small area that looked matted down and half a boot print in a patch of mud."

"Was it enough to get an impression?"

"Nope. Barely enough to know it was a boot but not size or style." He backed out, his arm around the back of my seat as he looked behind us, and then turned and drove down the dirt road that would eventually lead us to the main road. The faint smell of his cologne teased my nose, making me want more. "How are you doing?" He glanced at me and reached for my hand, holding it lightly.

I looked out the window of the car door. "Never better."

He gave my hand a squeeze. "Come on; it's me you're talking to."

I lay my head back against the headrest, hesitating so I could collect my thoughts before answering. "A little flustered, I guess."

"That's better," he said, caressing my hand lightly. "No one gets shot at and says they've never been better."

I was grateful for the comfort of his hand on mine. "You know—Cole mentioned something when we were out there. He told Claire it was a good thing Sydney hadn't been with us." I looked at him. "She comes home Monday, Levi. I need to find out who's doing this before she comes back, so it stops. That doesn't even give me two days."

He glanced over at me, brows knit beneath his cap, before looking back at the road. "I got the criminal histories for Henry and Norma. They were both victims of each other. Victim one day, defendant the next. Henry also had a history of criminal mischief, and he had been arrested for second-degree arson, but the charges were ultimately dismissed."

My eyes grew wide. "That can't be a coincidence. Did it say why it was dismissed?"

"No. But I've got Michael checking on it. He grew up here and has more ties to the community than I do. He's got plenty of people he can ask."

"Well, tell him to be careful. We know what someone thinks about me asking questions."

"He's equipped to handle it."

"Me too. I have my CCW."

He glanced over at me. I saw a slight twitch in his cheek.

"I realize that. But he has police training."

We pulled into my driveway and in front of my house. He put the car in park and left it idling.

"Do you think the fire was caused by faulty electrical wiring as the newspaper stated?"

He shrugged. "Not only wasn't I the investigating detective on the case, but I was also brand new to the department, so I don't have any first-hand knowledge of the case. The fire investigator said it was and he's the one trained to make that determination. There would be no reason to doubt his analysis." He looked at me. "Why? What are you thinking?"

"What if it wasn't an accident? You said Henry had been charged at one time with second-degree arson—"

"It could hardly be him that started the fire when he died in it."

"Not completely impossible though. Stranger things have happened." I looked at him, our eyes meeting. "Murder-suicide?"

Levi whistled and looked straight ahead out the window and over the field that led toward Claire's house. He reached for the keys and turned the car off. "That would be twisted, to do it by fire. But I've seen a whole lot worse than that during my time in the homicide unit."

I stared out the front window not seeing a thing. Levi's news kept churning around in my head. Was Henry Swanson cold-blooded enough to do the unthinkable? Sure, he had a rap sheet a mile long, but did that make him capable of being a killer?

"Could you find out who identified the bodies?"

"I already know the answer to that. The bodies were unrecognizable."

My head whipped around to face him. "Then how do they know it was them?"

"Dental records."

"For all three?"

"I would assume so. Mel, it's not my place to go questioning the results of someone else's tests from a time when I was wet behind the ears in police work."

"No, I don't suppose it is," I agreed. "I know better than to think you should. It's just that—well, I just want so badly to find out what happened to the little boy."

He took my hand again in his, his hand gentle and warm over mine.

"You're cold. Do you want me to turn the car on to get some heat?" he asked.

"Do you have to go back to work today?"

"No."

"Do you want to come in for a while?"

"Do you want me to?"

"Don't answer a question with a question. Would I have asked if I didn't want you to?"

"Got any soda?"

"Yes. And a beer or two."

"That stuff you call beer is carbonated water. Besides, I'm on call. But I'll take you up on the soda. Would it be pushing my luck and risk being uninvited if I bring up our conversation from last evening?"

"Maybe," I teased and winked at him. I opened my door and got out. "Come on, Detective. It's cold out here when I'm not biking to work up some body heat."

Levi offered to start a fire while I changed clothes into my oldest, most comfortable, shredded-in-both-knees jeans and oversized sweatshirt. I cleaned up the scrapes on my hands, putting antibiotic ointment and Band-Aids where necessary. Disney Princess decorated Band-Aids to be exact. I keep a good supply of them for Syd for when she comes to my house. I'm sure Levi was more than just a little impressed when I sat down, and he held my hands up to get a better look. His eyes twinkled with amusement.

"What?" I grinned.

"So which is your favorite princess, Princess?"

"Ariel, of course." He laughed and kissed each of the Band-Aids. "So were you kissing my boo-boos or the princesses?"

"About that talk—"

The ringtone, announcing Claire calling, sounded. I breathed out dramatically. "Saved by— the phone." I held it up and grinned. "Hi, Claire."

"Whatcha doin?"

I stood, walked into the kitchen and over to the window and looked across the open field toward her house. "Who wants to know, you or Cole? I see his car at your house."

"You're a voyeur?" She laughed. "Both of us want to know because we see Levi's car at *your* house." She laughed again.

"Oh boy, this could become a problem." I rolled my eyes.

"Want to come over for dinner?"

"How about you guys come here? Levi has a pretty impressive fire going."

"Just a minute." I heard her talking with Cole in the background, her hand obviously only half-covering the mouthpiece, then she got back on the line. "Okay. We'll be there in fifteen minutes."

"Deal." I got off the phone and went back to the living room where Levi was sitting the same as before I'd gone into the kitchen. He looked deep in thought. "Everything okay?" I asked. I sat down beside him on the couch, his nearness making me feel conflicted. While I felt safe from the outside world, I felt in danger from myself, where I wanted this to go and where it couldn't.

"How's Claire?"

"Another question with a question. I'll let you get away with it this time though. We're having company in fifteen minutes."

I absentmindedly leaned against him, my head on his shoulder. My muscles were starting to ache from the fall earlier, but the warmth from the fire began to help. He put his arm around me, pulling me closer. "We need to talk after they leave, okay?"

I wanted badly to say "If we have to", or "Maybe a later time," as in *much* later, but instead heard my voice say, "Sure." More than anything, I wanted things to stay exactly as they were right now. Talking, or anything at all, would upset that and make it different. I didn't want it to be different. Not yet. In fact, I'm not sure I wanted to be different ever. But I knew it wasn't fair to Levi or his son to put "the talk" off any longer than necessary.

We sat there silent, the two of us, watching the sparks in the fireplace and listening to the crackle and pop of the flames hungrily licking the logs. It was just barely dusk outside, but at this moment I forgot anything else even existed outside these knotty pine walls. Until the front door opened and I heard Claire's voice call out, "We're here."

Levi lightly kissed the top of my head before he removed his arm from around me so I could drag myself up. I love Claire to pieces, but this was one time, if not the only time, I would have been okay if she'd decided not come over.

We hugged, Claire a good half foot taller than me without my heels. I pulled back and held her at arm's length. "Have you gotten taller?" I asked as I stood on my tippy toes.

"No. You're just a little pipsqueak without your heels," she said.

"Very funny." I glanced around her and looked at Cole's feet.

"What?" he said.

"Nothing."

"No, Mel," Claire said, shaking her head.

"No, what?" Cole and I asked at the same time.

"You know what," she said looking straight at me.

"She may know, but I don't," Cole said. "Someone care to fill me in?"

"I know my friend all too well," Claire told him, then looked at me again. "She's checking out your shoe size."

Cole frowned. "Weird."

"Making sure it's not you that insinuated wanting me dead by placing my gravestone in Claire's backyard."

"Tell me you're kidding." Cole laughed, instantly stopping when he looked at me, realizing I wasn't.

"Well? How do I know? Where were you that night?"

"Melanie, stop it. Now!" Claire said. "We're not going to get into this tonight. We're here to have a good time with friends."

"I'm surprised you didn't check out everyone who was out on the trail today."

"Who says I didn't?" The fact of the matter was, I had. And there was one that looked like it could be a possibility. Michael's. I wasn't about to tell Cole that, though, not even Levi. Not until I've checked into the matter. I wasn't about to get my suspicion shot down because he was "one of them." "What can I get you two to drink?"

"Whatever you guys are having," Cole said.

"Club soda and Diet Pepsi?"

"Got any beer?"

"Depends," I said, smiling at Levi.

"She has carbonated water that says beer on the label," Levi said, now standing behind me.

"But I have an impressive bottle of wine if you'd like some of that."

"The Diet Pepsi sounds amazing," Claire said. "But I'll get it. Babe?" she asked.

"I've got mine, but thanks," I said.

"I was talking to Cole." She giggled, punching me in the arm as I walked by her, planting myself beside Levi again. "What do you want, hun?" she asked Cole.

"The same. Thanks." He winked at Claire then looked toward Levi and me. "So what have you two been doing, talking about today's events?"

"Good guess. You should think about becoming a detective," I teased.

Levi and I took our places on the sofa, Cole on an oversized chair and Claire on the floor at his feet, her arm resting on his leg.

"Not a guess. I just know my buddy over there and getting to know you, too. I think," he added, shaking his head slightly. "You're made for each other. God help us each and every one."

A round of laughter sounded delightful. "Something not so funny coming up," I said, "did

169

you guys honestly want me to make you something for dinner?"

"Do you get pizza delivery out here?" Cole asked.

"Nope. This is the sticks, my friend. Good old-fashioned country living."

"If you don't cook, what do you eat?"

"I'm at the salon more than I'm here, so I usually get food from the grocery store. And when I'm here I just dip into the neighbor's dog food." Claire let out a hearty laugh, a sound I haven't heard enough of late. "Don't look so horrified, Cole, I'm kidding. I don't like their brand." I grinned at him. "It's not that I don't know how to cook, in fact, my grandmother keeps working at teaching me her secrets."

"How about Levi and I make a quick trip into town and get something and bring it back?"

"There's a small burger place about four miles from here that has good food. They're only open on the weekends during the off-season, so we're in luck."

"It's a plan. Melanie, if you want to call in ahead, Levi and I can go pick it up and bring it back here. We'll go about—" he looked at his wristwatch and then at Levi, "in a few minutes?" Levi nodded his approval. "You on call tonight, buddy?"

"Yup."

"Figured as much." He looked at me and said, "You're good for him. You bring him business, and you give him a social life. Typically you won't catch him anywhere but home by the phone when he's on call."

"Is that so?" I asked as we exchanged a private look, warmth spreading all the way to my toes. Then it dawned on me what Cole had referred to, and I looked at him, my brows furrowed, eyes narrowed. "Wait a minute, what do you mean I bring him business?"

"I meant the homicide unit hasn't been quite so busy until you popped into the equation."

"Hm. Well, I like to do my part. Consider it a service to the community." I leaned over and nudged Levi with my shoulder, sat up and pulled my knees up to my chest, my feet resting on the edge of the cushion. His hand settled on my knee. "Have you heard any more about today, Cole?"

"Nothing more than Wescott would have heard. They'd report to him before they'd tell me anything. I'm just a little peon there."

"Are you his boss?" I asked Levi, amused. "How does that work?"

"Yup, he's the boss man," Cole said. "The big kahuna."

I looked at Levi who was clearly uncomfortable and not saying a word.

"Is that true?" I asked him.

"No."

"Sorry, buddy," Cole said to him. "Didn't mean to out you." Then he looked at me, a grin tugging at his lips. "He's not just the big kahuna, he's the big humble kahuna." Three of us laughed, Levi not being one of them. "Nah, I'm teasing. About the big kahuna part, not the part about being humble. He's head of investigations, though."

I smiled at him. "Should I be impressed or afraid?"

"You should be very, very afraid," Levi said, shifting slightly.

"And why am I first hearing this now? And from someone other than you?"

"Would it have made a difference?" he asked, shifting again.

"Heck yeah. I would have run like the wind in the other direction," I teased.

I was learning new things about him all the time. And I couldn't say I was disappointed about any of those things. Instead, it all felt so—right.

But it wasn't right. I couldn't let myself forget that. Our time hanging out together was limited. What I had to decide was should I make it easier for both of us by pulling away now or make the most of what little time we have together and worry about the rest when it happens. And was that even fair to either one of us? No, I had to do it sooner rather than later.

"We need to talk later," I leaned in and whispered.

"That's what I've been telling you," he whispered back.

An invisible weight tugged my emotions as I mentally prepared to tell him my decision

"You okay there, Blondie? You're miles away," he whispered close to my ear, startling me back to right here and now.

"Just thinking."

"About what?"

"About what I want you to get me from the restaurant."

"You'd fail miserably with a lie detector test."

The warmth of his breath tickled my ear. I shrugged and looked at him, quickly turning away again from those gorgeous, mysterious, yet

172

beautifully simple gray-green eyes. His hand circled mine.

"Anything on the camera you installed behind Claire's shed, Cole?"

"Who, me?" he said, poking his thumb in his chest, eyebrows raised. "Because for a minute there I thought the two of you forgot there was anyone else in the room."

"You're a real wise guy," Levi grumbled.

"No, nothing yet. When I bring Claire home, I'll check again."

"Why don't we stop on our way to pick up the food?" Levi asked.

"I have a better idea," I said. "Why don't we just all go to the restaurant, eat there instead of you guys bringing it back here to the house, and we can stop at Claire's on the way?"

"You're just worried we'll find something without you," Cole said.

"You got me." I chuckled. "But you have to admit it's a splendid idea."

"I don't mind taking you with me on police business. In fact, I rather enjoy it," Levi said, his eyes twinkling. "It's when you go investigating on your own, getting yourself into trouble and I'm not there to get you out of it that bothers me."

"I don't need rescuing."

"Oh, you so do too!" Claire entered into the conversation. "Once you decided to spread your wings and taste more of life, you've been doing a fine job of getting into pickles. You asked, God answered."

"He answered a little too well," I said, laughing easily.

"Have you heard anything from Jack?" she asked me.

"Not for a few days. I need to call and check in with him. It's gotta be hard going through what he's going through."

"Which is what?" Levi asked.

"He and Curtis are splitting up."

"What happened?"

"Curtis is a jerk." I shook my head and stared into the fire. "He's never been supportive of Jack having a life outside of the business. In fact, he's resented me from the get-go for Jack having a little fun."

I felt Levi's hot stare, and then he asked, "Exactly how much does he resent you?"

I looked at him when I realized what he was referring to and shook my head. "Curtis doesn't like me, but he doesn't have anything to do with any of this."

"How can you be so sure?"

"He has a point, Mel," Claire said, taking a drink of her soda. "It wasn't too long ago that Curtis was spying on Jack up here. In fact, that's when it all started to unravel."

"Whoever is doing this is doing it because I'm getting too close to finding out the truth about Zachary Swanson."

"And what do you think that truth is?" Cole asked.

"I don't believe the fire was an accident."

"What do you have to base that on?"

"My gut. Intuition." I pointed my finger at him. "Before you say anything negative about that, hotshot, my intuition is usually spot on."

Claire tilted her head back and looked up at Cole. "She's right about that one."

"If something bad happened to that little boy I owe it to him—we owe it to him—to make sure it's revealed."

Levi laced his fingers through mine and gave my hand a gentle squeeze before he stood up, pulling me with him. "On that note, let's get a move on and go check the camera in Claire's backyard."

17

When we got to Claire's, she and I went straight into the backyard. Cole went to the house to get a flashlight, and Levi casually walked behind us. But not before instructing us not to touch anything. Duh. Didn't mean I wouldn't though.

I turned to see him, hands in his front pockets, head down. I wondered what he was looking at, if it was something specific or if he was just trying to see where he was going to avoid tripping. Other than the beam of light from the flashlight bouncing around as Cole caught up to us, it was black out, the moon and stars out of sight, in hiding, frightened by what we may find.

A shiver rippled through me. Why did I feel like there were more than four of us out here right now? This was one time I wished my intuition wasn't usually so accurate. But if there was someone else in the vicinity, watching, at least Cole and Levi were both here.

The beam of light caught up with us, lighting the way until we reached the back of the shed. Cole went into the shed and came back out with a short ladder. He handed the flashlight to Claire as he set the ladder up and began the short ascent to the camera. After the shuffling sounds of getting to the back of the camera, the noise stopped, and it was eerily quiet until Cole whispered a curse word.

"What is it?" I asked

"The SIM card is missing. We've been made."

Now I was certain we weren't alone out here.

"Claire, I don't like that you're staying here tonight," Cole said.

"She can stay at my house," I said, going over to stand next to her.

"I haven't even completely unpacked yet, and already I'm being chased away from my house."

"Staying with you might not be the best choice either, Melanie. Whoever wants to keep the deaths of the Swanson family a secret—well, it's you they're trying to stop."

"No matter how they have to see to it," Claire said.

"Tell you what, why don't we go eat and we can decide then," I suggested.

"I'm not hungry," Claire said, looking around her. "What was supposed to be my new home has turned into a place that freaks me out."

"Well, since the seller obviously didn't give full disclosure, you need to rescind the contract."

"And how do you propose I do that?" she asked, sulking.

"It's far from easy and would take litigation," Levi said. "But it could probably be done under the circumstances."

My hand was on her arm, and I felt her shiver. "Come on, Claire, I'm not hungry either, and that's a first. But it will do us good to get into a well-lit, busy place to clear our heads so we can think more clearly."

"Always the practical one, aren't you? Even in the face of disaster," she said, her voice quivering ever so slightly. She covered my hand with her own and gave it a squeeze.

Cole finished looking around with his flashlight while Levi put the ladder back in the shed. As if on the same thought plane, the two circled to the back of the shed. The door creaked as Levi pulled it open.

"Why do you get to touch and I don't?" I asked. The air around us was tight with tension.

"Because I'm the cop," Levi said. If he knew I was in jest, he made no show of it. Of course, I didn't feel the lightness either. I was freaked out right along with Claire. "Let's get going." He led, the rest of us followed like obedient children. Nana would be proud.

The Fishing Hole Restaurant was hopping for a Sunday evening in late fall. There was a thirty-minute wait. Not that any of us minded. Especially Claire and me.

"Why is it that I'm more comfortable in a crowded room than with no people around?" she asked.

I looked at her and said, "Me too right now. Strange as it sounds, I'm not worried about being watched here." I looked at each of them around the circle high-top table as we waited for the host to seat us in the dining area. "Did anyone else feel like there was more than just the four of us out by the shed? Like maybe five of us?"

"Does anyone think it's weird that despite the person visiting my backyard they haven't bothered me? Mel has been the sole target of their hostility."

"I don't think it's weird at all," Levi said. "Melanie is the one who kicked the hornet's nest threatening to sting the person who's at the bottom of this."

"Well, it's not going to stop unless we find out who it is and stop them ourselves. Or myself," I mumbled.

Cole's eyes flashed with recognition as he looked across the room. He lifted his arm and waved.

"Hey, Mikey!" he called, still waving. Michael came over to the table and slapped Cole and Levi on the back in a friendly gesture and gave each of them a fist bump. "What are you doin' here, man?"

"Are you kidding me?" Michael said. "This place has the best fish and chips I've ever had. It's smoked salmon and fabulous." He looked at Claire and me and nodded at each of us. "Ladies?"

"Hi," we both said, enthusiasm lacking from both of us. Okay, just me. But including Claire in my lack of enthusiasm didn't make me feel alone.

"Where's your friend?"

"Rubie?" I asked.

"That'd be the one. Is she here?"

"No. We'll have to do. It's just us."

"That's too bad." He looked at Cole and then Levi. "I was supposed to meet my dad here, but it looks like he's standing me up. Mind if I join you guys?"

"Please do," I said, probably too quickly. Claire looked at me and raised her eyebrows. I didn't buy that he was out here for the fish and chips. But as long as he was here I was going to get what information I could. And what better way than when he had a beer or two, loosening his lips.

The host called our name, and we all stood and followed the waitress to our table.

"Can we please get an extra chair?" I asked her. "We have an unexpected addition to our party." I looked at Michael and smiled, a smile that I could feel didn't quite reach my eyes.

Levi put an arm around my waist, pulled me close, his lips brushing my ear. "What are you doing?" he whispered.

"Me?" I pulled back and looked up at him, my eyes wide with innocence I'm sure he couldn't quite see. "Nothing at all. Just being hospitable and inviting someone to eat with us, so he doesn't have to sit alone. He was stood up after all. So sad." I frowned.

Levi's eyes sparkled with amusement. I smiled, trying to look as cute as I could make myself out to be. "It's not working, Mel," he whispered in my ear again. "You're up to something. I can smell it."

"You're such a suspicious detective."

The waitress led us to a booth in the far corner, a sconce with a red shade hanging on the wall on the inside of the booth, a red tealight candle floating in a small bowl of water in the center of the table. Claire and Cole sat on one side of the booth, Levi and me on the other, and

Michael sat on the chair the waitress pulled from an empty table and put at the end of our booth.

"Can I get you something to drink?" asked the waitress.

We went around the table each taking our turn at giving her our order. When she got to Michael, he ordered seltzer water with a twist of lime.

"Wouldn't you rather have a beer?" I asked.

"I hate to be the only one drinking," he said.

"Levi's on call so he can't. But that doesn't mean you can't. Unless you're on call, too?" I asked.

"No, no. I'm not on call. I don't mind. I'd rather just have a club soda and—"

"How about if I have a glass of wine. That way you won't be the only one." I motioned at the server.

Levi stretched his arm loosely around my shoulders and said in a quiet voice with a forced smile, "Darlin', he said he doesn't want a beer."

"I was just thinking since it's a night of celebrating—"

"Oh?" Michael's eyes lit up. "What are we celebrating?"

"Just getting closer to answers is all." Levi's gaze burned into me like lasers, Claire choked on her drink, and Cole looked like he was waiting for a hand grenade to fall from my lips. "Answers to a problem we've been having with a co-worker, isn't that right, Claire?" I could swear I felt a gust of wind as each exhaled in relief.

"What kind of problem?" asked Michael.

I had to admit, he looked completely clueless. Either he truly was innocent of any wrongdoing, or he was a master actor.

"One of the girls at work insists on getting to the bottom of the Swanson family deaths. I told her to leave it alone, to let the past stay the past. But you know how we women can sometimes be," I said, smiling sweetly at him.

"Don't I know it," he mumbled, his eyes dark and distant before meeting mine again. "But I agree with you. Why dig up something that was put to rest a long time ago?"

I heard a sharp intake of breath and realized it was mine. I looked at Claire who appeared to be in shock, her eyes wide as could be. Levi cleared his throat, and Cole kept his gaze trained on me, no doubt fearful of what would come next. But I heard all I needed to. Pressing for more would only sabotage my efforts.

"Michael, have you heard anything more from the Hammonds?" Levi asked.

"Nope. Those two are going to kill each other one of these days. One of them is going to go missing, mark my words. And when they do, the other is going to act all surprised, but we'll all know what happened."

"I couldn't imagine living life with someone who makes you so miserable," Cole added.

"Well, we can't all have the perfect relationship like you and Claire do," I added.

"There's no such thing as the perfect relationship," said Michael.

"Then you haven't spent enough time around these two." I nodded my head at my girl and her beau and gave them an eye-roll.

"Perfect is completely subjective," Levi said, nudging me with his shoulder. "Perfect can happen if both parties are willing. Wouldn't you agree, Melanie?"

I felt my cheeks get hot. "I think I'm ready to look at the menu."

Levi's phone buzzed against my leg, and I jumped. He picked it up, looked at the display, frowned and sighed. "Looks like my fun just ended." He put the phone up his ear. "Wescott," he answered, suddenly all business. He listened to the caller talk, frowned again, and hung up. "I hate to say this, folks, but work calls."

"Literally. Need any help?" Cole asked.

"I'll let you know once I see what we've got." He shifted his attention to Michael. "Hey, buddy, could I impose on you for a ride to Melanie's to get my car? We took hers up here."

"We haven't ordered anything yet but drinks. Why don't we just all go?" Cole asked.

"I don't want to ruin everyone else's night," Levi said. "You guys stay and eat and feel sorry for me as I slave, starving and cold, working my butt off."

A round of laughter erupted.

"I'll take you," Michael said. "I should get going anyway. Obviously, my dad's not going to show. I should go check what's up."

Levi leaned over, grazing his lips on my cheek and whispered, "Call me when you get home, okay? I'm coming by to crash on your couch again as soon as I finish up at the scene."

Exhilarated tingling reached my toes again at his nearness. What in the world was I going to do about this situation? Ending it now seemed more and more impossible.

"Be careful out there," I said.

18

By the time we were done eating it was dark outside. Of course, this time of year it got dark far too early anyway, making me tired well before it's time for bed. After the third time yawning, I slipped my coat on.

"Thanks for letting me hang with you guys and be the third wheel. But I've had all the fun I can handle and need to get home."

"Am I staying at your house?" Claire asked. "Cause if I am, I'll just ride home with you since we have Cole's car."

"Or I could take you over to Melanie's when you're ready. I want to check your house anyway."

"Tell you what. You two take your time and work it out. Claire, you have the key to my house. Just let yourself in when you get there. I'm so dog tired I may crash and burn before I even get home."

"Okay. If you're sure. Not about the falling asleep at the wheel part." She started to nudge Cole to let her out of the booth. "I don't think you should drive if you're that tired. I'll drive your car."

"No. No, you won't. Apparently, Levi is crashing again on the couch, so I'll be okay. Really."

"Yeah, but who knows what time he'll get done and to your place. Call me when you get there, okay?"

"For heaven's sake, girl, it's all of four miles and still relatively early. What can happen?"

"After watching you in action tonight a whole lot can happen in a short amount of time," Cole felt the need to add.

"I don't remember asking you," I teased him. Well, kind of teased, anyway.

"What was that all about anyway?" he asked.

"Cole, how well do you know Michael?" I draped my scarf around my neck.

"Well enough to know he's a good man. He's one of us."

"One of us as in a link in the blue line? Or one of us as in one of 'us'?" I pointed to them and then to myself.

"Both."

"Hm."

"Why don't you like him?" Claire asked me as I buttoned my jacket.

"I don't know the man, so it's not that I don't like him." Cole slid out of the booth, and I leaned over to give her a hug. "Trusting him, on the other hand, is an entirely different matter."

Cole walked me out to my car, and once I was inside, he closed the door. I let my car warm up while I watched him disappear back into The Fishing Hole. The parking lot had cleared out significantly since we'd first arrived, and there were only a handful of cars left. Unusual for this place, especially since it was still somewhat early.

I watched as one of the tall parking lot lamps flickered on and off, finally sputtering out, like some horror flick.

I shivered, locked my doors and decided to get going despite my heating vents still blowing cold air. Not only was it creepy out here, but morning would come early, and I needed some sleep. Since it was hard to say whether Levi would be done with his call at a reasonable time, having Claire stay at my house tonight would be nice so I could get some sleep without worrying about her. Or about myself being alone, for that matter. Plus, if Levi did come by, it was a whole lot safer to have Claire there protected by him as well.

I had just turned the corner leading to the last two mile stretch to my house when bright lights appeared out of nowhere behind me, blinding me. As the lights gained on me, I pressed a little bit harder on the accelerator, but they only got closer, until they looked like they were right on my bumper. Visions of the accident I was in several years ago played vividly in my mind, and my heartbeat picked up its pace until I was sure it would propel me home in a nanosecond.

I tried to see if it was the same vehicle that had followed me around town the other night but it was hard to tell with the headlights shining right in my rearview mirror. I didn't think it was, though. The other night it was a sedan. This was a pickup truck of some sort. I was able to glimpse a bar high up across the entire width of the top of the vehicle. Yup, definitely a truck, and a big one at that.

My mind raced trying to think if I knew anyone with a truck, but I couldn't think of a single soul. What I knew for sure, though, was that I couldn't go home right now and lead this maniac to my front door. I had to turn around and get back to The Fishing Hole.

I sped up even faster, a dangerous decision on a country road after dark when a deer had been known on numerous occasions to dart out from nowhere, but my choices at this point were limited. It was either risk a deer or risk my life with this person intent on terrorizing me. I was safer with the deer.

My foot pressed harder on the pedal, and the phrase "pedal to the metal" became my reality. The space between my car and the truck widened, but only for a moment before it was right back on my bumper again. I felt my car jerk, and my phone, which had been in my shoulder bag, scattered to the floor with most of the contents of my purse. He hit my bumper! I felt another bump, and my body jerked forward, my seatbelt keeping me from hitting the steering wheel. Thank God I was better about wearing my seatbelt than I was about wearing a bike helmet.

I swerved to the left, grateful there wasn't any oncoming traffic, stepped on my brake and spun around to face the opposite direction, my tires squealing. I stepped on the gas again, the truck far behind until out of nowhere it was right on my bumper again, bumping into me harder than before. What the heck?!

Before I knew what was happening, the truck was pushing my bumper, and any control I had of my car was out of my hands and into this madman's. What was he going to do to me? Had I just eaten my last supper at the Fishing Hole? What would happen to my grandmother without me to watch out for her? Losing me would break her heart.

A million and one things ran through my mind at breakneck speed, yet things seemed to move in slow motion. The next thing I knew, my car flew headfirst into a swamp, the front end sinking into the muck, the rear end sticking up, and my airbags deployed.

When all was still, I opened my eyes to find everything was dark. All I could smell was the swampy stank of mud, moss, and stale water, which was now leaking into my car. There wasn't a single sliver of light anywhere around me. The front of my car inched a little further down. I took my seatbelt off and felt around the floor for my phone, grasping at everything, feeling with both hands until I found it. I felt for the little circle on the bottom of my phone and pushed. Nothing. Panic seized me, and I thought I was going to hyperventilate.

"Breathe, Melanie" I whispered. "Just breathe." I closed my eyes and forced slow deep breaths, one after the other until I was as calm as I was going to get. I touched the circle again, and this time my phone lit up. Thank God. Literally. And thank God I had Claire on speed dial, because my hands were shaking so badly I wouldn't have been able to punch in an entire number.

I heard Claire and Cole before I saw their lights. Judging by the sound of squealing tires, it was unmistakable how fast he was going, and I panicked again. They were either going to join me in this goopy swamp, and we'd all be up a creek, or they were going to drive right by me. Finally, his car lights illuminated the interior of my car through the back windshield that was still sticking up in the air. Another set of lights turned toward me. A truck!

I pressed the button to roll down my window, but nothing happened. *That's right, genius, electric windows.* I pivoted sideways and kicked one foot against the glass. Nothing. I attempted to start my car again. And, again, nothing. It felt like my brain was shorting out, leaving me without a clue as to what to do. Finally, finding strength I didn't know I had, I thrust both feet against the glass. My car door window shattered.

"Cole!" I choked, my voice hoarse, causing it to be quieter than it needed to be for him to hear me. "The truck—watch out!" I tried again to warn him. I poked my head out the broken window and looked toward the back of my car. Cole was talking and motioning something to another man standing in the stream of light. The extra set of lights I'd seen were from a tow truck. How had Cole managed to contact a tow truck and have him here so quickly? My phone lit up. *Now* it decides to work! I looked at the incoming number. "Cole?"

"Melanie, listen to me. Michael is going to pull out your car with his truck. I want you to keep your seatbelt on and—"

"Too late," I choked.

"Too late for what?"

"My seatbelt is already off. I kicked out my window."

"I heard it. But that's not the point, here, Melanie. Put your seat belt back on and brace as best you can. Michael's going to—"

"I know. Pull my car out." I swallowed hard, not sure if I felt relief or fear. One thing was for certain, I was going to feel pain. I touched my head gingerly with my free hand, wincing when I pressed too hard. "Michael's here?"

"Yes. His uncle owns a tow service, and he helps him out."

"How did he get here so fast?"

"You pick an awful time to ask questions, Hogan."

Leave it to Cole to find a polite, kind way to tell me to shut up. "So what do I need to do?"

"Nothing. You need to do absolutely nothing but buckle up and sit there. I know you're not very good at that, but I need you to try."

"Smart—"

"Man," he interrupted. "Smart man."

"That's what I was going to say," I said, trying hard to banter when it typically came so easily, like second nature. My head was splitting in half, and I couldn't stop violently shaking from the combination of fear and cold.

I heard a loud clank on my bumper. I jumped and screamed. I was too far gone to be calm at this point.

"That was just the iron hook from the tow truck connecting to your car. Stay on the phone with me, Mel. Talk to me until he gets you out of there."

"Is Claire with you?"

"Yup. She can't wait to talk to you. I told her to stay in my car where it's warm."

"Hey, Cole?"

"Yeah?"

"Thanks. For everything."

"Don't go getting sappy on me, Melanie," he teased lightly.

"Wouldn't think of it."

He said something to Michael, and I heard Michael's voice in the background. Guilt invaded my fear as I thought about how horrible I'd been to Michael earlier. Michael said something else, and then Cole's voice came across the phone again.

"Okay, he's ready to pull your car out. Hang on, okay? Looks like the front end is pretty stuck in the mud so it might jerk at first."

"Maybe I should get out first."

"Stay put."

"Then pull. I'm stronger than I look."

I heard him give a short laugh. "Don't I know it, Melanie. Don't I know it."

My car now back on the road, someone pried open my door, and I fell into the arms of the person who caught me, keeping me from hitting the pavement. I found it odd that my shaking increased now that I was safe.

The arms felt familiar and the hint of cologne unmistakable.

"I'm gone for all of an hour and a half, and you manage to get yourself into trouble," Levi said, holding me tight.

"Superman is here," I tried to tease through clattering teeth.

"Claire called me as soon as they got here and saw the pickle you were in."

"I'm glad she did." He held me until the shaking diminished enough that I could talk without fear of biting my tongue. "We need to talk."

"Yes we do," he agreed, still holding me, one arm around me, the other hand cradling the back

191

of my head. "I need you to tell me exactly what happened and exactly what you saw."

"I mean about us." I had to be delirious.

"Can't believe I'm saying this, but now's not the time. You choose the strangest times to want to have a conversation. Right now I need to find out who's trying to hurt you. The way it's going, I may as well set up camp in your guest room for a while."

"Do I get breakfast every morning?"

He chuckled a low, sexy sound. He was probably sure of my delirium now, talking about food at a time like this. I probably was for all I knew. Everything seemed skewed right now. My world was upside down. I needed a hot shower, a roaring fire in the fireplace, a cup of hot cocoa, and the company of good friends. I had one of four right now. Not bad, but I was aiming for four of four. Might as well shoot for the moon.

"Nope. I tried that, and you didn't eat it. Waste of food, if you ask me."

I held onto him tighter, wincing as pain shot through my head, my neck, and into my shoulder. "I'm glad you're here."

He pulled back slowly and looked into my eyes, both of us bathed in the lights of Cole's car. "I'm going to remind you of that the next time you try to run away from me."

"I've waited long enough," Claire's sweet voice sounded behind me. "It's my turn to give her a hug."

"Jeez! If I'd known I'd get this kind of attention with these things, I'd see that they happened more often."

"That's not funny!" Claire said, smacking my arm before she pulled me into a tight hug.

"Ouch!" I cried. "Careful. I discovered tonight I might be breakable. Or even broken."

One glance at Levi as I tried to pry myself free from Claire's grasp let me know he didn't appreciate my humor. *Oops. Some people were so sensitive.*

Red, blue, and white lights lit up the sky, sirens piercing the night, and soon two squad cars pulled up on the side of the road. I was sure to be on a first-name basis with the entire police and sheriff departments if this continued. Levi spoke with them, and they, along with Michael and Cole huddled together, each listening intently to whoever happened to be talking at the time.

When they finished, Michael began securing my car onto his tow truck. Water trickled from the window, and pieces of metal dangled where they should be firmly attached. The trunk had all but disappeared in a crunched up mess.

I watched as a piece of my past was put to rest. A part of my past I wasn't ready to let go of yet. It was so much more than just a car. It was a symbol of my independence after Cain left me. Something to prove that I didn't need him to complete my circle. I was enough all by myself. And not only was it a car that symbolized I didn't have to be Stable Mable all of the time, but I could also be fun and unpredictable and spontaneous if I wanted to be. And the best part? It was paid off. There was something beautiful to be said for not having a car payment. I groaned.

"Well? Which of you is going to give me a ride home?"

"Not only am I giving you a lift home, but I'm bringing you to the hospital. You need to get checked out," Levi said. "I can't believe you
193

wouldn't let them call you an ambulance. More than that, I can't believe they listened to you."

"They knew better. And I'm not going to the hospital," I argued.

"Oh, but you are."

"No, I'm—"

"Melanie," he said, exhaling loudly with exasperation, "I'm calling the shots here. I've seen your car, your forehead is bleeding, you're shaking like a leaf in a hurricane...need I go on?"

"Fine," I said, exasperated. "But I think you're overreacting."

"Be that as it may I, as well as Claire, would feel better if you got checked out. And that's not to mention your grandmother if she knew about this."

"Which she won't, will she folks?" I asked them, sounding sterner than I felt.

"When you're done at the hospital I'll bring you home and then go to my house and pick up a few things so I can stay and be sure you stay put and okay."

"Don't trust me, Detective? Claire said she would stay at my house."

"Why doesn't that make me feel any better?" He shook his head.

"Hey," Claire complained. "I take offense to that."

"Simply meaning that she won't listen to you if you tell her something anyway."

"*She* is standing right here, folks." I gave Claire a careful hug before walking to Levi's department car.

"It's the people whose world you upset that I don't trust," he said.

"See you at my house, Claire," I called over my shoulder, pain slicing through my head.

19

After being checked out at the hospital, Levi took me home so I could take a hot shower and change into my sweatpants and a hoodie and to get the hot chocolate I had been craving all evening.

I had just sat down with a cup of hot chocolate that he had ready for me when I heard Claire's key turn in the lock.

"Hey guys!" she called out. She came into the living room, slipped her coat off and sat in the chair. "Am I interrupting anything?"

"Nope," I smiled at her. It was nice to have her here in the safety of my home. "Levi was just waiting for you to get here before he ran to his house to pick up a few things. Apparently, he doesn't trust me to be alone. It's not like I can go anywhere."

He stood up, picked up his cap from the chair and walked toward the kitchen. "It's not Melanie I don't trust; it's the people she chooses to hang out with. Present company excluded, of course." He put on his leather coat and picked up his keys. "The people she lets into her life leave a lot to be desired."

"Yeah, I've been telling her that for over a year now," Claire said.

He looked at Claire. "Don't let her talk you into leaving the room. She has a mild concussion and whiplash. Doc says she needs to stay awake for a few hours and take it easy for a couple of days." He grazed my cheek with his lips and whispered in my ear, "See you in about thirty minutes, Blondie."

"See to it that it's not thirty-one." With a small chuckle, he was out of the house, locking the door behind him.

"The man even takes my keys. Like I'm going to go anywhere. I have no car."

Claire smiled at me. "Cole followed me over here and waited until I got in before he left. Are you drinking hot chocolate?"

"What a gentleman, that Cole." I mumbled. "Yup. Want some?" I got up and began making it for her without waiting for her to answer. I handed her a mug of the chocolate delight, topped with whipped cream and marshmallows.

"I finally get you to myself," she said as she licked the whipped cream, leaving a rim of white around her chocolate lips. "Seems like those times are few and far between these days."

"That's because your boy toy is always around."

"Not so. It's because you're always in the middle of some crisis that requires the entire community to get you out of." Our eyes met, and I noticed how tired hers looked. "You scared the heck out of me tonight, Mel." Her voice was quiet, and I could hear it shake ever so slightly.

"It's not like I did it on purpose." I finished off the last of my hot chocolate.

"You've had too many close calls lately. You've got to realize what that does to the people who love you. If your grandmother knew—"

"Which she won't," I interrupted, "right?" She didn't answer. "Claire?" I asked, my voice stern.

She looked down and then back up at me. "I won't tell her. For no other reason than I don't want her to worry more than she already does."

"I need to go see her tomorrow. What time is Syd coming home?"

"About that...Cole and I talked about that after you left..."

"And?" She stared at me as if trying to choose her words, something she's never had a problem with as long as I've known her. "What aren't you telling me?"

She looked into her mug as if watching something inside of it, but I knew her. She was avoiding looking at me.

"Claire?"

"I can't have her coming home with all this going on. It's not safe for her, Melanie."

The reality hit me, and a lump formed in my throat. "I'm standing in the way of your baby girl coming home."

Her head tilted to the side as she looked at me. "Not you, per se, but what's happening to you. I can't take that risk."

"I'll get to the bottom of it, Claire. I promise."

"Wanting to get to the bottom of it is what got us here in the first place."

I had nothing to say. What she said was entirely accurate. Finally, I looked at her and hung my head in shame. "I got nothin'."

"Well, then that's a first." She sighed, then continued. "Melanie, when you find yourself smack in the middle of things as you did with William and Violet, that's one thing. But when you insert yourself in the midst of things, that's entirely another."

I leaned back against the sofa cushion, put my head back, winced at the twinge in my neck, followed by stiffness. I sighed. "Claire, I'm sorry. I don't know what else I can say. All I could think about was Zachary and doing right by him."

"I get it, Melanie. The soft spot you have for kids, though, can be to your detriment. And to everyone around you. Just say you'll be more careful in the future." She leaned forward and picked up my hand, holding it in hers. "I would die if anything happened to you. And I can't even imagine what your grandmother would do. And Jack? Don't even get me started with Jack. He would have your hide if he knew what you got yourself into the middle of. We all count on you."

"I know." I looked down again and stared at the braided rug that covered the center of my hardwood floor. I felt like a child being scolded and waiting for my punishment to be handed out. When it was clear she was done, I looked at her, a smile tugging at one side of my lips. "Guess it's a good thing you have Cole to keep an eye on you and make sure you're safe, huh?"

"Yeah," she said.

I stared at her hair, kinky and wild. She rarely let it out of one of her brightly colored hair scarves, and when she did the freckles on her nose and cheeks popped out on her dark complexion, more noticeable than ever. Her mother being part Native American and her father African American gave her a gorgeous skin tone, more beautiful than I'd ever seen on anyone else in this lifetime.

"What's the scoop with Levi?" she asked.

"I don't know yet. We haven't had a chance to talk with everything that's been happening."

"What are you going to do?"

"I don't know that yet either." I sighed and slowly rolled my neck, working out the kinks. "We get along so well. He's fun, he's smart, he gets me—which I'll be the first to admit isn't an easy thing. I respect the man beyond anything I can even describe. He's kind, gentle...hot!" I added, wiggling my eyebrows.

Claire laughed. "It sounds to me like you'd be crazy to do anything other than hang onto him."

"Not crazy at all. I'd be selfish to hang onto him, Claire." My heart was heavy at the thought of giving up something amazing before it had a chance to develop into something more amazing. And I had no doubt it would. The million dollar question was at whose expense, though. His son's?

"If you give this a shot and it works out, his son won't be losing a father, he'll be gaining an incredible role model for a woman."

"What, are you reading my mind now? About his son, that is, not about the amazing role model thing," I said. "Although that part's true, too."

"Oh, brother!"

We laughed, and for a moment it felt like old times. Times I missed like crazy. But I've seen how happy spending time with Cole makes Claire, and I was glad for her. She deserves to be happy more than anyone I knew.

"I can go home tonight, you know, so you and the man can talk."

I snickered. "The man? Well, I'm not about to let you stay by yourself at your house."

"It's not me the freak wants, it's you. If anything I'm in more danger here than at my house."

"Good point."

"Hmmm, yes it is. Which is why I can't leave you here alone. Not even until Levi gets back."

"You're in the protection business?" I remembered how she'd saved by butt a time or two in the past when I'd had no idea she had it in her. "But then it wouldn't be the first time, would it?"

"Nope. Remember that," she said, grinning again, obviously quite proud of herself. "Hey, want a ride into work tomorrow?"

"That'd be nice since it'd be close to five by the time I got there if I had to walk." I thought about my car; no doubt totaled out. "Can I borrow your car tomorrow for a while? I guess I should go get myself a new car."

"Of course you can. Do you need me to help with anything?"

"Nah. I'll call my clients and reschedule who I can and see if Connie and Rubie can fit in a couple of them. Rubie's clientele is building quickly, but her schedule hasn't filled in yet."

"Here comes Levi." The beams of light from his headlamps reflected in the window on the opposite side of my house from the window that faced the front yard.

"I'll make myself scarce."

"You'll do no such thing." I stood to unlock the door for him, holding it open as he retrieved a small duffel bag from the passenger's seat. "Is that all you brought?" I asked him.

"We'll take it a day at a time as we figure this mess out."

"So the sooner I find out who's after me, the sooner you get to go back to your house?"

"That's not what I said, but, yeah, that's essentially it in a nutshell."

"Claire and I would have been fine on our own you know. You didn't need to put yourself out on our account."

"Yeah, I saw how that worked for you earlier tonight." I knew he was teasing but my cheeks still flushed with embarrassment. And I'd be lying if I said it didn't sting a little. He held the door as I let it go and backed into the kitchen.

He closed and locked the door, set his duffel down on the floor and put a hand under my chin, looking into my eyes. "I'm not being 'put out' as you stated. I would hope you'd know that by now."

"It just seems like I've caused a whole lot of upset for a whole lot of people."

"I don't see anyone who's upset here except the person who's trying to hide the truth from being found out."

"Claire's decided Sydney can't come home until we know who is doing this."

"Melanie, listen to me and please listen good. Until you made things uncomfortable for this person, he was roaming around free. And if that's the case, no one is safe." His lips brushed mine, and I got goosebumps upon goosebumps. "Don't get me wrong, I'm not saying I'm thrilled about this, but only because you're the one in danger."

"I'm glad you're here. I am." I turned away from him before he saw something I wasn't ready for him to see yet. If ever. "Can I get you anything?"

"Coffee. But I can get it myself. You go sit down and visit with Claire. A blind man could see you two aren't spending much time together these days."

How lucky was I? Not only was he all kinds of hot, but he was also sensitive and sweet, too. As my grandmother would say, Uffda!

I watched as he took his gun out of its holster and set it on the dining room table.

"Don't get any ideas," he said, not looking at me.

"I don't need yours. I have my own," I said, sounding like a spoiled five-year-old instead of the forty-one-year-old that I am.

"God help us all," he said, and I could hear the amusement in his voice. "How're you feeling? How's your head?"

"Still attached but aching like a son-of-a-gun."

He opened his duffel and pulled out a bottle of Tylenol and handed me two before he poured me a glass of water. I held them in the palm of my hand then set them on the end table. I couldn't decide if his being so attentive to my every need was sweet or uncomfortable. It would be easy to get used to this, but I couldn't let that happen. I couldn't.

My back stiffened with resolve I didn't totally feel. The tired, aching part of me wanted just to relax and let him take care of me. I needed some sleep so I could think clearly again instead of being weak, but he wouldn't let me sleep. *Darn ER doctor should have kept his mouth shut instead of giving Levi instructions. What did he know? Give the man a license to practice medicine, and he thinks he knows what's best.*

Levi sat down by me on the couch and looked at the cut on my forehead then the scrapes and bruises forming on my forearms and cheek.

"I'm going to be a real beauty come morning, huh? You'll both run out of the house screaming."

"We'll both just be grateful you're alive," Claire said.

I groaned and rested my head back against the sofa. "Man, I'm getting old. Feels like a truck hit me." My eyes popped open wide. "Oh! That's because one did!"

All of a sudden I started giggling, which turned into a fit of laughter that I couldn't stop no matter how much I wanted to. I had no idea why I was even laughing. I had lost control of my emotions, and despite seeing the concern in Claire and Levi's eyes as they watched me, exchanging glances, I couldn't stop. The laughter turned to a tear, then two, and then Levi held me as I sobbed.

After what felt like an eternity of Levi smoothing my hair and rocking me back and forth, the crying finally subsided, my breaths coming in gasps. I thought about when Violet left and after the door closed behind her how I cried until I was out of breath and gasping for air as granddad held me, my little arms wrapped around him, my face buried in his neck.

Claire held a tissue in front of me as she rubbed my back.

I took the tissue. "Thanks, but I don't need this. Levi's shirt worked great."

She chuckled as she continued to rub my back. "That cry was long overdue, my friend."

"Check that off my list, then," I tried to tease, my voice still quivering as I shook from the deepest part of my insides. "I'll need to get a new car tomorrow."

"Don't you need to wait for an insurance settlement?" Levi asked.

"I only had liability insurance on mine. And we don't know who crashed into me so I can't get his insurance information."

"Need to borrow some money?"

His question both shocked me and scared the living tar out of me.

"No," I said when I gathered my wits about me. "I have money in savings. I've got no one but Nana and Syd to spend my money on. And Nana won't let me buy her anything."

"Apple doesn't fall far from the tree," he muttered.

"I heard that," I said, my eyes narrowing. "But I'm proud to be anything like Nana at all."

"I can take you to the car dealer."

"Claire's letting me borrow her car."

"How about I take you?"

"I don't need—"

"Relax. I'm only taking you because the doctor said no driving for at least a day," he interrupted me. "It's part of that whole take it easy thing you're already having a hard time with."

"She neglected to tell me the part about the doctor saying no driving," Claire said, frowning at me.

"Fine. I'll take a taxi," I said, stuffed up from crying.

Levi let out a breath, long and slow and shook his head. "You are the most hard-headed, stubborn woman I've ever known. I'm taking you. End of story."

I gave him the old eye roll. "You don't have to be so bossy."

"You may want to think seriously about telling Rose," said Claire. "Otherwise how are you going to explain a new car?"

"That's right." I groaned and rested my head back again. "I hadn't thought that far ahead. I'll have to tell her, just not tonight. I'm too tired and just want to get some sleep."

"Can't let you do that," Levi said, taking my hand in his. "Doc told me to keep you awake."

"You're seriously trying to punish me, aren't you?" Pouting. Whining. I was getting pretty good at both. *Such an attractive woman when I didn't get my way.* "Maybe you could bring me over to Nana's after I find a car? I want to spend some time with her anyway."

"That'll work." He looked at Claire as he stood up. "I'm leaving her in your hands since she doesn't think you're so mean. I'll be at the kitchen table doing some work."

"Need help? I'm one heck of an investigator," I said.

He chuckled. "How about you leave that up to me and save all of us the extra work of worrying about you."

"Not funny." I made a face at him behind his back as he walked away.

I heard my phone ring on the kitchen counter. "Don't get up," he said. "I'll bring it to you."

"That's good because I don't think I have the energy to do anything other than sit here right now. I am stupid sore," I complained.

By the time Levi got the phone to me, the ringtone had stopped. A minute later it chimed, letting me know I had a voicemail. I looked and saw I had not one voicemail, but three, and I didn't recognize any of the numbers. I was tempted to put it aside since it wasn't anyone in my circle, that circle being Nana, Jack, Claire, Rubie, and now Levi, but thought what the heck, I wasn't being allowed to go to sleep anyway so I may as well listen to them.

I pressed play and put the phone to my ear, listening as the first message started. My mistake or good fortune—I hadn't decided yet. In fact, only time would tell. I set my phone down wondering what in the world I was going to do now. In fact, I thought I just might be sick. That or my head injury was worse than I expected.

20

"Melanie?" Claire's voice interrupted my speeding thoughts. "What is it? Looks like you've seen a ghost."

"No ghosts. Not yet, anyway." I looked at Claire and then to Levi who was standing in the doorway between the kitchen and the living room watching me.

"Who was it?" Levi asked.

"Which one?"

He frowned. "Meaning?"

"There were three voicemails. One was from Bryce, one from Zachary Swanson's kindergarten teacher." I took a deep breath. "The other from Cain." The room seemed to tilt slightly, and I wondered if I was going to wake up and realize it was all a dream. My pain in the neck or just wouldn't stay away. The resentment toward him I've yet to shake was bad enough. Now he decides to pop up?

Claire whistled. "Wow," she said in the middle of a loud exhale.

I looked at Levi, his eyes vacant and unreadable.

"First things first," Claire said. "What did Bryce want? And why would he call you knowing you're Jack's friend?"

"Hopefully not to talk about Jack, because I'd have an earful for him."

"I don't think it's a good idea for you to call him back tonight," Levi said. "Any of them. Getting upset isn't helping your recovery."

"I wouldn't call Bryce back without calling Jack first anyway. And whether I call him back at all depends entirely on whether Jack is comfortable with it. Zach's teacher I have to call back." I looked at Levi, my eyes pleading with him to understand.

"Cain?" Levi asked, his voice sounding quiet and distant. "The fact that he's calling now puts a whole new spin on things." I looked at him in confusion. "These attacks against you might have nothing to do with Zachary Swanson at all."

I shook my head, winced when it felt like a knife sliced through it. "No, Cain wouldn't physically hurt me."

"Yeah, because he's proven himself to be a real stand-up man," Levi grumbled.

"He's a manipulative, lying, cheating jerk, yes. But he wouldn't physically hurt me." Would he?

"What about the note she got on her windshield that night about leaving things with Zach alone?" Claire asked, looking at Levi.

"Leaving a cryptic note and shooting at someone and running them off the road are two entirely different matters." He tugged a kitchen chair into the room and straddled it backward, his arms resting across the back of the chair.

"Do you want me to call him?" Claire asked. "Jack, not Bryce or Cain." She shuddered.

"Yeah, that'd be great. But don't tell him about the accident because he'll be on the first road outta town and here within minutes."

"Isn't that his call to make and not yours?"

"Listen, friends, I don't have enough sleeping space for everyone. Before ya know it, the whole town of Birch Haven will be spending the night here."

Levi chuckled bitterly. "Well, I know of at least one I wouldn't want staying the night here."

"I draw the line there, buddy," I said. "Claire's staying regardless of what you say."

Claire tossed a pillow in my direction, realizing her mistake as soon as the pillow left her fingertips. "Oh my gosh! I'm so sorry!" Her eyes were wide, her mouth opened in horror.

"Relax. I've decided I'm not breakable afterall."

"Someone's doing their best in this town to prove you are," Levi said. "Not to minimize the importance of Bryce or Cain's call, but tell me what the teacher wanted. He or she has to be in their seventies by now."

"Said her name is Mildred Walker, she was Zachary Swanson's kindergarten teacher and that after tonight's incident she has information she thinks I'll find interesting."

"What I want to know is how she got your name and number. And how she knows about you digging into Zachary's life and death." His brows knit together as he seemed to disappear. "I don't like this."

"I'm going to call her back and arrange to meet tomorrow."

"I'll take you," Levi said.

"Trying to take over my investigation, Detective?"

"Relax. I'm volunteering to be the Watson to your Sherlock."

I gave him a half smile, my mind already traveling down various paths of what she could want to tell me, while a significant part of my brain couldn't get past hearing Cain's voice and wondering why he wanted me to call him. "As soon as possible, Mel. I need to talk to you," he'd said. It not only sounded urgent, but rather desperate. But why and about what?

I looked at my iPhone. It was late to be making phone calls, but anxiety nipped at my heels. If I could just get some sleep to block it from an outright attack, it would be great. But I knew the chances of that were zilch.

Only one way to find out what they wanted, late or not. I'd start with Mildred. I pressed the call-back button on my phone and listened to a generic voice message on the line telling me, "You've reached 320-555-5151, you know what to do. Leave a message, and I'll call you back." The message threw me off, and I nearly missed the beep that signaled me to begin talking.

"Oh! Uh, Mrs. Walker, this is Melanie Hogan calling you back. Please call me and—"

"Hello?"

"Is this Mildred Walker?"

"It is. Thank you for calling me back."

"I hope it's not too late."

"No, no. Just because I'm old doesn't mean I go to bed early. We need to talk. I think you'll be interested in hearing what I have to tell you," she said in a hushed tone.

Was she afraid of someone hearing? Who was she afraid of?

"What do you have to say that you think will be of interest to me?" I asked. "What is it that you know?"

"Not on the phone," she said quickly, her words running together. "Can you meet tomorrow?"

"What time?" I asked.

"Nine?"

"Just a minute, please." I put my hand over the receiver and looked at Levi. "She wants to know if I can meet at nine. Can I, Dad? Pretty please?"

Levi wasn't impressed with my sarcasm. I think it was the daggers that let me know. I smiled and winked.

"That'll work," he grumbled.

"Okay, Mildred. Nine will be fine. Where would you like to meet?"

"I can come to your house if you'd like. Otherwise, I can meet you at your salon."

"I can come to you if that works better." I looked at Levi, our eyes meeting.

"No, I'm afraid that wouldn't be a good idea," she said. "Your salon? That way it just looks like I'm getting my hair done."

"Mildred, is meeting with me going to put you in danger?" My gaze held Levi's.

"I'll be at A Cut Above at nine," she said.

The line went dead, and I looked from Levi to Claire. "Now that was the weirdest call I've ever had. The voice on her answering machine was a young woman. I thought I had the wrong number."

"Where are you meeting?"

"She wanted to meet here or at the salon. I didn't want her to come to my home."

"You must have hit your head harder than we even suspected," he said.

I made a face at him. "I may be stubborn and determined, but I'm not an idiot." I looked at Claire. "Would you mind calling Jack? If Bryce is acting like a jerk and Jack needs our help, I don't want to put it off. I'm just too exhausted to make the call myself."

"What do you want me to say?"

"That Bryce left me a voicemail asking me to call him back, but I wanted to check in with him first."

"And what if he asks me why I'm calling instead of you?"

"Tell him the truth, I don't care. It can't hurt. Just tell him not to get in his car and drive here because I'm very well taken care of by the medical Nazis."

I looked at Levi and wrinkled my nose before he disappeared back into the kitchen. After he gave me the most gorgeous, breathtaking smile ever. And take my breath away, it did. Unless it was the Percocet the doctor had given me for the pain. It all felt the same about right now. Delightful.

Jack answered mere seconds after Claire punched his number. I half listened to the one-sided conversation, fairly certain what Jack was saying on the other end of the phone partly by Claire's responses and partly because I just knew Jack that well to be able to gauge his responses.

I looked at Claire as she mouthed, "He wants to talk to you."

I pantomimed that I was sleeping and she gave me a dirty look. I knew better because I knew Claire. She hated lying more than just about anything on this planet. I held my hand out for the phone.

"Hi, Jack."

"Hogan, you're killing me."

As soon as I heard his voice, I began trembling inside again, another round of tears threatening a waterfall. I hadn't realized how much I missed him.

"You and everyone else I love." I sniffed. "But you still love me, right?"

"Are you crying? You don't cry. I can count on one hand the number of times you've cried since I've known you."

"Had you been here this week, you would have needed two hands." I sniffed.

"I need to come up there. I'm on my way."

"No, you're not. Stay put."

The line went silent until he said, "I'm coming up there, Melanie."

"No, you're not," I said again, swallowing my tears. "Claire and Levi are here. I'm very well taken care of."

"And you're letting them? Now I am worried."

"I miss you, Jack. It's just been an emotional evening, and I had a meltdown. But I'm good. You know nothing can keep me down. Tell me about you. Why did Bryce call me? Should I call him back?"

"That's up to you."

"No, it's not. My loyalties lie with you, not that—that—jerk."

Jack laughed a bitter sound. "It's amazing how something I thought was so wonderful could turn so sour and so painful."

"He never deserved you, Jack. I tried to be nice because I knew you loved him."

"Yeah, well, had you told me how you felt maybe I would have listened to you and wouldn't be in this place right now." I didn't say anything. "Girlfriend, I'm kidding! You know that, right?"

"Yeah. I'm just drained, and Nurse Ratched and Dr. Jekyll won't let me go to sleep. Or Mr. Hyde, whichever one it is at the moment."

I heard him laugh softly. "Karma."

I remembered when Jack was hit on the head and had a concussion, the doctor telling me to keep waking him at frequent intervals throughout the night.

"That was for your good," I said.

"So is this. For your good."

"So should I call Bryce or not?"

"He probably won't leave you alone until you do, so you might as well. Just not tonight. After what you've been through, that's the last thing you need to deal with."

"Or exactly what I need to keep my mind busy. I'll call you tomorrow. Love you, Jack."

"Love you, too. Get some sleep. Oh! That's right, you can't," he teased lightly, and we hung up.

I dialed Bryce's number before putting my phone down. I felt Claire watching me until I heard Bryce's voice and forgot about everything except how much I disliked this man.

"Bryce here."

"It's Melanie. I got your voicemail. What'd you want?"

"To tell you I hope you're happy for destroying mine and Jack's life."

"I'm flattered, Bryce, and I'd love to take the credit, but you did that all on your own."

"You think you're all that, don't you, sister?"

"I'm not your sister." Anger stirred in my gut.

"You'd do well to mind your own business and stay out of mine, or—"

"Or what, Bryce? Are you threatening me?" Levi suddenly appeared in the doorway to the living room, his forehead creased, the corners of his lips turned down. "Unless you have something worth my time to listen to, this conversation is over." I held the phone as the line went dead.

"Did he threaten you?" Levi asked, his anger hovering just beneath the surface.

"I think it's safe to say he doesn't like me, but what he thinks doesn't matter."

"If he threatened you, yes it does matter. To me."

"Me, too," Claire agreed. "What did he say?"

"To mind my own business. Seems to be a lot of people thinking I'm all up in their business lately. It's an epidemic."

"Sarcasm aside," Levi said, "given the state of things right now, I don't think that's something to take lightly. Someone is determined to silence you, and we can't rule anyone out at this point. Especially Bryce. And Cain," he said, his voice even. "I hardly think you're rational about that. You can't trust anyone right now."

I dismissed his comment about Cain. I wasn't ready to discuss that with him. "I can't trust anyone? Even you guys?"

He took a long, slow, deep breath and took his time exhaling while staring at the ceiling, one had on the back of his neck. I imagine he was counting to ten like Nana used to tell me to do when I was upset.

"Listen, Melanie," he finally said, "I don't think you're taking this seriously. This isn't a joking matter."

I looked at him with all the earnestness I could muster. "Sarcasm is my default, and it helps me cope. You know that by now. And while it may not be ideal, it is what it is. At forty-one years of age, I don't see that changing."

"Point taken." He shook his head slowly.

Clare had been quietly watching the exchange between us until now.

"We seriously need to consider Bryce or Cain as the threat. We're focusing so hard on it being a result of your digging into the Swansons' past that we may be totally missing something huge."

"Claire is right. I'm going to have Cole or Mikey take a look at it tomorrow and do some digging into Bryce's whereabouts." He looked directly at me, his eyes hard. "And Cain's."

I sighed and leaned back from the upright position to which I'd absentmindedly moved. "Can I please go to sleep? I'm exhausted, not to mention aching like none other." The Percocet was losing its effect. "I hate to be a pansy and complain and whine, but—"

"Yes," Levi said.

"I'll get you tucked in and wake you at hour intervals," Claire said.

"Every hour?" I said, my head pounding. "Even Jack got to sleep for a few hours at a time."

"You're not Jack."

I scowled at her. "You're mean."

"It's called tough love, baby."

"Yeah, cause you know so much about being tough."

"Come on, smarty pants, let's go."

I had just reached the top of the stairs to my bedroom up in the loft when I heard the ringtone from my phone. I turned to go down and get it.

"Uh-uh," Claire said, not budging from behind me. "You seriously don't need to take another call tonight. Especially the kind you've been getting."

"What if it's Nana?"

"I'll check when I go back downstairs. If it was her, I'll call her back and let her know you're not feeling well and are in bed."

"This is why I'm not married," I grumbled. "I don't like people telling me what to do. And I don't like being smothered."

Her answer was an arm around my shoulders and a gentle squeeze. I winced.

I lay there looking up at the ceiling and through the skylight when she went back downstairs. As tired as I was, my mind was spinning too fast, not allowing sleep to come. I could hear them discussing something, but couldn't decipher what it was.

I slowly rolled out of bed, landing light, careful not to cause a floorboard to creak as happened the other night. The movement after lying down made my head spin, and I held onto the edge of the bed to steady myself until the room stopped spinning, then tiptoed to the railing and listened carefully.

"Neither of us has gotten to know Bryce well," Claire told Levi, her voice barely above a whisper. "He only came up here with Jack a time or two."

"Do you think he's capable of what's been happening with her?"

"I don't—think—right—"

Dang! She was talking too softly, and I couldn't hear everything she was saying. I tried to listen carefully, my head feeling like it was about to split in two.

"...who called?" I heard Claire ask.

"I looked at the display when it was ringing, but it was a blocked number. They left a voicemail, but she can get it in the morning."

They were silent for a moment, and I was dying to go down a few steps to try and see what they were doing.

"I'm wondering if it was Cain again. Do you know him?" Levi's voice.

"Unfortunately."

"Meaning?"

"I can't stand that guy."

"You like everyone. Why not Cain?"

"Not everyone," Claire said. "And I was willing to give Cain a shot, because of being Melanie's husband, if nothing else."

"But?"

"But...then he came on to me. Told me Mel doesn't have to know because he didn't want to hurt her." Her voice got a little louder, letting me know she was still upset. But not nearly as upset as I was. She never told me that!

I felt my legs get weak and my head started pounding with sheer rage. My best friend? I sat on the top step, not caring if they saw me. I had to sit now before I fell and I knew I wouldn't have made it back to the bed fast enough. The floor was crumbling beneath my feet. Hot tears escaped down my cheeks. Great! I was turning into the world's biggest crybaby!

"So when she called him an arrogant jerk, she was nice."

"As far as I'm concerned."

"Does she know?"

"About what I just told you? No way!" she said in a harsh whisper, but loud enough for me to hear over the freight train rumbling through my head. "She already knows he's a jerk. I set him straight pretty darn fast and told him what I thought of him. Mel was way too good for that creep."

"Do you think he's capable of what's going on?"

"I would hate to think so, but probably."

Silence again. I couldn't tell if they were saying anything else or not. The roaring in my ears was too loud. Finally, it quieted and I heard Levi.

"I need to run and do something. Will you be okay for a while?"

"Of course. Where are you going?"

"I'd rather not say yet. But I should only be an hour."

I heard the door open, then close, and a minute later I heard his car driving out of the driveway. My bedroom windows face the back of the house, over the lake, so I couldn't see which direction he turned out of the driveway. Not that it mattered. I still wouldn't know where he was going. I stood then stayed completely still. I wanted to get to my phone, feeling like a prisoner in my home. As I tried to think of a way to get my phone, undetected, I heard the bathroom door open and close. Yes!

I tiptoed downstairs, holding onto the railing for balance, crossed the room, snatched up my phone and as quickly and stealthily as I could, I went back upstairs.

I'd just made it back into bed when I heard Claire's footsteps on the stairs getting closer. It couldn't have been an hour already. I closed my eyes to pretend I was asleep and kept my phone under my pillow. I felt her presence above me.

I opened my eyes wide and said, "Boo!"

She jumped back and screamed. "You're bad!"

"Well, that was good for a headache," I said with a grimace.

"Why aren't you sleeping?"

"Can't. Where'd Levi go?"

"I don't know. He didn't—" Her eyes narrowed. "Wait a minute, how did you know he went somewhere?"

I looked at her, the kid caught with her hand in the cookie jar. "Heard the car?" I said.

"Uh-huh." She sat on the bed and crossed her legs. "What else did you hear?" she asked quietly.

"Enough to know my ex-husband had the hots for you. Why would you keep something like that from me?"

"Doing my part in preventing a homicide. You would have killed him."

"It would have been justifiable."

"Yes, but I need you on this side of the prison bars."

I looked at her, studying her for a moment. "Seriously, Claire. I had a right to know."

"It was right before everything exploded. And then I didn't see any reason to add fuel to the fire." She looked at me, both of us trying to read the other in unchartered territory. "You have to believe me, Mel. I wouldn't have kept it quiet had I thought it would have done any good whatsoever to tell. I was only trying to protect you."

"I'm not—"

"Breakable, I know," she finished for me. "But you hurt just the same as everyone else. You bleed red just like me, like Levi, like Jack—I didn't want to do that."

I nestled my head into the pillow, pulled the covers up to my chin. "You're darn amazing, Claire Davis. Now get lost so I can sleep."

She smiled, stood and left the loft. I pulled the covers over my head, punched my security code for my phone, the screen lighting up, and listened to the mystery voicemail. I felt the color drain from my face as I listened to the voice on the other end, listening again, and yet again to be sure I'd heard right.

Finally, I put the phone back under my pillow. Sweet baby Jesus! There would be no sleeping tonight. My mind had other things to do. Like think about the bomb Cain just dropped on me via voicemail.

21

I managed to fall asleep about—well, I'll just say that the last time I remembered looking at the big green number display on my alarm clock, the numbers had just rolled over to reveal two thirty-three. I hadn't expected to fall asleep at all, especially when I heard Levi come through the front door at midnight, then Claire greeting him. Their voices were low as they discussed something, and then I heard the bedroom door to the guest room close and Levi talking on his phone in the kitchen. After dreaming up several scenarios of where he could have gone, I looked at the clock and fell into a restless sleep.

As I lay on my stomach, I lifted my head and looked to my left. Eight thirty! I had to meet with Mildred Walker in half an hour. If I was going to make it, I had to get my sore butt out of bed and get moving.

I groaned as I stood up, my muscles rebelling, screaming at me with every inch I moved. I finally managed to pull on a pair of jeans, slip into a sweatshirt and tennis shoes—there would be no heels today—brushed my teeth, pulled my hair back into a ponytail, avoiding the mirror, and went downstairs wondering what and who I would find.

I walked into the kitchen, and Claire looked up from her phone. She was dressed and ready to go, a bright orange hair scarf matching her skirt. "It's about time you woke up," she smiled. "How are you feeling?"

"Like doo-doo. Especially next to you." I looked down at my jeans. "Where's Levi?"

"He had to go. I told him since you're meeting Mildred at the salon you could ride with me."

"Huh. You mean he's going to trust me to talk with Mildred without him present? I must be dreaming."

"Yeah, I guess so. Not the dreaming part." She smiled at me, her eyes full of life. "I called Rubie and she said she'd get the salon open and manage until I get there. Levi wants you to call him after Mildred leaves and he'll come pick you up and bring you to Rose's."

"I need a car."

"You can't drive today anyway."

I groaned. Loudly. "You guys are both driving me crazy. You know that, right?"

"Yup." She grinned at me. "I saw you got your phone. Did you listen to the voicemail from last night?"

"Yeah. It was nothing." I hoped God was an extra forgiving God and didn't strike me down for lying. I needed time to process Cain's request without anyone else's input. Even Claire's. Not yet. "Ready to go?"

"Yup. I gave Levi my key so he could come back later and get his things. I didn't think you'd mind. I'll get it back from him later today. He left your key here." She pointed to the key ring on the table, adorned with three keys—that to my house, to the salon, and to Nana's house. The fob to my car was gone.

"If I can't trust a detective with the keys to my house, who can I trust?"

She stood, rinsed out her cup, slipped her coat on, and grabbed her shoulder bag from the chair by the door.

"When did you get a change of clothes?"

"Cole got them from my house this morning and brought them over."

I whistled softly. "Jeez! And here I didn't think I slept very well. Apparently, a tornado could have taken the house and I wouldn't have known it. I could have been in Oz with Dorothy."

"Still your favorite movie of all time?"

"One of 'em."

"Good. Because even with the wicked witch, Oz might be a safer place for you right now."

I pulled the door closed behind me, made sure it was locked, and climbed in the passenger's seat of Claire's car, making sure I fastened my seat belt. I shivered, remembering the previous night and how I was certain I wouldn't see another day. Now that I had, I had work to do so I could see another. And another.

When we got to the salon, an elderly woman was waiting by the front door. Rubie turned the closed sign to open, unlocked the door, and held it open for the woman.

"That must be Mildred," I said as I watched.

"Apparently. Do you want me to talk to her with you? My first client doesn't get here for another half an hour."

"Nah. I don't want you involved more than you already are, Claire. I started this whole mess, let me be the one to finish it." We both got out of the car and walked to the front door. "You can keep Rubie busy, though, if you don't mind. The less she knows, the better it is for her."

"Done."

I walked over to the woman who was standing by the product shelves, absently looking at the back of an Aveda bottle.

"Mildred Walker?" I asked.

She startled and turned to face me. "This stuff's expensive." She set the bottle back on the shelf.

"But it's very good," I said, looking at her frizzed mousy brown hair. She put her hand out for me to shake.

"Do you have someplace private we can talk?"

"We can go in the office. Follow me." I turned to walk toward the office and said over my shoulder, "You'll have to forgive me for being dressed as I am. I was in a car accident last night and not feeling quite up to par yet."

"I know. I mean about the accident, not about how you're dressed," she added quickly.

I vaguely recalled the part of her voicemail that mentioned the incident last night. I cleared Claire's purse and jacket off the chair so she could sit down, then skirted around the desk and sat down myself. "Coffee?"

"No, thank you. This really won't take long."

226

"Mildred, if you don't mind my asking, how did you hear about my accident already?"

"Word gets around in a small town."

"Yes, but this town's not that small. And this didn't happen in town. It was on a back country road. And considering it's only nine or so the morning after it happened—well," I sat back in my chair, "unless you've been out talking with people already this morning, you didn't likely hear it from the town gossip."

"You know how people talk." She looked down at her hands in her lap, averting her eyes.

"No disrespect intended, Mildred, but you left the voicemail on my phone last night shortly after my accident. So you and I both know you didn't find out about it from town gossip."

"I just wanted to ask you to please leave this whole curiosity about the Swanson family alone."

"It's not mere curiosity," I said. "That little boy—"

"Put it to rest, dear. It's best that way for everyone." She looked back up, her eyes pleading with me.

"And why is that? Don't you think my friend has a right to know about a family who's buried on her property?"

"It's not your friend that's doing the digging now, is it?" Busted. She got me there. "It doesn't seem to bother your friend. It only seems to bother you."

Her eyes turned hard for the briefest moment. I wondered if I saw it or only imagined it because the next moment it looked like she was pleading again.

"What do you know about this, Mildred? Why does it bother you that I have been looking into it? If you were Zachary's kindergarten teacher, I would think you would want justice for him if justice is to be had."

"I wouldn't say it bothers me." Defensiveness crept into her voice. "But why waste your time on something that's none of your business? I don't want you to get hurt. That's all."

Her words were running together again in a quick burst. Anxiety? Fear? Perhaps both. And why? I tried to get a read before speaking again.

"Who is it you think is going to hurt me?"

"Well, obviously someone tried to last night."

"About that—what exactly do you know about it? I'm quite certain you know a whole lot more than you're telling me."

"I don't bother repeating things that aren't my business, Mrs. Hogan."

"Ms."

"What?" Her eyebrows raised, her eyes trained on me.

"Ms. Hogan. I'm not married. But then you already knew that, didn't you?" I watched her carefully but couldn't get a read this time. "Why did you want to meet with me today, Mildred? Who are you protecting?" Mildred's hand flew to her chest, her eyes got wide, and her mouth formed a perfectly coral-lined O. Aha! I was onto something. "On whose behalf are you here today?" I asked.

"Why, mine, of course." She regained her composure. "I just wanted to ask you to please leave this whole thing alone. You seem like such a bright, nice girl. I don't want something happening to you like it did last night." She stood and slid the strap of her purse on her arm, bent at the elbow. "I need to get going if I'm going to get all my errands done. Thank you for meeting with me."

She'd just reached the door when I said, "Mildred?" She paused and turned to look at me. "You never did tell me who told you about my accident."

"I'm sure I can't remember, dear. Gossip is gossip and I try not pay attention to who says what." She looked down, smoothed the front of her jacket, avoiding my eyes, then sniffed and walked out the door.

I stared at the empty doorway. That visit was more than a little odd. Mildred Walker knew a whole lot more than she had any intention of letting on. And if she had no intention of telling me what it was, I would just have to find out another way.

I logged into the computer at my desk. Google was a fantastic tool and the perfect place to start. I looked at my cell phone lying beside me on the desk. Should I call Cain back first? I waffled back and forth, ultimately deciding I needed a fraction more time to think about that whole mess and then realized why. I didn't quite trust he didn't have anything to do with the attempts on my life. Not anymore. His voicemail changed my mind on thinking he wasn't capable. I was thinking about it the wrong way. No longer was I convinced he wouldn't have any reason to hurt me. He had a very good reason, in his twisted mind, anyway, to make sure no one else had me.

First things first. I turned my attention back to the computer screen.

22

I was waiting for the circle of doom that was swirling around on my computer as it thought about producing something on my search when Claire came into the office.

"So what did she want? She walked out in a huff."

"Because she didn't get what she wanted."

"Which is?"

"For me to drop my investigation into the Swanson family."

"Oh, Mel," she sighed. "Unfortunately, I think you're in too far to turn around at this point."

My eyebrows shot up in surprise. "Seriously? I thought you would be thrilled if I said I was backing off."

"I would have been thrilled if you'd never started. But you're in too deep now. I don't think the person who has been after you will just stop if you stop now, do you? You know too much."

"Yet not enough to put an end to it." I slouched back in my chair. "Nope, I don't think this person will stop now. Apparently, he or she has too much to risk."

She sank into the chair that Mildred had been in ten minutes before. Her eyes were pools of compassion. "How are you feeling? How's your head?"

"My head feels okay. It's the rest of me that hurts. I hadn't realized I was so out of shape."

"Being out of shape has nothing to do with it. You have bumps and bruises all over your poor little body after yesterday happened. But it wouldn't hurt for you to run again once in a while. Exercise always makes the bad tolerable and the good even better."

I laughed softly. "I know, I know. Coming from one who's a fanatic about working out, I would do well to remind you that moderation is key."

She sported a guilty grin. "I've cut down from what I used to do."

"Six days a week instead of seven now?"

"Four, sometimes five, smart aleck."

"I guess that's moderation. I work hard at moderately thinking about running. Does that count?"

She laughed loudly, and it made my heart happy, but my head hurt.

"What am I missing out on back there?" Rubie's voice called out.

"Melanie's sarcasm," Claire called back. "I know that surprises you."

I pulled a face at her. "Go back to work. I'm going to call Levi and see when he's able to pick me up to look for a car and then go to my grandmother's. After I pay a visit to the two headstone places in town. I want to see if I can find anything out on who purchased mine."

"Yikes." She grimaced. "That's disturbing. I don't think they'll tell you anything though."

"I have to try. Someone wants me six feet under."

She came around, gave me a gentle squeeze around my shoulders and then I was alone to ponder once again the weird conversation with Mildred Walker until Levi answered his phone.

"Hey, Blondie."

"What? No 'Wescott here'," I said in the best Levi voice I could muster.

"Since you're at my mercy for a ride, you might want to be nice." I could hear the smile in his voice. "Are you ready for me to come pick you up?"

"I am. But, Levi, I'm feeling fine. I can just borrow Claire's car, so I'm not taking you away from work."

"Let's see," he said as if weighing his options, "work or the company of a beautiful lady. That's a hard choice. Give me a minute to think about it, and I'll get back to you."

"I'm serious. I'm feeling perfectly fine," I lied.

"Even if that's the case, how do you plan to drive Claire's car back to her and your own, if you find one, as well. Do you have powers I'm not aware of?"

"Fine," I grumbled. "But you're sure I'm not interrupting your work?"

"Let me worry about my job, okay? What did the woman want to tell you this morning?"

"I'll fill you in when I see you."

"Be there in twenty."

Not a second past twenty minutes later, Levi's car pulled up to the curb next to the door. After saying my goodbyes to Claire, Rubie, Connie, and Babs—marveling at her new septum ring and shuddering at the thought of the pain—I pushed the door open and got into Levi's car by way of the open door he was holding for me.

"So are you always this polite, or does that end once you've got me hooked?"

"Depends."

"On what?"

"On whether I've got you hooked yet." He went around to his side of the car and slid in. "Where to, Investigator Hogan?"

"Birch Bay Auto. That's where I got my Nissan, and they were good to me there."

"Do you know what you're looking for?"

"Nope. I'll know it when I see it." I could feel him look over at me. I looked at him as he glanced my way again. "What?"

"You're telling me you haven't given a thought to what kind of car you're looking for? You don't do anything without a plan."

"I liked my little Nissan 370Z."

"You liked the car, or you liked what it symbolized? Because you don't need a car to symbolize your freedom and independence anymore. I think you've established that quite well."

I didn't answer him because I didn't know how. The truth was I didn't know what I liked about it except it made me feel different from what I had always been. "I've always dreamed of having a Mustang," I mumbled, surprised that it even came out.

"A Mustang, huh?"

I looked over at him. "Yes. Why do you say it like that?"

"Just surprised is all."

"About?"

"If you've always wanted a Ford Mustang, why didn't you get that instead of your Nissan?"

I snickered. "Because Cain hates foreign cars. Getting one was the obvious choice."

I heard him stifle a laugh. "Let's look at Mustangs."

I faced out the window, unable to contain the smile that revealed how happy I was at this exact moment. The sun was shining bright and warm on my face despite the chilly temperatures outside, and it felt like God smiling down on me.

"What did the woman want?" he asked, breaking the silence.

"For me to back off digging into the Swansons' lives."

"I think it's too late for that."

"That makes three of us. Claire said the same thing. It's odd though."

"What is?"

"She knew about my accident. She would have had to know about it last night already because shortly after the accident is when she left the voicemail on my phone."

"How do you know that's what she was calling to meet with you about?"

"Because her exact words were, 'I just wanted to ask you to please leave this whole thing alone. You seem like such a bright, nice girl. I don't want something happening to you like it did last night'." I did my best at mimicking Mildred's stuffy, prim voice. "The frightening thing was that she wouldn't tell me who told her. She just made a reference to the small town gossip. When I asked her who told her, she said she doesn't pay attention to who spreads gossip."

"Just what they say."

"Obviously." I looked at him. "Do you know Mildred Walker?"

"Heard the name, I think. But I don't remember where."

"I started looking up her name on the computer after she left but then Claire came in the office, and I got sidetracked. I'll look when I get home."

"The voicemail she left you said she was Zachary's kindergarten teacher?"

"That's what she said, yes. I'll see what I can find out about her." I looked out the side window again, zeroing in on a woman with two small children, a child holding each of her hands, walking down the sidewalk. "I have a feeling she's protecting someone, Levi. Finding out who that person is may very well lead me to the person behind all of this and it can finally be over."

"Cain?"

My pulse quickened, and my heartbeat felt irregular. "What about him?" I stared straight ahead.

"You call him back?"

"No."

"Are you going to?"

I didn't answer. If I said I wasn't, I would be lying. Maybe. If I said I was, I would be admitting to something I wasn't ready to. That he still had the potential to get to me. I noticed him glance in the rearview mirror. I wouldn't have thought anything of it if it hadn't been for the umpteenth time.

"What are you looking at?" I turned and looked behind us.

"We've had company since shortly after we left the salon."

"And you're just telling me now?"

"I didn't want you to worry. Or turn and look like you just did so whoever it is knows he's been made."

He got out his phone and punched in a number, waiting and glancing again in his rearview mirror. "This is Detective Wescott. I need you to run a plate for me, please. 275-ZW4. ASAP." He waited, and I held my breath, hoping this would bring us closer to a resolution. And grateful Levi was with me right now, especially after the close call I had last night. He sat up straighter, his body noticeably tensed, which made me follow suit. "Are you sure?" he asked. Silence as he listened, frowning. "Got it. Okay, thanks, Mary."

23

I waited, watching him. When it was evident he wasn't going to say anything, I asked, "Who is it?"

"The plate is registered to Phillip Donaldson."

"Does that name mean something to you?"

"Phillip is Michael's dad. He's also the fire chief."

"So maybe he wasn't tailing us at all. Maybe we're just both a little paranoid."

"Maybe."

But I knew he wasn't convinced. "Why would he have any reason to follow us?"

"Not so much us, but you," he mumbled as he glanced again in his mirror. "Hold on."

The car jerked to the right, and I grabbed the dashboard to keep myself upright, wincing as my sore and aching body rebelled at the sudden movement. I felt him look at me.

"I'm sorry." He took my hand in his, gently rubbing his thumb against the back of my hand. Even that hurt right now. "Considering what you've been through in the last twenty-four hours, I shouldn't have done that." He looked at me again. "You okay?"

"Yeah. I'm tougher than I look."

"Uh-huh. You don't look too tough there, Blondie." He glanced at me and frowned. "Especially with the nice bruise you're getting on your cheek. You're going to have quite the shiner there."

I pulled the visor down and looked in the mirror, gently touching the darkening circle. "It's a battle scar. Or should I say scar of honor?" I looked in the mirror at the emptiness behind us. "Looks like we lost him."

"We did. And just in time." He pulled into the parking lot of Birch Bay Auto and drove slowly around the lot as I scanned what was in view until he parked and turned the car off. "Let's get out and look around." Just as we reached the Mustangs, I heard two gentlemen talking a couple of rows over. I looked up and saw Levi watching them.

"Do you know them?"

"Not the salesman but the other man is none other than Phillip."

"As in Phillip Donaldson, the fire chief?"

"One and the same."

"But that means he—"

"Couldn't have been the one following us," he finished for me.

"Detective Wescott!" Phillip called and waved, then strode over to us. "Nice to see you, man." He extended his hand to Levi and then turned to me. "Who have we here?"

"Chief, this is Melanie Hogan, a friend of mine."

He smiled and shook my hand. "Hello, Melanie Hogan. It's always a pleasure to meet a beautiful lady."

I felt my cheeks flush. And not from being flattered, that's for sure. Something about the guy annoyed the heck out of me. He was loud and obnoxious, and I could only imagine what he'd be like with a drink or two under his belt. I shuddered.

"Nice to meet you," I lied.

"Well, I've taken enough of this good man's time," he said, patting the salesman on the back. "He was showing me the new inventory they've gotten in. Some mighty fine looking cars. I'll let him get on with making some money instead of keeping a poor old man entertained."

"I've never known you to be poor, and you're certainly not old," Levi said, an unmistakable chill in his tone.

Phillip laughed, an annoying sound, oblivious to anyone other than himself. "It's been too long, Detective. We'll have to get together for a beer one of these days."

"You take care, Phillip." Levi watched as Phillip thanked the salesman then walked across the lot to his Lincoln SUV.

"Everything okay?" I whispered, hoping the seller wouldn't hear.

"Nothing to worry about." He looked at the salesman. "The Chief been taking all of your time, has he Peter?"

"He's been here about an hour browsing all the vehicles deciding what he wants to buy next." He watched Phillip pull out of the parking lot and then turned to us. "What can I do ya for?"

"I'm in need of a vehicle," I said.

"You the one that totaled your car last night?"

Levi and I exchanged a look. "Well, word sure travels fast around here," I said.

"You know how it is with small—"

"Towns," I finished for him. "Yes, I do. But it seems to be getting worse. Mind if I ask how you found out?"

He shook his head slowly. "You know how gossip is among the locals."

"Everyone seems to be reading from a script in this town," I muttered.

"Ma'am?" he asked, clearly confused.

"Nothing. I'm just going to look around if you don't mind. I'll find you when I'm ready."

"I can just hang out here in case—"

"No need," Levi said, "she told you she'd find you when she's ready."

"Sounds good," Peter said as he walked backward, watching us. "Just give me a shout then." And he turned to walk into the building.

"So what do you make of that?" I asked him. "Him knowing about my accident."

"Sounds like the whole town probably knows by now."

"I think it's odd. By the time I'm done buying a car, I'm going to find out who told him about it."

"I have no doubt you will," Levi smirked, knowingly.

Levi hung back as I looked at four different cars, three of them Mustangs. I went back and forth between them comparing all of the details on the pricing sheets taped in the windows, then back again to compare the physical details of each before I finally narrowed it down to one and crossed the lot to go back to it.

"So, just curious," Levi said as he walked beside me, hands in his jeans pockets. He'd been so quiet during the search, I'd nearly forgotten he was with me. "Exactly how did you go from always wanting a Mustang to deciding on a Jeep Renegade? They're miles apart."

"Some dreams are better left as dreams. A Renegade is all-wheel-drive, which in Minnesota you know as well as anyone is necessary. And the Renegade is more practical and has a higher consumer rating."

"Consumer rating?" He cocked his head to one side. "You've looked at consumer ratings?"

"Well, Detective, I'm a lot more than just a pretty face," I said and winked.

He grinned. "And the white? Why white instead of black?"

"Venturing outside of my comfort zone." I smiled at him. "Would you mind staying here while I test drive it with Peter? He and I have some things to discuss."

"I wouldn't dream of interfering with your investigation. I just wish you'd do me the same favor."

I looked at him, my eyes narrowed. "I'll do my best, Detective. But I can't make any promises."

"Just for the record, you're not even supposed to be driving today. Do you think test driving a new vehicle is a good idea?"

"I don't feel dizzy, my headache is gone, I'm not nauseated...I'm fine except the rest of me being beaten up. But thanks for being concerned, Doctor Wescott."

My curiosity had gotten the best of me before I turned the corner out of the parking lot of the car dealership.

"When did you hear about my accident, Peter? Just curious, because it just happened last night."

"My wife was doing some shopping, and someone told her about it."

"Shopping, huh? Last night or this morning?"

"She ran out late last night for some last minute stuff. You know, milk, eggs—"

"Bread," I said, finishing the all too popular list everyone uses as an excuse. "She tell you who it was that told her?"

"I don't remember."

"Seriously?" I glanced over at him trying to get a read. "You're too young to forget things that happened less than twenty-four hours ago."

"Didn't pay attention. It was late; I was already in bed. Besides, I didn't know her. Turn left here unless you want to get on the highway."

Her. "I thought you couldn't remember, so how do you know you didn't know her?" I looked for the turn signal and flipped it on to make a left onto the street that would lead me to the highway.

"Are you interested in buying this vehicle, or did you just want to ask me questions? Why is it such a big deal, anyway? About how I found out."

"Both. I am interested in buying this vehicle. In fact, I love how it handles. This is probably the fastest decision I've ever made in my entire life." I looked to my left and merged into traffic. "But it's important to me—critical, actually—to know who told you about my accident.

Why I need to know wouldn't make sense to you anyway." If it did, that would be a whole new concern.

I looked out of the corner of my eye and saw his hand grip the handle on the door. "Fine, I was with my wife, and we weren't shopping, okay? We were just—out. I suppose she was about sixty-five, seventy. Somewheres in there. Glasses, salt and pepper hair, not completely gray, but plenty of silver. And orange lipstick. Why do women think orange is a good color for lipstick?"

I looked as he grimaced and shook his head and I couldn't help but snicker. "I think it's called coral."

"Coral, orange, whatever. It's all just orange and shouldn't be worn on lips."

No matter, I had my answer. "Thank you, Peter. You seriously have no idea how much you just helped me."

I turned off at the next exit, went over the bypass and back onto the highway going back to the dealership. "Love this vehicle. Let's start the paperwork when we get back." I heard him sigh. Relief? Probably because he now knew for a fact that I wasn't wasting his time, stealing his opportunity to make a buck. "So does Phillip Donaldson come to the dealership a lot just to browse the inventory? Must be frustrating to see customers come and go, other sales people getting the sales when you're stuck with someone who just wants to look."

"Nah. He buys all of his cars from me. But then again, since he's my uncle, he'd better or I'd kill him." He chuckled. "His wife and my mom are sisters."

24

Levi and I were sitting in Peter's office as he went to check with his manager about the offer I made.

"I'm impressed with your bargaining skills," Levi said, lacing his fingers through mine.

"Careful. You know how word gets around in this town."

"Does that bother you?"

"That everyone is in my business? Yeah," I said, shaking my head slowly. "It's not like I have an exciting life or anything."

"Maybe you didn't, but that doesn't seem to be the case anymore."

"Are you pouting?" I snickered.

"You never told me how you learned to bargain so well. You surprise me every day."

"Learned from the best. My granddad." I took a moment to bask in the memory. "Hey, did you know Peter is Phillip's nephew?"

"I did not know that." His brows knit together. "Wonder how that works."

"Well, typically it happens when someone's brother or sister have kids and—"

"Okay, smart aleck." He rolled his eyes and shook his head slowly. "Guess I asked for that one. What I meant was—"

"I know what you meant. Peter said his mom and Phillip's wife are sisters."

"Hm. I didn't know Selena had any family." He took his cap off and balanced it on his knee.

"Does Phillip have any brothers or sisters that you know of?"

"He had a brother or a sister who died a long time ago. I don't know which though. I've never had a lengthy enough conversation with him, and that's not something you just come out and ask someone."

"So how did you even know?"

"You know how small towns—"

"Gossip." I chortled. "Yes, that good ole' small town gossip. There seems to be a lot of that in Birch Haven. A whole lot more than even I thought and I'm a hair stylist. We hear as much as a bartender or a shrink does. I just didn't realize how fast word travels in the general population. Outside the walls of my salon."

"Maybe the population who knows about your accident isn't so general, but more specific."

"Exactly what I was thinking." Our eyes met and held. "Peter finally admitted he found out from an older woman wearing orange lipstick. Mildred was wearing coral lipstick when she came to talk to me this morning."

"I thought he said orange lipstick."

I shook my head and mumbled, "Men."

Peter came back in the tiny office, and we put our conversation on hold.

"What does your wife do, Peter? Does she work outside the home?" I asked.

He looked up from the paperwork he was preparing to pass across the desk for me to begin signing my life away. "She sure does. We don't have kids yet so...she teaches at Crestview Elementary."

Levi's and my eyes met, eyebrows raised.

"What grade does she teach?"

"Kindergarten."

By the time I left the dealership—after convincing Levi I would go straight to my grandmother's and nowhere else, despite my efforts at telling him I felt fine—it was two o'clock. I had time to make one quick little stop. Or two, depending on what I learned at the first one.

I maneuvered my new Renegade into the graveled parking lot of Birch Haven Headstone Company. I was impressed with how smooth this baby ran. Sitting up higher than I did in my little sports car was a pleasant surprise as well.

I took in the sample headstones that ornamented the grass around the building, searching for one similar to mine. I shivered at the thought. That was just way too weird.

"Can I help you?"

I jumped, my hand flying to my mouth, taking a minute to catch my breath.

"Sorry, miss. Didn't mean to scare you."

I turned and looked at a short man, advanced in age, with thin, silver hair and wire-rimmed glasses. His eyes looked enormous through the magnification of the bifocals in the round lenses.

"Looking for something in particular?" he asked. His hands were clasped behind his back, and his neck protruded forward. Made me think of what the product of an owl and a turtle would look like.

"Do you keep records on who makes purchases?" I scanned the lot around me.

"That information is confidential." His neck leaned forward a bit more, accompanied by the slight jutting of his chin. "I'm a professional."

"Yes, of course, you are. I didn't mean to insinuate anything other."

"Are you looking for anything in particular?"

"Yeah, my headstone," I mumbled before looking at him again. "I just had a rather...well, a disturbing event where someone purchased a headstone and had my name put on it."

His brows knit together. "Where did you find this headstone?"

"Long story." I sighed. "And one I'd rather not get into."

"Say, aren't you the girl that got into that fender bender last night?" He squinted through his glasses, studying me.

"Yes. And let me guess, you heard it through the town's gossip."

He shrugged, disinterested in my assumption. "Guess you could say that. A customer that was just in earlier today was tellin' me about it. It's dangerous out there. But," he sighed and shrugged his shoulders again, "job security for me, I suppose."

I was speechless. What an odd little man. With a sick sense of job satisfaction. I pulled out a business card and handed it to him. "Mr.—"

"Jones."

"Mr. Jones. If you come across anything that can help me, could you let me know? In the meantime, I'll head over to the competition and see if they're a little more helpful." I began to walk away and stopped, turning to see him still watching me. "You know how it is," I said, "the way you treat people today could bring you business tomorrow. Or not."

I strode to my car, opened the door and pulled it shut, sitting behind the wheel for a moment. I was chasing my tail here. No business is going to give out information on past customers.

I reached to start my car and jumped as knuckles rapped on my window. Mr. Jones stood there, ever so prim, expectantly. I rolled my window down.

"Yes? Did you remember something?"

"Well, seems I have. I looked at your card here, and it seems...well..." he leaned forward, his nose nearly touching my partially rolled down window, "you didn't hear this from me, but a gentleman recently bought something from me. Said it was urgent and didn't want to go through ordering and have to wait, so he bought it right off my lot."

"Do you have another like it that I could see?"

"I only keep a sampling on my lot. So, no."

"What makes this man unique to the other customers you've had? Other than the fact that he needed it fast."

"It was his name. It was the same as your last name here on your business card. Hogan. First name of Abraham. Or maybe it was Cole."

Cole?!

"Maybe it was Abel...I just can't remember right now."

"Cain," I said, almost to myself.

"Yes, yes. Cain. That was it. Cain."

"Thank you," I mumbled as I rolled up my window. I felt like I'd been sucker-punched. Levi was right. It was Cain all along. The person who wanted me dead was not one and the same as that who wanted me to leave the history of Zachary Swanson alone.

I inhaled long and slow, slowly exhaling before I found the strength to start my car. I pulled out of the parking lot and started toward my grandmother's before making a detour to go home and pick up my shears so I could trim her ends.

The drive to my house was fraught with tangled up thoughts about how it had come to this. The last voicemail he left insinuated he needed me back. That he'd had time to realize the mistake he made and needed to see me ASAP. Did I make a life-threatening error in understanding what he meant? Did he mean see me dead rather than alive? And why now? More importantly, *why*? I picked up my phone and punched in Claire's number. She answered on the first ring.

"Hey, Mel." She laughed at something someone was saying in the background. "Hey, can you hold for just a minute?" she asked me.

"I suppose."

"I'm just cashing out one of my—" She stopped talking to me as I heard her talking to her client.

"Hey, Claire?" Nothing. "Claire!"

"Yeah, just hold on a second, hun."

"I'll call you a little bit later, okay?"

"You okay?"

"Fine. I just got home so let me call you back in a minute."

"Wait," she said, suddenly all ears to me. "What are you doing at home? I thought you were going to your grandmother's."

"I am. I just wanted to come home to grab my shears so I can give her a trim."

"Coming to the salon would have been quicker. And what about the pair you keep with you?"

"I didn't call you to get scolded. I called because—" Turning into my driveway, I saw a car parked in front of my house. Who did I know that drove a Lincoln? No one in my circle, that's for sure.

"Because of what?"

"Let me call you back. I need to see who this is at my house."

"Stay on the line with me."

"Don't you have a client?"

"Not one who's more important than my best friend. Stay on the line. That's an order."

"Usually it's me giving orders," I said absently, trying to see in the darkly tinted windows of the Lincoln. The door opened, and I gasped. "Oh my—"

"Mel, who is it?"

"Cain."

"Do not hang up, Melanie," she said, her voice filled with concern. "Stay on the line. He doesn't need to know, just keep the phone in your hand so I can hear."

I was frozen in place as I watched him make his way over to my car and open the door for me. I sat motionlessly.

"Hello, Melanie."

"Cain," I whispered. "What are you doing here?" I asked, finally mustering up some authority. "You have no business coming to my home."

"It used to be our home, Melanie."

His voice was gentle, but I knew him too well to believe for a second that it was genuine— actually, after what I just found out at Birch Haven Headstone, I learned I didn't know him well enough.

"Used to be, Cain. Not anymore."

He looked at the house then back at me. "I like what you've done with the place."

"You didn't answer me. What are you doing here?" He reached for my hand, and I shrank back. "Don't. Just answer the question. It's not that hard."

"I left you two voicemails, but you didn't call me back."

"As hard as this may be for you to believe, you're not a priority to me. I was in a car accident last night, but I'm sure you know all about that, don't you?"

"How would I know about that?"

"You seem to be the only person who doesn't know about it. So either you live under a rock or you're lying. And if I remember correctly, you're superb at lies and deceit."

"About that..."

"There's nothing to be said about that, Cain. It's all been said and done. And over. You can leave now." I got out of my car, ignoring the well-manicured hand he held out to help me. I shut the door behind me.

"Can I come in?"

"No." I looked at him, feeling myself soften at the pained look in his eyes. "What you can do is get back in your car and go back to your wife."

"I can't." He nearly choked, sadness in his eyes beyond what I thought he was capable of feeling.

"Why? Did she leave you? Karma, my friend." I knew I was less than gracious, even hurtful. But all kinds of ugly was brewing in me right now.

"She died."

My eyes popped open. "I'm sorry, Cain. How are the kids?"

"They're with my aunt and uncle right now."

"How?"

"We were hiking, and she fell off the side of the trail into the river and hit her head on a rock. I'm not sure what the actual cause of death was, blunt force trauma or drowning."

Or murder. "Were you guys having problems?"

"Why would you ask that?"

"Curious."

"No, Melanie, I didn't do it." His tone had a glint of something hard, then sadness returned.

"I didn't say you did."

"You didn't have to. I know you well enough—"

"That's where you're wrong. You don't know me at all. Where did she die, Cain?"

"Not far from here."

That could explain his purchase of a headstone. But the timing, the urgency.

"Melanie?"

"Just thinking."

"About?"

"How are the kids doing with her death? The oldest is old enough to understand losing her mama. She's what, about eight now?" I could taste the bitterness seep in, creeping into the back of my throat. "Go home, Cain. Take care of your children."

"They're where they need to be right now. I want to know if we have a chance of getting back together."

I laughed aloud at the absurdity. "That would be a loud, resounding no!" I finally managed to say.

"Melanie, I messed up. We were good together."

"Not anymore, Cain. Now go."

"My aunt and uncle always loved you, you know."

"And I them. That didn't change because of your infidelity."

"They've agreed to leave me their estate, which is large if you remember, if I patch things up with you. Said our divorce was the biggest mistake I made. I agree with them."

The clouds of confusion completely cleared and rays of clarity forced their way in.

"You agree with them because you think it's a mistake or because you want the inheritance?" I shook my head slowly, seeing him in yet a new light. This man had a million sides to him, none more flattering than the other. I felt nothing but pity for him and his kids.

"If you change your mind—"

"I won't," I said, my voice quiet, firm. "Goodbye, Cain."

I stood and watched him sulk back to his less than impressive Lincoln before he stopped

253

and turned back toward me. "You'll regret this, Melanie. Someday you'll see what you've lost out on."

At this point, I just hope I'll see someday. I watched him drive out the long driveway. I stood motionless for a few moments, trying to absorb what had just transpired. Oddly, I felt peace I'd been waiting many years for. It was finally, really over. It was then I remembered I still had Claire on the line.

"Oh man, Claire, I'm sorry. I totally forgot about you." I said before realizing she had hung up. My phone began to play its ringtone.

"Hey, Claire," I said without looking at the number.

"I thought you told me you'd go straight to your grandmother's."

"Levi." I slumped down on the front porch step. "I came home to get my shears so I could give my grandmother a trim."

"So I heard. What were you thinking to get out of your car with a potential killer there?"

"He's not my assailant. If Claire had stayed on the phone and listened, she would have known that, too. Not that I blame her for hanging up."

"She hung up to call me."

"Of course she did."

"How do you know he's not the one that's after you?"

"Oh, I didn't say he wasn't after me." I rubbed the back of my neck, feeling a headache coming on. "He's just after me alive, not dead." I filled him in on his aunt and uncle's proposition to get his inheritance. "The headstone he got was for his wife, who just passed."

"What headstone?"

254

It occurred to me that he would have no idea what I was talking about since I did exactly what he asked me not to do. Make any stops before going to my grandmother's. Busted not only once, but twice. And then a much larger issue occurred to me. I gripped the phone tightly, my breathing increasing its pace.

"Levi, what if he killed her?"

"Hogan, you're killing *me*!"

I sat up straighter. "No, listen to me, Levi. His wife fell to her death when the two of them were hiking. If his aunt and uncle gave him the condition of his inheritance, maybe he wanted her out of the way. They wouldn't have allowed for him to get it by way of divorcing her."

"We, as in you, me, or any combination thereof, are not doing this right now, Melanie. Get to your grandmother's. Please," he begged.

"I'm going, I'm going. I was just—"

"Getting in your car to go," he interjected. "Getting in your car to go to your grandmother's."

By the time I got to my grandmother's house, I was more than ready to have some down time with just Nana and me. I couldn't wait to kick off my shoes and settle in on the sofa with a blanket and talk with her. It had been a couple of days, and I missed it here. One of her famous cooking lessons sounded like heaven about now, too. She'd put in countless hours trying to teach me how to cook, but secretly, I think we both enjoy it so much because of the bonding time. And what better place than in the kitchen with its warm, welcoming atmosphere and all the fantastic aromas. Not to mention the kitchen table that has held endless private, intimate conversations between Nana and me. Her kitchen is my favorite place in the world. Even more so than my house, which I love like crazy.

Nana met me at the door and wrapped me in a hug. She was strong for a woman of her age and right now her strength made me wince in pain. She pulled me back and looked at me, her hands still on my upper arms.

"Are you okay, dear?" She brushed my cheek with her fingers. "What in heaven's name happened to your cheek?"

"I have something to tell you."

"Well come in, dear. Come in." She stepped aside so I could walk past her, and she closed the door. "Whose car are you driving?"

"That's part of the story I need to tell you."

"Melanie Hogan, it sounds like you have a lot to say. Let me get us a cup of tea, and you can start."

I watched as she moved effortlessly, filling up the teapot with water and retrieving two Chamomile tea bags. Minutes later she set a white ceramic mug of steaming tea in front of me on the table and one in front of her.

"Okay, talk. It looks like you're going to have quite a bruise on your cheek if not a shiner on that eye."

"I was kind of in a car accident last night. Which is why the new car."

"Kind of in a car accident?" Her eyes glistened with concern. "Either you were, or you weren't. How did it happen and why haven't I heard about it until just now?"

"You seem to be the only one in town who hasn't heard about it," I muttered. "You and Cain."

"Cain?" she asked, incredulous. "Where did you see that man?"

"I'll get to that." I took a breath, trying to think of the right way to tell her about what happened, finally deciding that if I didn't just tell her the truth she'd be able to tell I wasn't forthcoming anyway. I took a deep breath and started from the beginning when we got to Claire's and found out someone had found the wildlife cam we set up and ended with the part of Peter being Phillip's nephew.

"And Cain?"

"Yeah, then there's Cain." I filled her in on the bombshell he dropped on me.

When I came up for air, I took a sip of my cooling tea and waited for Nana to say something. Anything. But she remained perfectly silent. Her nearly ever-present smile dimmed a whole lot.

"Aren't you going to say something?"

"I'm not sure there are any words suitable right now, don't cha know."

"You're angry, huh."

Her eyes were tender and warm as she sat back in her chair. "Not angry, dear. Concerned, but not angry."

"Levi and Claire both stayed at my house last night."

"I don't know why Claire didn't just move in with you. I would feel a whole lot better about you living out there if she lived in the same house. Besides, it would probably be good for her to have help with Sydney."

"She has plenty of help with Syd. Between her parents and Tyler's parents, she only has Syd about half time the way it is."

"I wish you two would at least consider it."

"It's too late, Nana. She's already got the house."

She sighed. "I suppose that's true. But she could always rent it out, you know. Just an option."

"Yes, it's an option. And we're going to talk to someone about seeing if she can rescind the contract. But the way things are going with her and Cole...well, let's just say she probably won't be alone at that house very much longer anyway."

"Do you think it's heading that way so fast?"

"No, you're probably right. It is too fast. If I know Claire, and I do, she wouldn't move any faster than at a snail's pace in having another man around Syd. Heck, she still thinks she's successful in making Syd believe they're just friends." I snickered. "Syd's smarter than Claire if Claire honestly thinks Syd doesn't know better."

"How about you and I watch *The Good Witch* tonight. It starts in just one hour and will do both of us good to watch a little light TV, snuggled under a cozy blanket on a cold night."

"I should get home, Nana. I'm not sure I'm brave enough to drive home after dark yet after last night."

"Can you just stay here with me tonight?"

"I could, but..."

"But what?"

"Let me call Claire and see what she was planning for tonight."

Nana's eyes brightened, and she perked up. "Ask her to come and stay too. We can all watch *The Good Witch* together. It'll be just like when you were younger when you'd invite granddad and me to watch movies with you and your friends."

"The fact that my friends thought you were cool enough to want you to watch movies with us says a lot about you, ya know."

"Tell her I'll make the popcorn."

"Put Ranch seasoning on that popcorn, and she'll be over before it's done." I smiled as I stood to find my phone. I asked her over my shoulder, "Speaking of *The Good Witch*, have you heard anything from the bad witch?"

"Melanie Hogan," she scolded me gently. "Violet is your mother. I thought you'd forgiven her."

"I have. But it doesn't mean she gets to be my mother." I waited for Claire to pick up and saw the look Nana was giving me. "Okay, maybe calling her a witch was a little over the top."

I left a voicemail for Claire when she didn't pick up, telling her Nana wanted her to come. That, even more than the popcorn, would get here there. She loves my grandmother almost as much as I do. Almost.

As soon as I finished the voicemail I heard a loud thump outside. Nana and I looked at each other. "Stay in here, Nana, I'll go check it out."

"The heck you will. Not by yourself." She grabbed the broom and walked behind me to the door. I unlocked the door and opened it slowly, poking my head out and peeking around the front yard. I kept the porch light off so whatever it was that made the noise didn't see me.

Seeing nothing, I stepped out, holding the door open with one hand, leaning out slightly so I could get a better view. I felt something on my ankle, and I screamed then froze, barely recognizing my voice, startled that the sound came from me. I heard Nana's giggle and dared to look down and saw Callie, Nana's giant calico cat rubbing against my leg. I sucked in a deep gulp of air and picked up the cat, putting my face right up to hers. "You were almost squashed by a very dangerous weapon, Callie cat. A broom."

My grandmother laughed and ushered me back into the house. "Why don't you go relax, and I'll make some dinner."

"I can help. What are we making?"

"I can do it. You should go get off your feet and rest."

"Nana, I'm not an invalid, you know. I'm perfectly fine."

"Let me do this for you, okay? Let me take care of you."

I gave her a hug, and she hugged me back, more gently this time. "You may be retired, but you still have the nurse in you." I picked up my phone. "I'm just going to make a phone call first."

"To Claire? I thought you already called her and left a voicemail."

"I did. I want to call a woman who was a good friend of Norma Swanson. Mildred mentioned her name to me. I don't think she expected me to remember it."

"Then I'd say she underestimated you."

"Yup, I'd say she did."

"Do you know her number?"

"No. But how many Selena Olmstead's could there possibly be? I have the Internet on my iPhone. I'll look it up."

"What do you want to meet her for?"

"To see what she knows. I'm convinced someone killed the Swanson family, Nana, and it wouldn't surprise me at all if it were none other than Henry himself."

"How could he do that when he was killed in the fire, too?"

"I don't know. That's why I want to talk to Selena."

"Melanie..."

"I'll be careful," I said, looking into her worried eyes. "I promise."

"What if careful isn't good enough?"

"I won't let my guard down. I'll see if she can meet me in a public place, okay? At the salon, if that makes you feel better."

"It would."

"Then it's a plan. But first I need to call her and see if she'll even agree to meet with me."

It didn't take much searching to find her in the electronic phone book. Just as I suspected, there was only one Selena Olmstead in Birch Haven.

25

By the time Claire got to my grandmother's, we were twenty-five minutes into the movie. But we'd all seen it so many times she didn't miss anything accept half of the popcorn that was already gone. After filling up on Nana's delicious chicken soup with homemade dumplings, followed by her scrumptious chocolate zucchini cake, I suspected I'd succumbed to nervous eating when it came to the popcorn. I was so stuffed I was sure I was going to pop.

I'd talked with Selena while Nana made dinner. We were set to meet the following morning. Not only did she sound a little wasted, but she also seemed completely disinterested in knowing why I wanted to meet with her. For the rest of the evening, however, I, too, was disinterested in anything other than where I was at that exact moment. With two of my favorite people in the world. The third, Jack—and Nana's favorite, I think—was missed, for sure. Next time, Claire and I promised Nana, we would make sure Jack was with us, too.

Claire and I both left the house at seven thirty the next morning, Claire to go home and get ready for work, and me to go home and prepare to meet with Selena. Despite telling my grandmother that I would meet with Selena in a public place, Selena said she wouldn't have a car, so I arranged to go to her house, conveniently forgetting to mention it to my grandmother. I felt guilty, but not enough to make me not go. It was senseless to worry Nana needlessly. At least that's what I told myself until I believed it. I needed answers before the person who was trying to shut me up tried yet again and succeeded. I shivered.

I called Levi on my way over to Selena's house letting him know where I was going to be just in case something happened. Given the weird things that had been going on and what people were saying, I didn't know who to trust at this point except for my inner circle.

As I drove I inhaled the exhilarating new car smell, trying to relax my jumbled nerves. The sun was out again for the fourth day in a row, and I took it as a sign of promise that it was going to be a good day. Or maybe that was my way of telling myself what I wanted to hear.

Whatever the case may be, I hadn't expected to see the large colonial style house that loomed before me as I pulled up the drive of the address Selena had given me. Did I have the wrong house? I looked at the large black wrought iron numbers on the house alongside one of the three garage doors then back at the slip of paper I'd written the address on last night. Nope, according to this, it was the place, alright.

I looked out my windshield and studied the house for a minute before opening my door and

263

stepping out, standing there for another minute as I took a deep breath and closed my door. I walked up the red brick walkway, up the red brick stairs, and to the oversized barn-wood door. The long narrow window in the door had black wrought iron bars that crisscrossed over it, no doubt to prevent someone from being able to break it and reach the lock to open the door. Like that would stop anyone who was intent on breaking in.

I rang the doorbell, and the song it played sounded through the door. For a moment I thought I'd stepped onto the set of the Addams Family. When the door opened, and I was looking into the face of Morticia—gaunt, pale, and black dress to boot—I became convinced I'd stepped out of reality and onto a television set. I instinctively looked over Morticia's shoulder, searching for Lurch, telling myself I'd run like the wind if I saw him.

"You must be Melanie," she drawled.

I hadn't remembered the drawl in our phone conversation the night before, just slurring of words.

"Are you Selena?"

"The one and only." She smiled, showing white teeth against pale skin. She opened the door wider, keeping her hand on the door handle, stepping aside to allow me access. After I was inside, she closed the door. My heart thumped when I heard the lock click into place. If I made a go of it right now, I could probably make it out safely. And then just as quickly as the thought came to mind, I chided myself for being so ridiculous, grateful I'd filled Levi in before getting here.

At the top of the five steps inside the entryway was the kitchen. I'd just stay right here, thank you very much. No need to go in any farther.

"Tea? Wine?" she asked.

Wine? It was only nine o'clock in the morning! "Uh...no, thank you."

"Come on in. I'm just doing a bit of ironing. I can finish up while we chat."

Despite my plan to go no farther than the kitchen, I followed her until we reached the living room, a monstrous fireplace along the far wall. "You know, maybe I'll have a cup of tea after all if it's not any trouble." I wanted to get my snooping done and get the heck out of Dodge.

"No trouble at all." She set the iron back down. "I'll be right back."

"Thank you." I breathed in relief.

The second she was out of sight, I crossed to the fireplace and began looking at the photographs on the mantle, starting on the far right, working my way to the left. There was one of an older couple, in sepia tones, resembling that of being from the forties or fifties. The next was a baby that looked eerily familiar. Try as I might, I couldn't place from where I remembered it. Next in line were three kids, two boys and a girl, all between the ages of five to ten. The boy with the red hair looked like a miniature version of Michael. Could it be? What would be the chances? No, I was grasping, and I didn't have time for that. It would do nothing but distract me from getting to the truth.

I shuffled down a few inches and looked at the next one, an old picture of the Swansons, the same picture that showed them alive and well in the newspaper article as it described the horrible events of the fire.

When I got to the last one, a family photo, I looked at a more attractive version of Selena. There was a girl of about sixteen positioned in front of her, a boy to the girl's left. As I looked at the next boy, and the man standing behind him, I froze, and the hairs on the back of my neck stood up. I looked back at the Swanson family photo again.

"Nothing like family pictures, is there?" I jumped, stifling a scream. "We don't get them done nearly as often as I'd like to."

"This family picture—Phillip is your husband?"

"Yes." She smiled and handed me my tea. "Do you know my Phillip?"

"We met briefly. Just yesterday when I was buying my car."

"Yes, I heard you were in an accident. Poor thing. How are you?"

Of course, you heard about it. "I'm doing fine, thank you for asking. You and Phillip don't share a last name. How long have the two of you been married?"

"Shortly after he lost his sister. The Swansons died about the same time, and we met in a grief support group."

"How did his sister die?"

"Heart attack. And so young. I guess heart problems run in his family. Scares me to death for him, you know."

"I'm sure it would. Michael is a good kid. I've met him through my friend, Detective Wescott."

Her eyes lit with recognition. "Oh yes! Detective Wescott." She looked at me and whispered as if she were telling me the secret of a lifetime. "That man is so handsome! If I were single and younger, I'd give him a run for his money." She took a guzzle from her wine glass. The way she was talking, I wasn't sure she hadn't had a drink or two before my getting here. "Mikey isn't mine, you know."

"No?"

"His mother left Phillip when Michael was just a little tyke. How in God's creation can a mother leave her child?"

"I think it happens a lot more often than one would think," I said, my mouth suddenly dry. She was getting into dangerously personal territory. "Does he ever see his mother?"

"No," she shook her head, her eyes taking on a distant look. "The woman has never tried to call, stop by, has never even sent a single letter."

"That must have been painful for him." Michael and I had more in common than either of us knew.

"He doesn't remember anything about her. As far as he's concerned, I'm his mother."

"He's fortunate to have you." I hoped that was the truth.

"You said you had some questions about Norma Swanson?" she asked, changing the subject.

"Yes. From what I've heard, you two were best friends."

"We were. Her death ripped me apart. She was such a good woman, and that good-for-nothing husband of hers—well, let's just say there wasn't a whole lot of tears shed when he died. I know it's not nice to speak ill of the dead, but that man had no redeeming qualities."

"Was he ever violent with Norma or Zachary?" I asked. I knew the answer from the newspaper articles, but I wanted to hear it from someone who may have witnessed it.

"He was. I think she had what they call—oh, what is it—battering syndrome, or something like that."

"Battered women's syndrome?"

"Yes! That's it! Battered women's syndrome."

"Was he violent with Zachary, too?"

"I don't know. As close as me and Norma were, I only saw Zachary once, and that was when he was just a baby, covered in one of them little receiving blankets. She hid him from everyone. I think she was afraid people would see what was going on."

"Did she ever try to leave Henry so she and Zachary would be safe?"

"Thought about it, sure. But it don't work that way. Unless you're living it, you can't possibly understand." She took another drink of wine, her eyes sparking with anger. "That good-for-nothing loser told her he'd kill her if she ever tried to leave and take his son. She figured if she left and took him, Henry would kill them both. If she left by herself and left Zachary with that monster, she wouldn't be there to protect him when Henry went into a rage, which happened every time the man drank. And let me tell you, that was more often than not." The irony of that didn't escape me at all—those words coming from someone who was well into the wine at nine o'clock in the morning. "She figured as long as she stayed she would at least be able to protect Zachary. So, in the end, doing what was best for them turned out to be the worst for them."

"She didn't have any family to help her?

"She had a couple brothers somewhere, but I never met them. And didn't care, if you want to know the truth. Like I said, I only saw little Zachary once."

"Hm." I was trying to figure out their relationship. Claire and I know everything about each other. And Sydney is like my child. Apparently, it's not like that between all best friends.

She took another guzzle. If she didn't ease up a little, I was going to end up scooping her up off the floor.

"Do you think the fire was an accident?"

"Don't know what else it coulda been. If Henry had made it out alive, I would have bet money that he was the one to start the fire. He'd been busted for starting a fire or two in his past. But since he was found dead, too, it ruled that idea out."

"Did either of them have any other enemies that you can think of?"

She laughed a bitter sound, choking on her wine. "Shoot, take your pick. Henry had more enemies than there were people in this town. And Norma? Well, people were quick to judge her. They'd say, 'Why does she stay and let that man do that to her and the kid?' Or, 'If she's gonna just stay and let him do that then she deserves it.' People are just plain cruel, you ask me."

Her slurring rose to a slightly higher level. It was hard to tell if it was because she was so angry or the fact that she had now drained the last of her glass. She excused herself to go into the kitchen. To pour another, no doubt.

I looked at the photos again, doing mental gymnastics to figure out what it was that was bothering me about the photo of the little boy, the Swanson family photo, and the Donaldson family photo. I was missing something big. I could feel it. But what was it? Thinking so hard was beginning to bring on a headache, the first significant threat of one since right after the accident. Headaches were no stranger to me, thanks to the car crash I was in several years ago. Thank the good Lord I have a hard head.

Selena came back into the room holding a coffee mug. My guess was wine disguised as coffee. I'd seen Violet do that when I was a little girl and still remember it to this day. She hadn't fooled me then, and Selena wasn't fooling me now. From somewhere within me, I felt pity for Selena but didn't quite know why. I suspected she was an unhappy woman.

"I suppose I better be on my way. Thank you so much for your time. I'm so sorry to have dredged up such painful memories for you."

"Don't be sorry. It helps to talk about it. Especially since I can't talk about it with my husband."

"Why's that?"

She waved her hand and sniffed. "He doesn't think it's good for me to go getting all worked up over something that's done and over. He said I can't change it anyway."

"Have you talked to someone else about it, Selena? A professional?"

Her eyes grew wide. "No, no. I couldn't do that."

"Because?"

"Phillip doesn't believe in counseling."

"What would happen if you went anyway?"

She looked shocked that I suggested such a thing. Then just as quickly a blank look replaced the shock. "Hm. I suppose I don't know."

"Since Phillip's not the one that would be going to counseling, perhaps it wouldn't be an issue with him if you did." I watched as she appeared to be processing the information, tilting her head to one side, the corners of her lips turning down.

"No, no, I don't think that would work," she mused. "But I'll have to think about that."

"Good." I smiled at her and touched her arm. "You take care, Selena."

She stayed in the same spot, not moving. I went to let myself out, opening the door at the same time someone pulled it open from the outside, nearly causing me to fall into the arms of the culprit. I looked up, surprised.

"Michael!"

"Hi Melanie," he said, his usually pale cheeks pink from the cold, his blue eyes dancing with mischief. "What brings you here?"

"I came to speak with your mother."

"Selena?"

"Yes."

"I wasn't aware you knew each other. What a small world."

"Birch Haven isn't exactly a metropolis."

"No, no, that it's not. How long have you known Selena?"

I thought carefully about how to answer. My grandmother has always drummed into me that honesty is the best policy, but sometimes a little fib fits better. And a fibcould potentially be a lot safer.

"I just had some business to discuss with her." Not totally the truth but not exactly a lie either. "What brings you here? Do you live with your folks?"

"Nah. I just like to check on her whenever I'm in the area."

Apparently, he was aware of her...habits. I thought it best to play dumb. "Has she been ill? She didn't say anything about not feeling well when we talked."

"She's been tipping the bottle lately. A lot," he mumbled, pantomiming swigging from a bottle.

"Oh?"

"Well, not just lately. It's been going on for quite a while. And when she's drinking she says things that aren't true. You can never guess what's going to come out of her mouth. So that you know."

"Is that so?"

"It is. So whatever she may have told you today, you'd probably do best just to let it go as fiction."

"I'll remember that," I said as I began walking away backward, continuing to face Michael. I wasn't about to turn my back to him. "And Michael?"

"Yeah?"

"Thanks again for taking care of my car last night." As soon as the words were out of my mouth, I realized how Selena would have found out about my accident. *Jeez! Paranoid much, Melanie?* I turned and finished walking the last few steps to the driver's side of my Renegade. I took a minute, squeezed my eyes shut and took a deep breath, screaming when I opened them and saw someone standing right outside my window. He bent over slightly and looked at me, motioning for me to roll down my window. I sighed with relief and rolled my window down. "Yes, Michael?"

"Like your new wheels." He smiled at me. He was close enough for me to notice his slight under bite, reminding me of a modified version of a Pekingese dog I had when I was a child. "You have good taste," he said, snapping my attention back from the gut feeling that something obvious was right before me and I couldn't put my finger on it.

"Thank you."

I rolled up my window, did a three-point turn and drove out of the driveway, waving back at Michael who was still standing there watching. As I pulled onto the highway, I looked back and saw him disappear behind the front door.

26

On the drive home I tried my best to relax and think about things other than the case I'd become so wrapped up in. The very one that nearly got me killed on the bike path Sunday and again that night.

I focused on the scenery rolling by outside my window, the sun playing hide and seek as it took shelter behind the increasing clouds. Halloween decorations littered people's yards out in the country every bit as much as in town. I marveled how Halloween is such a popular holiday, favored by kids and adults alike, when I had never particularly liked it. As a kid or now as an adult. It always held a certain creep factor to it, and the horror movies didn't do anything to persuade me otherwise. Violet never had the time to take me trick-or-treating, and when Nana and Granddad did...well, I loved the dressing up part because I could be someone other than myself. Someone a mother would want. Like a princess. What wouldn't mother want a princess? I dressed up as a princess every single year until one year I decided I wanted to be Prince Aladdin. It was then Granddad began to worry about me. I smiled at the memory, missing Granddad more than ever.

Heading home, I thought about the salon and how much I missed life-as-usual, going into work, laughing with Claire, Rubie, Connie, and now Babs. I missed spending time looking at the stars through the skylight in the roof directly above my bed, sitting on the balcony with the sun beating on my face and reading a good book, even doing the bookwork at the salon.

Suddenly I had an epiphany like a boom of thunder. The red sea parted, and the mystery surrounding the photos on the Donaldsons' mantle and the Swanson family became apparent.

My foot pressed harder on the gas pedal, and I drove as much over the speed limit as I could and still feel confident I wouldn't get pulled over by Birch Haven's finest. I'd just turned off of the highway and had gotten no more than a mile down the back road when I saw flashing lights coming up behind me. I looked around me expecting to see whoever it was the police car was after. When he caught up to me and trailing behind my car, lights flashing, siren wailing, I sucked in a deep breath. I slowed to see if by some miracle he'd pass me to chase the person he was after. But when the patrol vehicle slowed, staying close on my bumper, I pulled off on the shoulder.

When I saw the uniformed body beside my window, I fumbled for the button to lower the window, surprised to see one of the officers I'd met one of the many times I'd gone in to meet with Levi over the last year.

"Officer," I stated in my best there-must-be-some-mistake tone I could muster to deceive my

275

shaking self into believing I was completely in control. "What's the problem?"

"I received a complaint about you driving carelessly." His tone was flat, yet dominant.

"Me?" Now I was shocked. "There must be some mistake. I was just coming from—"

"No mistake. The person calling in the complaint gave me the license number that's on your temp tag there." He jerked his thumb toward the back of my car. "Mind telling me what's going on?"

"Nothing's going on. I was just on my way to the police station to—"

"License and registration please," he said, interrupting my fib. He held out his hand, palm up.

"Of course." I reached into my purse and pulled out my wallet, then went for the glove box."

"Slowly," he ordered, hand on his weapon.

I stopped and put my hands up. "I'm just getting what you asked me for." He stood alert, hand resting on his gun, the other motioning me to continue. I slowly opened the glove box. "Do you mind telling me who called in the complaint?"

"The caller wishes to remain anonymous."

"I'm sure they do. Because the report wasn't accurate."

"The world is full of guilty people who didn't do anything. If you don't believe it, just ask them, and they'll tell you."

"Jerk," I muttered under my breath.

"No need to be hostile. I'm just doing my job."

Oops. I need to learn to control my mouth. "What did this person report that I supposedly did? Is the caller even dependable?"

"You could say that."

"What did I supposedly do?" I asked again. "I have a right to know."

"You have a right, all right. A right to remain silent."

My mouth dropped open. "Am I being arrested?" I asked, my voice an octave higher than just a moment ago. "For what?"

"Not yet, but for obstructing an officer if you continue to keep me from doing my job." I reached for my phone. "Put your phone down. You can use it when we're done here."

He inspected my driver's license carefully, followed by my registration, then walked around to the back of my car to look at the temp tag taped to my back window. I watched through the back window as he called someone on his phone. *Odd. Why wouldn't he just use his radio?*

He came back to my window, leaned over, peered at me for a long uncomfortable moment. I shifted in my seat. He handed me back my license and registration. "I understand you're causing quite a ruckus around town snooping into things that are none of your business." His eyes locked on mine. "If you care about what happens to you, you'll stop and let the past stay in the past."

"Is that a threat, officer?" I said, my voice quiet and steady, my eyes daring his to break the stare. Now I was just plain mad, and I could feel my insides shaking. If there was one thing I disliked more than almost anything, it was a man who resorted to intimidation.

"Take it as you will. I'll let you off with a warning this time but—"

"A warning for what exactly? You still haven't told me what I did."

277

"Next time you won't be so lucky." He tapped his hand on my door and stood up. "Good day, Ms. Hogan. And wherever it was you were going, you might want to think twice. Go home."

Before the words were even out of his mouth, I began closing my window and locked my doors. I shuddered, lay my head back against the seat, and as soon as he pulled away, I closed my eyes and took a deep breath before grasping my phone from the seat beside me. I punched in a number that was getting to be almost as familiar as Claire's. Now that thought scared the snot out of me.

"Wescott here."

"Levi, it's Melanie."

"What's wrong?" he asked. "Are you okay?"

"I just had the weirdest encounter with one of the officers from the police department."

"Where are you?"

"On the side of the road."

"Which one?"

"Lakeside Drive. I'm pretty sure he just threatened me."

"He did threaten you, or you *think* he did? And which officer?" The hard edge in his voice was unmistakable.

"Shaw."

"Who?"

"Officer Shaw."

"Melanie, are you still sitting on the side of the road?"

"Uh-huh."

"I want you to drive."

My pulse kicked up a notch when I heard the urgency in his tone. I sat up straight. "Where?"

"Anywhere. Come here. No," he added quickly, "go home, and I'll meet you there."

"Levi, what's wrong? You're scaring me."

"Officer Shaw was fired over six months ago."

I felt the color drain from my face. "Do I want to know why?"

"Taking bribes and official misconduct."

"Was he charged?"

"For the official misconduct. The charge for taking bribes was mysteriously dismissed."

"Who supposedly bribed him?" I started my car and looked around me, making sure Impersonator Shaw was nowhere to be seen. He didn't say anything, and I feared a lost connection. "Levi?"

"Chief Donaldson."

Ka-Ching! I swallowed hard and realized I was holding my breath when things around me started to get fuzzy. I gulped in a deep breath.

"Melanie?"

"How fast can you be at my house? "

"I'm on my way. Are you okay?"

"Better than okay. You're going to be so jealous."

"Why would that be?"

I heard rustling in the background and then a loud bang. I winced and yanked the phone away from my ear, slowly putting it back again. "What was that?"

"Sorry. Dropped the phone. Why am I going to be so jealous?"

"Because I just solved the case."

Rather than park in my detached garage and risk another encounter with Mr. Personality, aka Impersonator Shaw, on my walk to the house, I pulled into the front yard, a few steps away from my porch. I barely reached the front door when Levi's car came barreling in the driveway, his car door open before the car fully stopped. Despite being at least fifteen minutes further away from my house than I was when we spoke, he was only mere seconds after me.

He scanned the area while I took comfort in seeing the bulk of his service weapon under his jacket. A lot of good mine did keeping it in my nightstand drawer. I got my concealed permit after an encounter with darkness little more than a year ago. After today's encounter with darkness, I would fare far better if I kept it in my car with me.

Levi's hand rested on the small of my back as I unlocked the door. He closed it behind him and turned the deadbolt.

"Am I in that much danger that the door has to be locked even when you're here?"

"It's a habit you should get into whether someone is here or not."

"I live in the country. There aren't a whole lot of people out here."

"Yeah? Well, you could have fooled me." He slipped his jacket off and hung it over the back of a chair. "Since I've met you, you've had more unwanted visits at your house than I've had the entire time I've lived in my house in town. And I've been there seven years."

I took off my coat, poured a glass of water, set it in front of Levi, poured one for me and sat down at the table across from him.

"You said you solved the case. Start talking."

"Remember when I went to see Hank and Gertie?" He nodded his head, signaling I could continue without losing him. "Well, Hank was such a crotchety old man, and Gertie the sweetest little thing, and—"

Levi's department issued phone rang, and he held up a finger as he answered.

"Wescott."

I watched as he listened, the corners of his lips turning down. There were a few uh-huhs and okays before he said, "I'll be right there," and hung up. He stood and grabbed his jacket.

"That was Michael. Emergency. I gotta run and take care of something. I won't be gone long." He bent over, kissed my cheek and looked at me, our eyes locking. "Lock the door behind me and don't let anyone in. Do you hear me?"

"Yes, sir!" I said, emphasis on the sir and giving him a mock salute.

"This isn't a time for jokes, Melanie. I'm serious."

"So am I. I'll lock the door and not let anyone in. I promise." He stared at me like he wanted to say something but held his tongue. "What? I will!" He was just about to pull the door closed behind him when I said, "Hey, Levi?" He turned around, his hand still on the doorknob. "I'm going to head into town and see Gertie. There's something I need to ask her."

"I don't think—"

"Keeping me here against my will is considered kidnapping, is it not? Or false imprisonment—something like that. Besides, I'd be safer in a senior living facility than here."

"You have a valid point. Get your keys. I'm going the same way, so I'll follow you until we get into town."

Twenty minutes later I went one way on one of the few streets that run through town, and Levi turned the other way, giving me a short honk and a wave.

I pulled into the parking lot of the facility and drove toward the back where I found one empty parking spot. Apparently, there was a lot going on today or else someone had some celebration. It wasn't mealtime, so I was betting there was entertainment of some sort for the residents, bringing in family members. I hope Nana never has to be in a place like this. I won't let that happen. As active as they keep these folks, Nana would be lost without a private kitchen and her gardens. I would move her in with me or else go live with her if I had to before resorting to moving her into a multi-housing facility.

When I opened the door, I was greeted by Roy Acuff's "Wabash Cannon Ball" streaming from the dining room, accompanied by a lot of laughter and voices talking.

"What's going on here today?" I asked over the sound of the music and smiling at the girl behind the desk.

"It's our monthly mingle. The folks love music and dancing."

"It's all fun and games until someone breaks a hip," I joked. One look at the girl told me she didn't appreciate the humor. *Oops.* "I'm here to see Hank and Gertie."

"Are they expecting you?"

"No. Can you tell me what room they're in and I can surprise them?"

"I can't do that. It's against our policy. I can call them for you though and let them know you're here."

"Okay." I leaned my hip against the desk, one arm bent at the elbow and resting on the counter as I watched the shenanigans in the dining room.

"Apartment 238. Gertie asked if you could please knock softly, though. Hank is resting."

"Of course. We wouldn't want to wake up Hank." I smiled at her. *No sir, we didn't want to wake Hank.* "Thank you—" I looked at her nametag. "Thank you, Rita."

She smiled at me as if using her name made us long time buddies. "My pleasure—" she looked at the sign-in sheet, "Melanie."

Huh. First name basis for us both. Guess that seals the buddy deal.

27

The door whipped open just as I'd reached up to lightly rap my knuckles against the worn, thin mahogany wood veneer. I was surprised to see Gertie standing there. Her swift movements and strength for someone who gave the impression of being weak made me reassess her abilities. I was impressed. She wore the same sweet grandmotherly smile she'd given me the last time we met. Or maybe it was the apron.

"Hi, Gertie. Am I interrupting you?" I looked past her expecting to see a small kitchen.

"Just watching my soap operas is all."

"Oh, I saw the apron and assumed—"

"No, no." She waved her hand. "We don't have kitchens here. I was doing some crafting while watching *Young and Restless.*"

"How nice," I said, trying to sound enthused. I had no idea *The Young and The Restless* was even on television anymore. And crafting—well, crafting is something I not only have no patience for, but I also have absolutely zero interest in it. The extent of my crafting was to craft poetry, which I hadn't been doing enough of lately.

"Yes." She peered at me over the rims of her glasses, looking me over from head to toe. Self-conscious, I looked at my high-heeled black boots, my faded jeans, and my black sweater. Nothing appeared out of place. On the contrary. Normal as normal could be. "Come in, come in." She waved me in, then smoothed her apron, her hands lingering on her hips.

"I understand Hank is resting?"

She rolled her eyes and huffed. "Yes, he is. He's been such an ornery old coot. One of these days he'll be gone and I'll miss him I suppose." She narrowed her eyes and leaned in. "But I couldn't imagine that happening lately, let me tell ya." She shook her head and walked further in, away from the bedroom that was just off to the left when coming in the door. "That man is going to drive me plum crazy."

To say I was surprised was an understatement. Gone was the sweet storybook woman I'd met the last time I was here. But as quickly as I thought about checking on Hank to be sure he was just sleeping, she was sweet as pie again.

"What drags you in to see an old woman?" she crooned. "Can I get you a cup of tea?" she asked without waiting for me to answer.

"Sure, that would be wonderful."

It's not like I was in a hurry to get back home anyway, given someone had a price on my head. I planned to stay in town until Levi called me to let me know he finished whatever business called him away. I'm not often scared, but I'm not known to be foolish either. Although if one asked

285

Claire, she'd have a very different opinion. Nana, too, probably. The poor woman probably thought I'd gone completely bonkers lately.

I busied myself with being nosey, poking around at the photos displayed in the cluttered apartment. I slipped out of my coat, laying it across the arm of one of the two chairs. It sure was toasty in here.

I was zeroing in on an all too familiar photograph that sat atop a pink and blue crocheted doily. I inhaled sharply. What in the world was the connection? I thought I had it figured out but this sure threw me a curveball. Could there be a simple explanation and I was looking for what wasn't there, suspicious of everything? Anymore, I wasn't so sure. At least not as sure as I was an hour or so ago when I was talking with Levi.

"Whatcha looking at there?"

"This picture of Zachary Swanson. The same one used for his obituary photo in the paper."

"Is it?" Her eyebrows raised in surprise.

"You didn't know that?"

"I must have plum forgot." She handed me a mug of steaming tea, set hers down and shrugged her shoulders. "That was so long ago, you know. I couldn't possibly have remembered that photograph. Getting old is heck on the memory, don't cha know. "

I took a sip of my tea, keeping an eye on Gertie over the rim of my cup, trying to read what was in her eyes. Raspberry. I puckered at the tartness.

"Sugar, dear?"

"Yes, please."

She disappeared into an adjoining room and returned seconds later. "We're not supposed to have microwaves in here," she whispered when she handed me two sugar packets, "but what they don't know won't hurt 'em." She winked at me, and I suppressed a laugh. She was quite pleased with herself for sneaking one in. A real lawbreaker, this Gertie.

I tore the corner off of both packets at the same time and poured them in my tea, stirring with a plastic spoon she'd given me. I took another drink, this time savoring the sweetness, the warm liquid bringing me to the point of overheating.

"These places must be insulated very well. It stays quite warm."

She waved her hand. "When you're old, dear, you like it warm. Circulation's not what it used to be, don't cha know."

I took another drink, Gertie watching me. I looked at her and raised my eyebrows in question.

"Well, are you gonna tell me why you're here? I'm sure you have better things to do than visiting an old woman without a good reason."

The heat was apparently affecting me because the room seemed to tilt slightly. I scooped my hair up with one hand and lifted it off my neck. Beads of perspiration dotted the nape of my neck, my forehead, and along my upper lip. "I'm sorry, I'm just terribly warm."

I let my hair fall and began to fan myself with a newspaper that lay on the little table beside my chair.

"Oh dear, I certainly hope you're not coming down with something. Try to take another sip of tea and see if that won't help you a bit."

I did as told just as a wave of nausea passed. Thank goodness it passed, I thought. "I think my head injury from my accident may have been a little more serious than I thought." I closed my eyes and took a slow breath, trying to regain my senses.

"Gertie, how well do you know Chief Donaldson and his son?"

She paused, one corner of her lip curling upward ever so slightly. "Quite well, I'd say. Why?"

I had a good sense that the good little grandma, here, was hiding something. And yet I couldn't pin it down. It was just so danged hot in here!

"Well enough to know that Michael and Zachary are one and the same?" I managed to get out before the room began to sway and another wave of nausea came and passed. My eyes searched hers and a cool smile played on her lips. "I'm not telling you anything you didn't already know, though, am I, Gertie?"

"How did you figure it out, child? Hadn't you been warned over and over and over again to mind yer own business? This family is none of yours."

"What have you done?" I whispered, barely able to make the words escape my lips.

"What have I done?" she said, that same evil smile still playing on her lips. "The question is, child, what have you done? You done went and got everything that we worked so hard for all in a giant mess. What business was it of yers whether Zachary is still alive?" She effortlessly removed the cup from my hand. "Here, let me help you. We wouldn't want you to spill that on yourself now, would we?"

"Gertie—" I said, my breath coming in short gasps. "What did you put in my tea?"

"Pretty soon it won't matter none what it was. Just relax and let go child. It'll be easier for you that way. You shoulda done that a long time ago. We gave you plenty of warning but you didn't listen."

She began stroking my hair, now damp with perspiration. Try as I might to jerk my head away, I couldn't get it to coordinate with what I wanted it to do. My head felt completely detached from my shoulders.

"So how did you finally figure it out?" she asked, still stroking my hair. "You know I didn't want to do this. You seemed like such a sweet child, you did. But too curious. We can't be having curious now, can we?" She tugged my hair. "Now, I asked you how you figured it out? And who did you all tell about it? Come, child, tell Grandma Gertie all about it."

"The—chip—chip—chipped tooth. The same—cowlick—the hair," my words were a mere thready whisper, and she leaned in to hear.

I severely underestimated this seemingly kind old woman. She wasn't weak at all. Not only did she outsmart me, but she also overpowered me, someone half her age, even if she resorted to slipping something in my tea to do it. The bottom line is she did it. My head was hanging loosely, one hand clutching my stomach, the other hanging onto the chair as the tilting room threatened to dump my weakening body to the floor. "Chief—Donaldson—"

"Is my son. My other child—"

"Nor—Norma..."

"I lost one; I won't lose another."

"The—fire—" She was leaning in closer now, struggling to hear what was barely a whisper coming from my lips. "Phillip—did—it."

"Yes. Phillip did it. Working for— " Her voice silenced but I couldn't focus to see what she was doing. "Oh, what the heck. It won't matter what I tell you now, because you won't be around to tell anyone none, will you." She sat on the chair by me, her hand on my back.

"Hank," I tried to yell, but as in a bad dream, nothing came out but a whisper.

I heard her chortle. "Don't you be bothering callin' that old coot. He can't hear you. Not anymore anyway."

A surge of adrenaline came from somewhere and I panicked. "You didn't."

"Didn't what, child?"

I managed to gather enough strength to look at her. I thought I saw sadness reflected in her eyes. But maybe it was just the heat and the swaying of the room.

"Phillip couldn't bear to see what that man was putting that sweet young boy through. And Norma was letting it go on. Don't you worry none, though." Her voice sounded like she was trying to comfort a hurting child. "He showed compassion for his sister, yes he did. He gave her a dose of something that made her have a heart attack, so she didn't feel the fire. He woulda took good care of her if he could of. See, I got pregnant with Norma while I was in school. I had to give her up. My Pa made me. By the time Phillip was born, well, Hank wouldn't hear a having Norma live with us. The world's better off now..."

Her voice faded into nothingness.

His sister died of a heart attack. Levi's words about Phillip's sister played through my mind.

"Gertie—call—call—"

"9-1-1?" She chortled a heavy sound. "It's too late for that, child." She stroked my hair again. "Just let go. Let go," she crooned.

Somewhere, I couldn't tell where, or whether it was even real, there was loud pounding and hollering of some sort. So much noise but I was too tired to care. I was just...so...tired. And everything went black.

I woke up to the smell of antiseptic, my head pounding like someone was clanging symbols inside of it. Each breath hurt and I struggled to open my eyes just enough to let a sliver of light through my eyelids, light that felt like it would slice my head wide open. I closed them again, noticing comforting warmth covering my hand. I gasped in panic, fearing Gertie wasn't done with me yet.

"No," I squeaked out. "Get away...from...me."

I turned my head to the side and squinted as I tried to see who it was. But as I regained consciousness a wee bit more, I knew by the touch who it was before I fully saw.

"Levi?" my voice croaked. I poked my tongue out to try to moisten my dry lips.

"Hey, Blondie," he whispered, kissing my hand and holding it to his lips.

"Thirsty," I whispered, my eyes closed again. I felt a cool straw touch my lips. I opened them enough to let the straw between them and sucked, my throat hurting as I did. I winced in pain. "Hurts."

"You gave us all a scare, there, kiddo."

I felt warm lips on my forehead, followed by a gentle hand stroking my hair. This time I didn't want to pull away. I wanted to lean in. A hot tear slid down the side of my face and soaked into the pillow beneath my head, followed by another and then another. Try as I might, I couldn't stop them.

"Hi, Nana."

"Melanie Hogan," she said trying to sound strong, but I could hear her voice waver, "don't you ever pull a stunt like this again. Do you hear me?"

"I love you, Nana." This time it was more than a near lifeless whisper. Not much more, but at least a little. Little progress was better than none at all. "You, too, Levi." Wait! Did I just say that? It had to be delirium. Or maybe I was dreaming all of this and I was actually in a coma. I opened one eye just enough to see Levi's face. Yup, I'd said it alright.

"Get some sleep, Blondie. We have lots of catching up to do when you wake up."

"Looking—forward to it." My eyes closed and everything went black again. This time, though, I felt each of my limbs relax. I was in good hands. And I had a strong sense that I was a lucky woman. In more ways than one.

28

It was Thursday, two days after my near death experience—the last one of them, anyway. I lay in my bed recovering as Levi brought in fresh water and a new bouquet of flowers, the majority of them daisies.

"I'm not sure I've ever seen a nurse wearing jeans. You know, Fredericks of Hollywood has nurse costumes that would fit your new role."

He chuckled that low, husky sound I loved so much. "Melanie Hogan, I think you're on the fast track to getting back to normal."

"Lucky for everyone who knows me, I'm sure."

"Yup, the sarcasm is returning quite nicely." He leaned over to kiss my forehead then ever so gently on my lips. "You feel up to talking?"

"Depends."

"On?"

"What you want to talk about." I smiled at him, knowing I owed him my life. He couldn't reach me on my phone and figured out the family drama puzzle. It was then he knew he needed to get to me. And fast. Thank goodness I told him where I would be or the talk he wanted to have would have been a non-issue. So, yes, as much as I didn't want to talk, knowing how uncomfortable it might be, I owed him at least that. "I'm listening." I took a sip from the straw, set my glass down and settled into my pillows.

"I've decided to turn down the job in New Hampshire."

"Why?" I asked, feeling conflicted, knowing the answer before he had to say it.

"I think you know why. You and I—"

"You need to be with your son, Levi."

"And I need to be with you, too."

"Not at the expense of your son."

"Well, now, that's just insulting. The fact that you would think I wouldn't have my son's best interests at heart."

"That's not what I said."

"It's what you insinuated."

"That wasn't my intent, and you know it."

"I finally found someone I want to share my life with, and whose life I want to share. My son can be part of that if you'd stop being so stubborn, making him the reason we don't have a future."

I lay my head back against my pillow and closed my eyes, processing the words I wanted to say. I opened my eyes and looked into his.

"Your son isn't what's stopping us, Levi, it's the fact that it's several states away. You know by now how much I love kids. And that's exactly why I will not be the reason to take you away from yours. I don't want to be the one your son looks at as 'that woman'. The one who took his daddy away." His eyes got hard for a moment before sheer frustration took its place.

"There you go again. You're not taking me away from my son, but you're too hard-headed to hear what I'm saying. I wouldn't let anyone take me away from my son. Or take my son away from me, for that matter."

I exhaled long and slow. "I don't see this working out. We're coming at it from two opposite angles."

"It doesn't have to be that way."

I stared at the framed photo on the wall in front of me, the one of the sun rising over the lake the summer after Cain left me.

"I have an idea," he said.

"I'd love to hear it."

"Lighten up, Blondie." He took one of my hands in both of his. "How about we meet in the middle?"

"That would be about, what...Ohio?"

"You're just a laugh a minute. How about I take the job out there on a one-year trial basis. My chief has already told me I've always got a place back here whenever I want it."

"As head of investigations?"

"What can I say? He likes me. I'm likable like that." He gave me that boy-grin.

"And so humble." I shook my head slowly. "But—"

"It would be long distance for us, but I believe we could make it work. After that first year, we'll re-evaluate."

"You'll have dumped me by then for some east coast hot mama."

He scowled. "That's not even the slightest bit funny."

I snickered, trying to trick myself into feeling better. It didn't work. "Let me sleep on it.

295

I'm exhausted." I settled back into the bed, tossed and turned, trying to get comfortable. Levi stood, walked around to the side of the bed and began to sit down.

"Relax and don't be so nervous," he grinned. "I'm fully clothed and on top of the covers."

"What makes you think I'm not relaxed or that I'm nervous?" I asked defiantly.

"Oh, I don't know. Maybe the fact that you were holding your breath." He laughed softly and settled in beside me, putting his arm around me and pulling me gently against him. He held me and stroked my shoulder.

That wasn't from nerves, my friend. That was something entirely different. And that was the last thought I had before I fell into the most comfortable, restful sleep I remembered having in a very long time, if ever.

When I woke up the room had darkened considerably, and I heard voices in the kitchen. Claire? I got up, my hair disheveled, my black sweatpants and black and white sweatshirt as far from attractive as one could even imagine. Oh, well.

Claire and Cole were sitting at the kitchen table while Levi was filling their cups with coffee. As soon as Claire saw me, she jumped up and had me in a hug before I could utter a single word.

"It's good to see you," I said, my voice muffled against her shoulder. She released her grasp, and I looked at the clock above the stove. "Seven o'clock?" I gasped. "Why did you let me sleep so long?" I asked Levi.

"Because you needed it."

"Don't you have a job you need to be at rather than stay here and babysit me?"

"Babysitting you is my job. And a full-time one at that." He winked at me. As Nana would say, Oofda!

"How's the salon?" I asked Claire.

"Believe it or not, we're getting along without you."

"Ouch!" I scowled.

"I'm kidding. We miss you like crazy and can't wait for you to be back."

"I can't wait to be back. I miss life as usual. Boring, normal..."

All three had exchanged looks before three sets of eyes trained on me, Claire's mouth in a perfectly shaped pink "O."

"Mind if I tape that statement?" Levi asked.

"No need. Davis doesn't forget a single thing. Ten years from now she'll remember this whole conversation verbatim."

The laughter that erupted around the table was the exact medicine I needed and which had been lacking. My spirits lifted, my soul soared, and my energy peaked.

"Has anyone talked to Michael?" I asked.

"He's taking a leave of absence from the department," Cole said. "He said he needs to get his head straight and try to make sense of his whole life which was virtually a lie the entire time."

"Do you think there's hope for him and Phillip to reconcile?" I asked.

"Not likely," Cole said.

I went to stand by Levi, leaning into him. "I hate to see crap happen between a parent and child."

Levi stretched his arm around my shoulders and squeezed. "I think he could have looked past the fact that Phillip took him and raised him as his own without ever telling him he was adopted. What he can't, and probably never will get past, is the fact that Phillip killed Henry and Norma, that he hired Shaw to threaten you, and that he tried to kill you."

I felt horrible for ever suspecting him in the first place. "So you think he didn't know about any of it the whole time?"

"I'm convinced of it," Cole said. "Mikey's decent people."

"On the bright side," Claire said, grinning, "Michael and Rubie have a date Saturday night."

"Lord help him," I said, rolling my eyes. I tucked a strand of hair behind my ear. "So has Levi here told you about our plan?" I looked up at him, met the question in his eyes with a smile. "We're officially going to give this thing a try."

"This thing?" Claire asked.

"Yeah, this thing. I stink at relationships, so we'll just call it a thing." Levi hadn't even blinked as I kept my eyes trained on him. "It'll be long-distance for the first year, but that'll be a good thing."

"How so?" Claire asked.

"Because it gives me more time to solve crimes without him interfering in my investigations."

His eyebrows raised and it got so quiet in the room I thought someone pushed the pause button. Until Levi laughed a very nervous sound. Finally, he rolled his eyes and said, "And you guys thought Mikey should be worried."

I laughed, circled my arms around his waist, stood on my tiptoes and planted a light kiss on his lips that came down to meet mine. "I'll be good. I promise," I whispered against his lips.

"I guess I have a year to find that out, don't I?"

Nana's Scrumptious Chocolate Zucchini Cake

½ c softened margarine
½ c vegetable oil
1 ¾ c sugar
2 eggs
1 tsp vanilla
½ c sour milk (see below)
2 ½ c unsifted flour
¼ c chocolate chips
4 tbsp cocoa
½ tsp baking powder
1 tsp baking soda
½ tsp cloves
½ tsp cinnamon
2 c finely diced zucchini

Cream margarine, oil, and sugar. Add eggs, vanilla, and sour milk. Beat well with mixer. Mix together all dry ingredients and add to creamed mixture. Beat well with mixer. Stir in diced zucchini. Spoon batter into greased 9 x 12 x 2 pan and sprinkle top with chocolate chips. Bake at 325 for 40-45 minutes.

- To make sour milk, add 1 tbsp vinegar or lemon Juice to milk.

Acknowledgments

Special thanks to:

First and foremost, my Lord and Savior Jesus Christ. My everything.

My family. For being the wind beneath my wings. Your support and encouragement is the foundation on which my writing life solidly stands. This wife, mother, and grammy is the most blessed in the world.

Tiffany Carter, Becky Shadlich, and Holly Hutson. You ladies are invaluable.

Dominique Abeyta. Thank you for gracing the cover of my book. Your beauty is breathtaking.

Rocky Mountain Fiction Writers and Sisters-in-Crime Writer's Groups, especially my Colorado sisters. What a gift to belong to such a talented, helpful group of writers. I'm never alone in the solitary act of writing because of you fun, knowledgeable sisters and misters.

My Brighton Group. Without all of you, I wouldn't have completed my first book, much less my fifth. Thank you for helping me to bring my dream to fruition and always keeping it real.

About the Author

Rhonda was born in northern Minnesota but now resides in Colorado with her husband and her dog, Roxie, and close to her children and grandchildren. Though she fully enjoys the Rocky Mountains, a piece of her heart will always belong to the woods and lakes of Minnesota.

Her love of writing took flight at the tender age of four when she was caught writing with her crayons on the knotty pine walls of the family home. In her teens, she tested her hand at journalism by writing an article or two for the city newspaper about school events. She completed an online Journalism/Short Story Writing course and was a stringer for another local newspaper, writing about school and community events. It was then she realized writing fiction is her first love and true calling. She has written poetry through the years, some of which have been published in poetry anthologies.

Though her love of writing travels back many years, it wasn't until she completed her paralegal degree and her boys left the nest, that she threw herself into all things writing. When she's not at her day job as a Restitution Advocate in a District Attorney's Office, she can be found hibernating in her home office creating characters, settings, and stories. When she's not writing, she's reading books on the craft of writing, and is typically reading more than one fiction book at a time. Mostly mysteries, of course.

Her online home is at www.rhondablackhurst.com and her blog is at rblackhurst.wordpress.com. She would love to have you visit her there.

Made in the USA
Columbia, SC
25 May 2020